# CRIES OF THE FORSAKEN

# CRIES OF THE FORSAKEN

## Book 2 of The Broken Pact

A Tale of Gods and Men

By

KRISTOPHER
JEROME

DARK
TIDINGS
PRESS

*Cries of the Forsaken* is a work of fiction. Names, characters, places, and incidents are the products of the author's imagination or are used fictitiously. Any resemblance to actual events, locales, or persons, living or dead, is entirely coincidental.



Cover art by Milica Celikovic
Maps by Sanjin Halimic

Hardcover ISBN: 978-1-951138-04-2
Paperback ISBN: 978-1-951138-02-8
eBook ISBN: 978-1-951138-03-5

First Edition, September 2019

Dark Tidings Press LLC
PO Box 593
Albany, OR 97321

darktidingspress.com

For Grandpa Doug.

I know you would have found it just as funny as I do that my son hears your name every time he gets into trouble.

The Rim of Paradise
The Great Chasm
Illus

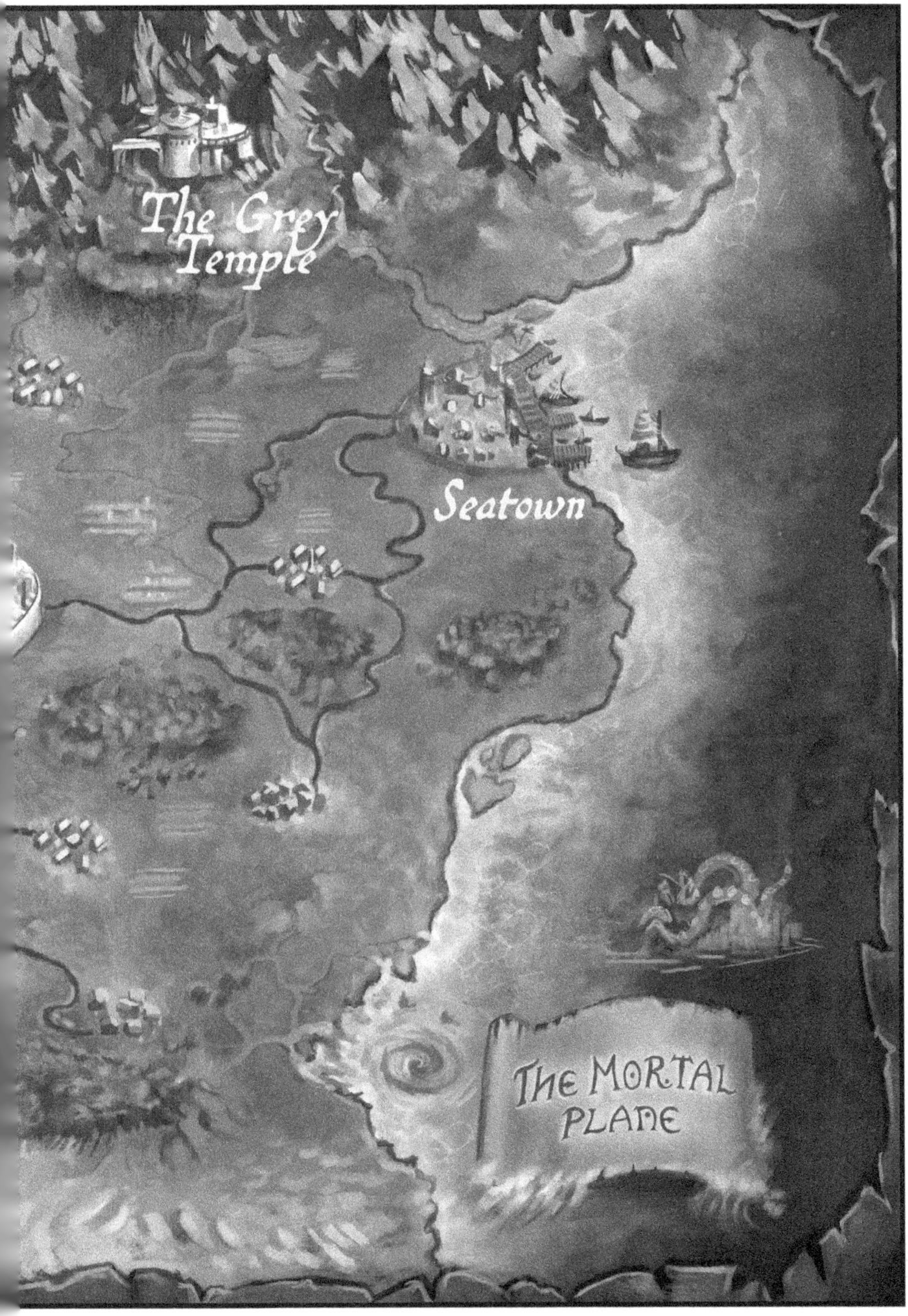
The Grey Temple
Seatown
THE MORTAL PLANE

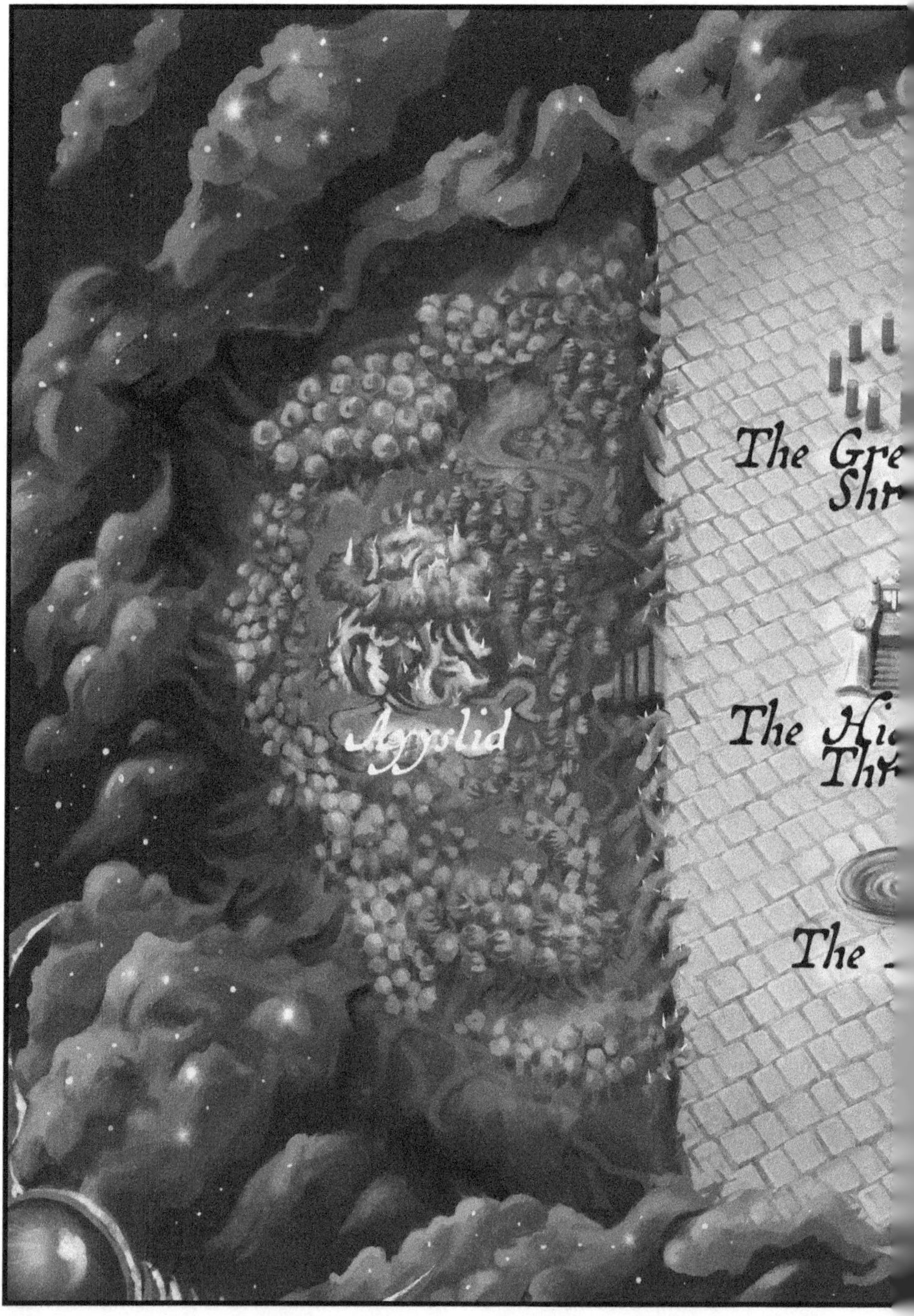
The Gre
Shr
The Hi
Thr
The

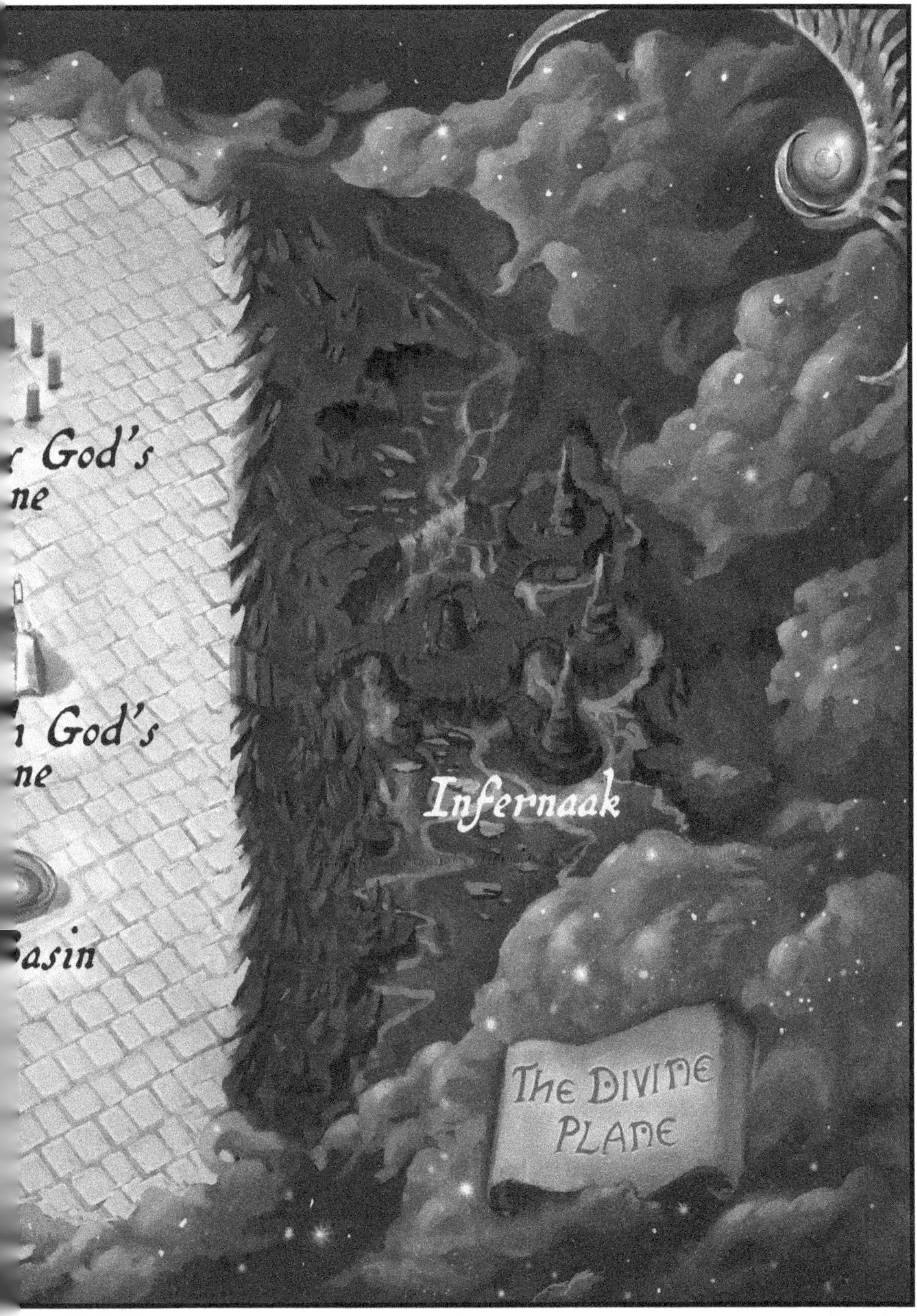

God's
ne
God's
ne
asin
Infernaak
THE DIVINE
PLANE

"So it was said that those who betrayed their brothers and sisters would forever be tarnished. Unfit to sup at the table of the Gods of Light or Darkness. Damned beyond any salvation, except that of a quick death."

—*Excerpt from Canticle of the Forsaken Ones*

# CRIES OF THE FORSAKEN

# PROLOGUE

High above him, the clouds boiled, and if there had been stars, they would have wept. The world no longer held the glory that it had in ages past, but if one knew where to look, ancient powers could be seen stirring. So it was this day. Aenna was dimmer now than it had been, for another of the betrayers must have met the justice that had eluded them for some thousand years. It had taken lifetimes but, finally, the world was beginning to right itself.

He knew only bits and broken pieces of what had transpired on the Divine Plane above, but the rest he could guess at. No word filtered to him from Illux or the villages outside his walls, not to this hidden place. How long had he been kept secreted away in this village, away from the goings on of the outside world? Lifetimes. Lifetimes beyond lifetimes. Only one being yet lived outside this glade who knew of his existence. The last to have seen him draw breath had fallen with him into the sea and rejoined the High God's side.

*Fiora. At least you saw the light in the end.*

Merek turned his gaze from the sky and looked earthward at the forest-covered village below. Small, squat homes were placed this way and that, peeking out from beneath the foliage. Looking from lower down the mountainside this place was completely hidden from view, and from the air—like Merek was now—it was all but invisible. He made sure of that. A decade of persecution and fleeing from the so-called followers of the Gods of Light had taught him what true safety meant.

He cried no tears for those who had betrayed him, then or now. There was a darkness in him he hadn't been able to shake since the others had commanded the deaths of his friends and the banishment of his god. He had not fallen to his knees like so many others had, however. He had raged against them with the anger and power befitting of his silver blood. Merek was many things, but he was no coward, and he was no traitor.

Below him, the small village of the last truly faithful champions of the Light was continuing with its day as if there had been no change in the heavens. The village was nestled away in a glade to the northwest of Illux, high in the Rim of Paradise. At its heart was a giant tree of golden bark and amber leaves. There was power here, power that would be needed in the war to come.

Merek had founded Liorus in the years following his final disappearance, selecting this spot because he knew that it would be avoided by any minions of Ravim or the three betrayers. He had also been charged with the care and safekeeping of the tree at the village's heart in order to keep those locked beneath it safe from any possible threats. After Fiora had fallen he had lain low for a generation at least, eking out an existence in the Rim and the lands beyond, making sure no one who saw even a glimpse of him lived long enough to utter a word to gods or men.

Once he had settled in the glade, he knew that he was finally in his ordained place. The faithful had come to him slowly at first, but soon he had gathered a small fighting force of those who still remained loyal to the one true God of Light. Their Lord had come to them in dreams, they had claimed, and sent them north, past Demons, bandits and worse to find salvation.

*Soon it will be up to them to repopulate the world. Soon it will be time to remake the Mortal Plane as it should have been in the beginning.*

The Seraph made his slow descent earthward toward the houses below, his short white hair ruffled by the currents of wind that claimed dominion over these heights. He often took to the air the survey their surroundings, making sure the peoples of the world below weren't encroaching on the edges of his dominion.

Merek was the last of his kind, from a time before even the Pact of the Grey God had been created, from a time before the war between the gods was more than a shadow of what it had once been. He had walked with gods, monsters, and legends, and for a short while, he had been one himself.

He had been one of the greatest champions of Lio then, second only to his childhood friend Daniel in his rank and valor in battle. But that was before his god had been betrayed, before the Seraphs had been butchered, leaving only Fiora to guide the world of mortals.

Slowly, he landed upon the earth between the trees, feeling the moss-covered ground softly give under his weight. He found himself spending more time in the air as of late, enjoying the freedom that flight brought him. It reminded him of better days. His life had become shackled to this one place, hidden at the edge of the world. After Fiora had hunted down and killed the last of the Forsaken Ones, those Seraphs who had remained loyal to Lio and refused the Grey God's sentence of death, he had gone into hiding and faithfully followed the commands that Lio has communicated to him.

Merek had never lost his link to Lio, even when the God of Light had been cast down, a fact that both had kept secret from the other gods. He had been made Seraph in a time when only one God of Light imbued the winged servants with blood, meaning that he could speak to Lio alone. Fiora had been the last in the unbroken line of Seraphs in Illux to also share that trait, but in her case, it had been through the traitor Arra. Since her death, each Seraph shared the blood of the remaining three Gods of Light, giving each of them equal access to the mind of the holy warrior. This came to pass because none of the other Gods of Light had been able to communicate with Merek or the other Forsaken Ones when they had defected. After that, it had only been a matter of time before they learned to mask their presence from the watchful gaze of Aenna and the Basin to which it is connected.

Merek walked through the spiral pathways that webbed between the small houses of the village, heading to the tree at the center of the glade. Those he passed all bowed before him, some even stopping to kiss the ground upon which he walked. They knew they were in the presence of one of the original champions of the faith. They knew that to not show the proper reverence to such a figure was blasphemous. And blasphemy was death. These were not the weak mortals of Illux, those who would abandon their faith when they were threatened and faced with death, these were the followers of Lio, who still knew him as a God of Light.

The Seraph had known of his gods' plans for dominating the Mortal Plane for some time, a revelation that he had kept to himself alone. None of the others were quite ready for the reality that was unfolding even now in the world beyond. In order to regain his status as a God of Light, and to bring justice to the betrayers, Lio had to continue on in his guise as the Fallen One, a bitter and weak God of Darkness. This meant that he must use the tools of his enemies to bring destruction upon them, even if it sickened him. Demons. Accursed. Divine Beasts that he had fought so hard to destroy. Some of the very creatures that had killed his friends and loyal servants now fought under his banner.

Lio had told Merek that he would never defile him by asking him to command Demons and Accursed, even if it would lead to the victory they both craved. This was why he had taken the time to ensnare that wretched Herald into his service. None of the dumb brutes knowing that even as they worked to destroy Illux they sowed the seeds of their own destruction.

And so, Merek had waited.

Now, the time was coming for him to take part in things. Lio had told him just that morning after a week of silence. Arra, the first traitor, had been wounded, but it had not stopped her from physically journeying to the Mortal Plane and killing the Herald, routing his army and sparing the false Seraph and her surviving forces. After that Lio had remained silent. Merek did not know what else had transpired to dim the window Aenna, but he knew that it had been the work of his master. The gods once again walked the Mortal Plane. This would change things, of that Merek was sure.

By now he had reached the giant tree, its golden bark giving off an evanescent glow. It throbbed under his touch, the bark moving under his fingertips as if it was itself a living, breathing thing. The surface of the tree was not rough like natural trees, but smooth as if it had been worked over by a masterful carver. The tree had grown from a branch of Ayyslid, a final gift to mark the place that the first casualties of the Light's betrayal to Lio were interned. Even now, Merek could feel the stirring of the other within the wood, hungering to be released upon the world that had wronged him.

*Soon, my friend. I promise you.*

"It may even be sooner than we had thought, Merek," a familiar voice whispered from behind.

The Seraph spun about and fell to his knees, prostrating himself before the shinning figure that appeared behind him. Even in his current state, Lio was a sight to behold. It mattered not that Merek remembered him as he once was. He loved his god no matter what form he took. Lio's once golden skin had greyed from years of hiding within Infernaak, and his white hair had turned a sickly yellow color. One of his eyes was ruined, a white orb set in a fissure that split his face. Even so, he exuded a strength unlike that of any other being on or above the Mortal Plane. When Merek finally looked up he saw that

Lio's face had been marred by several deep cuts that were forming scars. They almost looked as if he had been struck by the claws of some mighty beast.

"My lord," Merek said as he stood. "Who has done this to you?"

"Some pet of Arra's," Lio said, flatly. "The beast attacked just as she was about to face the killing blow. It matters not. They can do nothing to me that has not already been done. Even the fool who once sat in that throne holds no power over me. Not now."

The God of Light moved in closer and examined the tree. His black armor reflected no light, but rather seemed to absorb it. Even the natural glow of the tree dimmed and faded as he approached. Merek found that after several moments he had to avert his eyes. The sight of his god in such a state sickened him. He quickly wiped away a tear that was forming and returned his gaze to Lio. Lio raised his hands and placed them on the tree, closing his eye as he did so.

"Is he comfortable?" he asked, distantly. "Does he struggle to be free of his prison?"

"No, my lord. He recognizes my presence, and I think it brings him comfort, for he no longer rages against his prison as he once did. Even so, I can sense an…emptiness in him that was never there in life."

Lio stood silently for a time, breathing deeply as he held his hands in place. Merek thought that he could see the expression on the fallen god contort into one of immense grief for the briefest of moments. Finally, Lio opened his eye again, stepping back from the tree.

"That is…unfortunate," the god said. "And what of the other?"

Both Seraph and god looked down at the smooth earth beneath the tree where the other being was shackled. Merek tried to think of him even less than the prisoner of the living wood.

"Of him, there had been no sign all of this time. But once Aenna dimmed and we knew that Ravim had fallen by your hand I began to notice him stirring as well," Merek replied.

"It is not yet time for him. He would not understand the evil that we must subject ourselves to in order to restore the world to the way that it should be. It pains me to leave him so ensnared, but I fear we have no other choice. Damn them!"

Lio seemed to then fly into a fit of rage, his fists striking at the tree. The angered god was able to stop his blows just before they connected with the glowing bark, inevitably freeing that which was locked within. Neither he nor Merek was prepared to face what had become of *him*, again. Not yet. Not for a long while.

After a time, Lio seemed to have returned to himself, and turned back to face Merek, a smudge of silver blood forming around his white orb. He looked more determined now than he had before, almost as if something had returned him to the place that he hadn't inhabited since his fall. The sight filled Merek with anticipation. Their enemies would quaver in fear if they could see the look that now crossed Lio's face. The God of Light wiped away the silver blood and placed his hand on Merek's shoulder. The contact was exhilarating, as if every muscle in Merek's body vibrated from the touch. He felt the same feeling that he had felt when the blood had been given to him at Daniel's recommendation.

"Arra is dead. The Divine Plane reacted to her passing just as I knew it would. The wounds that we visited upon her had been too great. Even when she played that little game with our armies, she knew she was doomed. Still, her actions have slightly altered our plans. With the Herald dead it is necessary that I create another, lest I rely on you to lead the armies of Darkness to the gates of Illux, which I dare not do."

"You know I would never deny one of your commands, my lord," Merek said as confidently as he was able, while fighting his own revulsion.

"I know," Lio said softly. "But it is not yet time for you to make yourself known. Once the city has fallen to my armies and the Gods of Light lie dead then it will finally be time for us to restore the world to that way that it was. Just when the forces of Darkness think themselves victorious, I will slaughter their gods and you will gather the remaining forces of Light and smash the Demons and Accursed just as you always have. We will awaken the Divine Beasts and set them upon those few enemies that survive. It will be a glorious day, of that I am sure.

"Still, we must take caution now, in light of recent events. Arra saved the false Seraph, taking her to Ayyslid before she died. I do not know what knowledge they will have armed the woman with, but she cannot be allowed to interfere. I have a feeling that somehow she will find her way here, in order to try and awaken Tyr. That cannot be allowed to happen."

"I understand, my lord. What shall I tell the faithful?" Merek asked.

"Tell them that the time of judgment is finally upon us. The day of glory, just as you have promised them, is near, and they may be called upon to fight both men and Demon alike. It will not be as simple as the true forces of Light killing the forces of Darkness. The Light must purify itself. Make them ready for me Merek, for I may need to call upon them and you sooner than either of us had hoped. And when I do, those who betrayed us will finally learn what justice is."

In a flash of light, Lio was gone again, leaving Merek to stand alone in silence. He would begin the preparations that very hour, for he felt that Lio's fears were correct. He had planned for some time to ask the people to mark themselves in a sign of faith, weeding out what few weaklings had inevitably joined with the others. It seemed he would need to bring this about before the enemy found them. It would not be long before they would be forced to fight all of their enemies. Again, he placed his hand upon the tree.

*Soon, my brother, you and I will bathe in silver blood.*

# CHAPTER I

The smell of smoke and burnt flesh clung to his nostrils. It was sour and foul. It was sweet and sickening. He doubted he would ever rid himself of the stench, if he even survived long enough to care. He supposed he would keep smelling it long after his spark left his body and returned to the High God.

They had been screaming, all of them. Running and screaming and bleeding and dying. And burning. That monster had gutted some of them, and burned others. Villager and Paladin like were butchered like they had been animals. All of his brothers and sisters had been killed by that *thing*. It had taken the girl, and it had taken his arm.

Gil looked down at the stump of what remained of his right arm, just below the elbow.

He vomited again.

It didn't matter that the maiming had been days ago. It didn't matter that he had healed the wound as best he could. The bleeding in the beginning had been overwhelming. He nearly ran out of time before he was able to stop the bleeding with the healing magic bestowed upon him by the gods. Yet he had stopped it, he had forced the warmth of the magic to stop the warmth of his blood from emptying into the soil he died upon. None of that made any bit of difference to the revulsion he felt in the pit on his stomach when he looked upon the stump.

The Herald of the Gods of Darkness had taken his arm when they had battled over the young woman. Gil had fought bravely, but no amount of bravery could stand against such wicked power. Even power like that which he wielded.

*Jaina.*

Gil was a Paladin of Illux. A holy warrior charged with the protection of those humans who worshipped the three Gods of Light. He had been stationed in the village of Marna, the most southern settlement that humans dared inhabit. Any farther south would have put them deep into Demon patrolled territory. The road to Illux was perilous, beset by attacks from the wretched creatures and bandits both. Still, until that night their village had flourished. Marna had survived under the protection of four Paladins. Gil, Jakob, Clarissa, and Albert. Marna was the last bit of fertile land to the south, and they had worked every inch of it, sometimes sending more grains and vegetables to Illux than many of the villages near the Rim. Now it was nothing but ash and cinders.

The smoke rising in the distance had been the first sign that something was wrong. The night stars had been blotted out by a dense fog, yet the smoke was still visible from the faint glow that illuminated it from below. Gil had felt uneasy the entire night, as if someone had been watching him. Then he saw the magnitude of the flames and he knew that something wicked was among them. While his brothers and sisters had gathered many of the villagers to hunt the creature, Gil had begun evacuating those whose homes were threatened from the blaze. He was no coward, but saving lives always took priority to ending them. It was during his efforts to get as many of those in charge to safety as he could that he stumbled upon Jaina, hiding in the burning house where the beast had left her.

She would barely speak when he found her. He knew that it had killed her family. She thought that it wanted her for some reason, and she feared that it would return. That was reason enough for Gil to personally take her to safety. Little good it had done her. It hadn't taken long for the Herald to find them and attack. Gil stood his ground, but the thing was too fast for him. It played with him for several agonizing minutes, moving too fast for him to hold any real defense. Then, without warning, it removed his arm and left him for dead. Before he passed out the last thing he heard was the sounds of Jaina screaming as she was carried off into the night.

Gil awoke minutes later, nearly dead, but he was able to use what little strength he had left to close the wound. That effort pushed him back into the blackness and he awoke late the next day when the fires of the village had finally begun to die down. The smell of the place pressed down on him like an iron net. His armor was blackened, his cape a ruin, and his blond braid was singed. Gil pulled himself to his feet and stumbled down the hill into the charnel grounds, hoping that whatever twist of fate had spared him had spared another. If the High God had saved Gil then, perhaps, he had saved more villagers also. He found no one. Wandering through the smoldering ruins had only added to his delirium.

He had been wandering ever since.

How many days it had actually been he wasn't sure anymore. Before leaving the village, he had gorged himself on the charred remains of the livestock. At least that is what he told himself. Since then, he hadn't had anything to eat beyond some roots and fetid water. The wounded Paladin could already feel his weight loss from the continued diarrhea and lack of sustenance. He was still dying, but slower now than if he had simply bled out in the muck.

*If you are listening, just let me die.*

He thought he was stumbling northward toward Illux, but he didn't actually know. Direction was meaningless to him. The grasses continued on as far as he could see, with only sparse trees scattered in the distance. He vaguely remembered that Ryun was nearby—the next village between Illux and Marna. Perhaps he could find help there.

*If they yet live.*

The thought made him retch again, but he held it back. Paladins guarded the villages in case Demons or Accursed were to attack. They stood between the shipments to Illux and the bandits that preyed upon them. Nothing would prepare any number of Paladins for the scale of evil he had witnessed. Nothing like that had happened since the Purge of Illux at least, if not before.

The only other time a village had been burned that Gil knew of was when the Paladin Cecilia had gone insane. There was no way for him to be sure this hadn't simply been the first strike in some larger offensive orchestrated by the Gods of Darkness. Or possibly, this had not been the first strike but the last. Surely, if Illux had fallen they would have known, but if the city was besieged, it was possible that no word had gotten out.

He noticed the feeling of nausea too late. His lunch of roots was on his feet before he could aim away.

Wiping his mouth, the Paladin collapsed onto his haunches and stared at Aenna. Somewhere up above him the Gods of Light were battling for his well-being on the Divine Plane. At least that is what he used to tell himself. His view of the gods who watched over them all was certainly brighter than some of his companions from the city. Once, that is. Now he wasn't so sure. His previously cheery outlook was what growing up in the villages had done for him. Though the people of the city were more openly pious and lived in the shadow of the Grand Cathedral, they had lost the appreciation for the simpler life, they had lost an honest connection to the glory of creation and the gods. It was an outlook that Trent and Devin would never understand.

*I'll never see either of them again.*

Losing Trent would have been hard, but it was Devin he would miss the most. They had loved one-another since meeting up during their training, long before their initiation. Devin was loud and bombastic, while Gil had been more reserved, still awestruck by the city at that time. He almost wheezed out a laugh when he remembered he thought Trent and Devin had been together. When his feelings for Devin had begun to manifest, he started to get jealous of their red-headed friend. Those two were inseparable. For all of Trent's deep-seated anger, Devin counterbalanced it was unbridled confidence that bordered on carelessness. Gil had been smitten. His eyes unfocused as he pictured Devin's dark skin.

Then Aenna dimmed.

He almost didn't notice the change, so engrossed in his fantasy was he, but something had caught his attention. Dumbly, he blinked and tried to wipe his eyes to make sure he wasn't mistaken. There was enough sanity left in his mind to recognize he was careening wildly from delusion to reality. The Paladin needed to be sure that what he saw was real. After staring dumbly into the sky for several minutes he was certain that one of the gods had died. Everyone knew that any changes to the window to the Divine Plane meant that something had befallen one its denizens. Not since Lio had slain Xyxax nearly a thousand years before had Aenna ever changed its luminance. This was surely connected to what had happened to his village. This meant that war had truly begun again, like it had in the days before the Pact.

Gil retched again, collapsing into his own vomit. All thoughts of Aenna faded like the window itself.

It was the sound of crickets in the darkness that finally woke him. When his eyes first fluttered open they were greeted with a nearly starless sky. Dark clouds obscured all but the faintest bit of light. Stunned at the late hour, Gil dumbly sat up and looked around in disbelief. The Paladin was too weak to stand without help, so he leaned forward to push himself up with his hands. Once his stump made contact with the ground he was painfully reminded of the reality he found himself in. He collapsed again, gritting his teeth and trying to keep his eyes from watering.

Until now he had kept himself moving forward because he couldn't bring himself to give in. Not to his pain. Not to despair. But what could he do now? There was no way he could make it to Illux in this condition. So far, his prayers had gone unanswered, and the gods were ignoring his plight. Aenna dimming meant they had more pressing concerns than the life of a single Paladin. Prayers were rarely answered in the best of situations. Perhaps, he should fall on his sword and be done with it?

*Jaina.*

No. He may not have been able to save the people of Marna, but that didn't mean he couldn't avenge them. No, he would not give in to death, he would grab it and deal it to those who slaughtered his people. And what of the other villages? Ryun nearby? Or Amel of his youth? There were other places in need, villages that needed to be warned. He would not fail them like he failed Marna. He could not. Alyssa, from his time in Rinwaithe, flashed through his mind's eye. She would not end up like Jaina had.

Gil kept his stump close to his chest as he rolled over and used his good hand to push himself upward. Gritting his teeth, he stood and began stumbling in the direction he assumed was northward again. The clouds parted, showing the stars twinkling lightly above him, sending down enough light for him to see the ground beneath his feet.

*I'll see Devin again, and then I'll track down the Herald. Gods, give me strength. We'll do it together.*

He didn't know how long he traveled, but it seemed like the night was dragging on longer than any night before it. While the Paladin trudged along, his thoughts returned to Amel, the village he had grown up in as a boy. Life had been difficult for farmers in the village, many of whom felt as if they were enslaved by the demands of the citizens of Illux. Amel was known for being less receptive to what they saw as the yoke of the city than other villages. Still, they found safety from the brave Paladins that were stationed there. Gil remembered the woman, Kirin, who had been the senior Paladin of Amel while he lived there. She had been a caring woman and had inspired Gil to travel to Illux to begin his training.

Once he had passed the Initiation, he had forgotten why he had become a Paladin in the first place. City Paladins didn't think about the well-being of the villages. They never knew anything beyond the immediacy of the war. Many of them cared so little for the villages that they didn't even take the time to learn their names. Every child in the villages knew of Illux and Seatown, but few from within either location thought of the villages as anything but nameless sources of food. Trent and Devin weren't the worst, but even they couldn't think much beyond the walls of Illux. Gil didn't break from this mindset until the three of them, along with that Balance Monk, tracked down a bandit blood cult in the Rim and destroyed it. Rinwaithe, the village closest to where the bandits had been operating had suffered many horrors through the ordeal, horrors that Gil had never wished them to experience again. That was when he decided to return to his roots, and he asked to be stationed at Rinwaithe where he spent the next few years.

That was a lifetime ago.

Ahead was the shadowed form of a ruined tower. This tower must have been one of the outposts that once covered the lands beyond Illux before the time of the Pact. These towers at one time served as a means of communication in case armies of Demons and Accursed marched on the city. None remained manned after the Seraphs were culled. Fiora had ordered all of them abandoned.

Weariness finally overcame him, and he knew he would need to rest again. This tower would give him shelter for the rest of the night, and possibly the next few days if he didn't start to recover.

Scattered stones from the tower littered the countryside, remnants of an older time. Gil climbed through an opening at the rear of the tower and slowly made his way up the winding steps inside to the second floor where he collapsed onto the stone and closed his eyes. Sleep came quickly, but it brought with it dreams of blood and flame.

Sounds from below woke him with a start. Sounds of men talking.

Gil bolted up and looked out the little window to the ground below. A small makeshift camp was being assembled by four well-armed men. They looked dirty and unshaven, each looking over his shoulder at the others, clearly refusing to be caught unawares. Several horses were hitched off to a tree just beyond the last of the scattered stones. The horses were weighed down with several hefty looking bags.

*Bandits.*

It had been some time since Gil had needed to draw steel against another human, and unlike his old companions, he hated to do so. Even if he still had both of his arms he would have hesitated to make himself known to these men. Still, men such as these often brought death upon themselves. Slowly, he dropped away from the window before he was seen and slumped against the wall. They hadn't seen him yet, which was their only hope. Still, it could be days before these men left. He didn't have that long.

Gil gingerly pulled free his sword and looked it over. He wasn't left-handed, and he certainly hadn't taken the time to practice without the use of his right hand. That meant that his only other option was to rely on magic. The Paladin knew that there was no way he could survive using such energy—not in his current state. A Paladin's magic was a gift from the gods, but it used the life-force of the Paladin as a conduit. The physically weaker or more exhausted the Paladin, the less powerful and more dangerous the magic. What hope did he have?

"What do you think is in `ere?" a voice called from below.

"Haven't you seen one of these outposts before? They're all from ancient times," another voice answered.

"I want to take a look around."

Gil backed into the far corner of the room, away from both the window and the stairwell. No furnishings had survived the centuries of disuse, so he found no places to hide. The uneven masonry clanked against his armor loudly as he pulled himself across the room. Once he reached the place where he would make his last stand, he propped himself up as best he could. Weakly he held his sword before him, the weapon looking odd in his off-hand. There wasn't much hope for him now. He moved his cracked lips and tried to form words.

"Give me strength."

Footsteps echoed up the stairway. The first bandit stumbled up the steps, apparently tripping over the last few before spilling onto the landing. Cursing, the man pulled himself up and looked around the room. His clothes were a mismatch of dark browns and blacks, sharply contrasting with his pale skin. He spotted Gil and cursed again, louder this time. Dirt-covered fingers ran across his shaved scalp before falling smoothly to his side. The man unclasped the axe that hung there and faced Gil, weapon raised.

"Who the fuck are you?" he rasped.

The Paladin struggled to speak for several moments, trying his hardest to wet his mouth. Finally, after dumbly moving his lips for what felt like several minutes he was able to talk in a hoarse whisper.

"I was a Paladin in Marna. The village has been destroyed by the Forces of Darkness," Gil said. "I need to get word to Illux, or even reach another village. People must be warned."

"There is no way I'm letting a Paladin, even a crippled one, get away from me alive," the man spat.

*I must convince him. I have to.*

The Paladin tried to sound strong when he next spoke: "When men wage war the gods hardly notice. But when the gods wage war, it is mortals who suffer the most. Please, don't make me do this."

"Save the sermon for the High God."

"So be it."

The man ran at Gil, swinging his axe wildly before him. Gil staggered as he brought his sword in front of him, trying to enter some kind of defensive stance. He was able to deflect the first blow of the axe, but the contact with the weapon caused him to lose his grip and drop his sword. It clattered to the floor, echoing through the empty chamber. The beleaguered Paladin balled his hand into a fist and smashed it into the jaw of the man as hard as he could. The force of the blow sent both men falling to the floor. Once on top of the bandit, the Paladin could smell the reek of the open road on him. Gil started to wheeze, but he continued to strike the man, first with his fist, and then with his stump until both became bloodstained.

The bandit's axe bit hard into Gil's shoulder, bringing with it a fire that burned deep into the muscles of his arm, tightening them. Gil opened his mouth and screamed in pain. Then he bit the other man like he was an animal. Teeth sank into flesh on the bandit's neck and shoulder. Skin gave way with the littlest bit of pressure. The blood that filled Gil's mouth sickened him but, still, he clamped down. His stomach churned like a tempest, causing him to shudder. He continued shaking even when the other man stopped moving.

Gil rolled off the bandit and vomited all over his corpse. Blood and bile mixed in a scarlet tableau upon the floor. By now there was almost nothing left in his stomach but his own fluids, and his body rejected even those. Distantly, Gil thought he could hear the patter of footsteps rising up the stairway. He lifted his head in time to see a dark shape bounding from the stairs, making incomprehensible noises as it did so. Darkness filled the room as it entered, obscuring Gil's vision. The shadowy thing looked like a Demon to Gil's eyes, bringing forth a rage from within him that he didn't think would ever surface again.

Blue light erupted from Gil's hand, hammering into the dark shape, and sending it careening out the window behind it. The Demon cried out quickly before being silenced by a loud crash. Below, the sounds of whimpering horses arose, followed by the shouts of fearful men. Gil pulled himself back into the corner away from the corpse, once again clutching desperately at his sword. He propped himself up against the wall, trying to focus his wandering mind onto healing his bleeding shoulder.

Somehow, Gil knew that more Demons would not enter the tower. His last display of power had scared them off. They knew he was coming for them now. He was coming for all of them.

# Chapter II

Edmund hadn't seen so many people together in all his life. Hundreds pressed against each other in the struggle to get through the open gates. The sound and the smell of them was almost as overpowering as seeing them pour in for the first time. They came from every village in the wilderness, answering the warning sent out by the Seraph some days prior. The call had gone out on horseback with some of the city's fastest riders, and the people had wasted no time in following. It didn't matter to them that Illux would be the most likely target of any large-scale attack. It didn't matter that there wasn't room in all of the city to house them, even if they would be given access to the inner city—which they wouldn't. All that mattered to them was that Marna had been razed, and the Seraph had raised an army to mete out justice. What happened after they arrived was unimportant.

Edmund of the City watch stared blankly at the crowd, losing himself for a moment as his eyes flitted from face to face. He had no family name—almost no one had one of those save for a few of the old Paladin families from the inner city. Some of these very refugees could be relatives, and he would have no idea. His people, whoever they were, had come from the slums. They had no history beyond a single generation back, like most of their neighbors. No, Edmund was just Edmund, a man of low birth and little distinction. Except that right about now he was possibly the third most important man in the city. With the Seraph gone, along with most of the senior Paladins and army commanders, Castille had been left in charge of the City of Light and its defenses. Other than Castille and his few Paladin cronies, the city was being run by the City Watch. In times of peace the watch protected. In times of war it defended. The Watch was commanded by Captain Redrick; his first lieutenant was none other than Edmund.

*Poor Edmund about now. I should have ignored Trent.*

He shoved a man back who pressed against the line of watchmen a little too vigorously. There was no malice in the action, but they could not allow the line to break, or the flood of refugees would stampede into the city like scared livestock. The destruction that would bring could threaten to be more than just property damage. These people were afraid, and fear armed the mob like the knife to the cutpurse.

The Watch was funneling people through the gates into the slums that ringed the city, pressing up against the outer walls like a tide of filth and shit. Edmund tried to keep his revulsion at bay. He had no qualms with taking in the people from the villages, but he knew better than most what would happen to his old home once they were in. Already, other men and women of the watch, as well as a few Paladins, were lining up at the inner city boundary to make sure that no one accidentally stumbled past the areas where they were meant to be housed. Keeping the villagers away from the Cathedral and the cleaner, more open spaces of Illux was Castille's idea, and Edmund hated him for it.

Castille was a man from the inner city, most likely born to some ancient family with a name and a history they traced back to a time when the gods walked the Mortal Plane. Those types looked down their noses at the people of the slums and the villages like they were a lesser race. Captain Redrick was cut from the same cloth, although his chosen profession had certainly earned him the ire of his brethren who no doubt wished he had been armored in white plate like his forebears. Paladins didn't beget lesser men, after all.

*Damn the lot of them.*

Edmund had joined the City Watch to help ease the suffering of the people in the slums, an insurmountable task if there had ever been one. A few months ago he had decided to forgo the entire ordeal and enlist with the Paladins, something he wanted to do since he had just been a boy. Only fools and cravens joined the City Watch, he had been told growing up. Sometime over the course of his training he had sparred with the recently minted General Trent, another man who was once a boy from the slums. Although they hadn't known each other before they each took service to the city, their paths had crossed once or twice prior to that day. After easily defeating the lesser warrior, Trent had convinced Edmund he could do more for the people of the slums as a member of the Watch than he could as a Paladin. Looking at the burden that the slums were facing today, and being powerless to do anything about it, he wasn't sure that Trent had been right.

A woman in the crowd tripped and fell, a wailing babe clutched desperately in her arms. She braced herself to prevent the child from taking any harm from the fall, at her own expense it seemed. The pressing mass seemed to be ignoring her as they continued into the city, most walking around her, though Edmund thought he saw one or two step over, or even on, her.

"Fill in!" he shouted over the cacophony at his closest two men.

Leaving his sword sheathed, but hoisting his shield, Edmund fought his way through the throngs of refugees to the woman, knocking people back where he had to. He meant them no harm, but he wanted the others to know that they needed to stay out of his way. There was no other hope of saving the woman. When he reached her, he saw she was battered and bleeding, though the child seemed to be unharmed.

"Get back!" he shouted. "Make way! Damn you, make way!"

His shield connected with a man's nose, rending flesh and sending blood spurting. That got the attention of most of the passersby who now gave the woman ample space. The wounded villager stumbled back cursing, but his companions bore him off before he could attempt to retaliate. Edmund reached down to the woman and gave her his hand, pulling her to her feet. Her baby was wailing, he noticed finally; the sound had until then been mostly drowned out by the murmur of the crowd. Edmund didn't release the woman's hand when she had fully risen, instead keeping his iron grip to pull her from the river of people to the line of City Watchmen and beyond.

Once they were away from the crowd he spoke to her. "You were hurt. Do you require any healing? The child?"

"Oh no," she muttered. "I will be fine. I have been through worse. My son is just hungry. We left with little food as soon as we heard what happened to Marna. Will we be safe here?"

*I doubt it.*

"You and your son will be safe from Demons and Accursed here, miss. It's the slums you ought to worry about. You may stick with me today if you need. What's your name?"

"Willa," she said dejectedly. "And my son is Ajax. Where will we be staying my lord?"

*Don't start with the titles. I'm no better than you.*

"The people of Illux have been instructed to allow refugees from the villages to quarter with them. The City Watch will be erecting makeshift tents in the streets for those who don't find lodging."

As the look on Willa's face turned even more distressed Edmund remembered someone he had promised to look after while the army was gone from the city. He had too many responsibilities at the moment.

"Are you able to work? Can you wash clothes?"

"Yes, my lord. Why do you ask?"

"I have a friend, or at least the mother of a friend, who might take you and your boy in. She's an older woman named Elise. I will take you to her when the crowds stop pouring in. Until then, stay behind me, and keep up."

Willa nodded and fell into step behind Edmund, quietly cooing to Ajax under her breath. The red-faced little boy didn't seem to want to stop fussing. The trip to the city had likely been hard on them both, and it was doubtful they had had much to eat in the last few days. Edmund's stomach twisted in knots when he thought about telling her that the food ration would be just enough to keep you alive, but never enough to stop the hunger. The city barely had enough food to feed itself, let alone another several hundred people. It was likely that the refugees had eaten better on the road than they would in the coming days. It wouldn't be long before the rations were distributed, and once that happened the members of the City Watch would see just how loving the followers of the Light really were.

The trio moved back toward City Watch's line, where Edmund could better observe the influx of refugees. He wished they had planned for this contingency earlier. Above, the sun was starting to lower itself—soon they would need to close the gates for nightfall. There was no way that Castille would authorize leaving the gates open past dusk, no matter how many villagers were camped outside. It was simply too dangerous—if the men and women on the walls couldn't see an approaching enemy, it might be too late for them to shut the gates by the time it arrived. Edmund imagined the people on the far side of the city had begun filing into homes that weren't theirs, or setting up tents on every side street and privy trench.

This woman and her son would be much better off nestled into that tiny hovel with Elise. Trent had been right of course, that old crone had not taken lightly to his attempts to relocate her to somewhere more secure before the villagers arrived. It hadn't helped that he didn't come and talk to her himself, and those he had sent had been chased off in their attempts. As a compromise, Edmund had stationed one of his men to stand watch near the entrance of her house—without her knowing of course—to prevent anyone entering without her consent. He wasn't about to let some ruffian from outside the city to take over the childhood home of Trent, not after he gave his word to keep her safe. Edmund imagined that the hardest part about getting Willa and Ajax to safety would be convincing Elise to take them in. From what he had been told, she was a handful, and had been somewhat embittered that Trent hadn't seen her off himself before he had marched off to war. A fool's errand she had called it. A trap.

*That woman should be the one running the city.*

A watchman named Jarl approached Edmund with a scowl plastered across his face. He rubbed his beard thoughtfully as he walked. When Jarl neared Edmund he nodded in deference before speaking.

"This comes straight from the top, sir. Captain Redrick has been ordered by Castille himself to seal the gates."

"What? Why? There must be hundreds still outside!" Edmund gasped.

"They say we won't have the room, or the food, to support any more refugees. The rations that we are going to hand out today are already going to be less than what we thought."

"You leave the gate open. I need to see Redrick about this myself."

Edmund spun about and began making his way toward the inside of the city. The Captain of the City Watch would most likely be just inside the barriers keeping the inner city separated from the slums. He was no coward, but Edmund knew he couldn't stand to be so close to such riffraff. Even so, there was no way he could honestly wish to leave that many people outside to die. Redrick was a hard man, but he was not a cruel one. Castille on the other hand…

"Will we have enough to eat?" Willa shouted over the raucous crowd.

"I'll make sure of it," Edmund muttered.

*Even if they have to eat from my own table.*

Ahead where the cluttered and leaning houses of the slums began to thin and the paving stones began to show, Edmund saw a tight cluster of watchmen. They were gathered beyond the wooden barricades that had been hastily erected in the street. The wooden wall could be removed from the inside if need be, but Edmund had the feeling that Castille was going to try and make these barricades permanent. As he approached, several of the guards turned and rushed the barricade, thinking at first he was a lost villager looking for a home. When they recognized him, several stood at attention and pulled the barricade apart at the center to make way for him.

"Where is Redrick?" Edmund asked when they were through the barrier.

"The *Captain*," a man corrected, "is just up the street, issuing orders to the men preparing the food dispersal."

"Stay here," Edmund said to Willa and Ajax. Then, turning to the man who had spoken before, "Take me to him."

The man turned and led the way up the street, away from the tumult behind them. Here the city was unnaturally quiet, most of the civilians having cleared the street at the orders of the Paladins and the Watch. Castille was taking no chances that they would get in the way of his men corralling the new additions to the city as efficiently as possible. The silence was only broken by the sounds of the cobblestones under their feet and some carrion birds above. Even Ajax seemed to have stilled.

"Captain!" Edmund shouted when he saw the man.

Redrick turned and grimaced at him. He was an older man, his dark-brown skin lined and wrinkled from too many years managing this city. His once black beard was lined with snow, tracing his face like a small glow. He motioned dismissively at the men beside him, dispersing them in an instant. As Edmund approached Redrick crossed his arms over his chest and sighed.

"Edmund. Why are you not overseeing the closure of the gate?"

"Because the gate isn't being closed."

Redrick ground his teeth but didn't respond. Instead he turned to the man who brought Edmund to him. "Make sure the gates are closed immediately. We cannot bear anymore villagers."

"Are you a servant of the Light? Why then would you leave the innocents out there to die?" Edmund asked.

"Castille was very clear. We do not have the food, nor do we have the space. The gate must close." Redrick nodded and the other man ran off with the message.

"We would have both the food and the space if we allowed them into the inner city. The slums alone cannot hold the influx—"

"I know because of your history you have a different perspective than I, but the truth here is that we have few options. With any luck, the Seraph and her army will return victorious in a few more days."

Edmund's heart sank. He hadn't wanted to admit it before, but he knew deep down that things would not be that simple. Life in the slums had taught him that much. The Seraph and her armies had been gone for days, and there had been absolutely no word since they had left. No outriders had come bringing news of the battle, no wounded had been sent back to recover. The only news had come from the western villages early that day when they had flooded into the city. It sounded like nothing had gone according to plan.

"What do we tell the people locked outside the walls? What do we tell those inside who we don't have the food to feed?"

"We tell them that war is painful, and this is price that the faithful must pay to be victorious."

The two men stared at each other in silence for several moments.

Suddenly, there were shouts in the distance back toward the closest barricade. From where they stood, neither Edmund nor Redrick could see what was happening. There was no wind to carry the words that men yelled to them, but the anger in the sounds was nearly palpable. Redrick motioned to Edmund and began sprinting toward the source of the disturbance. For his age, Redrick was able to keep pace with the far younger Edmund better than the other man would have assumed. When the two City Watchmen reached the barricade they saw throngs of villagers and city-folk alike pressing against the wooden structures and lobbing stones and other less desirable objects at the men on the other side. They shouted and snarled like beasts, but when Edmund looked into their eyes, he only saw starving men. Edmund looked over his shoulder and noticed Willa was cowering in the entryway of a house, clutching Ajax desperately against her breast.

Redrick quickly pulled a man away from the barricade and shook him violently.

"What is happening here? What are they doing?" Redrick barked.

"T-they began to attack our men when the gates were closed. Some of them had family locked on the outside. Then some of them heard that there wouldn't be enough food for them all and Infernaak broke loose."

*How did they not know this would happen?*

"Well don't just stand there you fool!" Redrick yelled. "Push these savages back! We have been ordered to keep them from the center of the city! By the order of Castille they will not enter these sacred streets!"

Almost at the same instant that the barricade broke under the force of the pressing masses, swarms of yelling civilians began to surround them from the rear as well. Before any of the City Watch realized what was happening they were surrounded. Some of the villagers sported broken pieces of wood or loose stones, while others had gathered weapons that most likely had come from fallen members of the Watch. Edmund cursed. It hadn't taken long for it to become complete and utter chaos.

As he was drawing his sword, Edmund heard the screams of Willa over the sounds of the violence. Edmund twisted about to look for her. Mobs like this never showed mercy to the helpless. Behind him an angered man raised a blunted blade to crack Edmund over the head. The City Watchman struck the blunted weapon with his own sword so hard that the weapon fell from the man's hands. Edmund followed through by crunching his attackers nose with the pommel of his sword. Blood spurted everywhere. The villager cursed and staggered back, falling into the crowd.

*I cannot kill them. I must not.*

Another villager charged him, swinging wildly with a wooden pole. He cut the pole in two and kicked the woman in the stomach, sending her to her knees. Tears streamed down her face and a string of curses flowed from her lips. Her eyes looked at him like he was one of them. Like he was from the inner city. Pushing past her, Edmund made his way toward where he heard Willa screaming moments before. Most of the villagers he shouldered past moved away from him with little resistance, cowering from the raised steel and the look in his eye. He wasn't from the inner city, and in this instance that made him more dangerous.

Finally, he reached the doorway when he saw Willa. Blood covered the ground around her body, a large stone lying close by, covered in gore from her head. As he got near, he almost slipped on the slick paving stones of the entryway. She wasn't breathing. There was no sign of Ajax. Quickly casting about, Edmund spotted a man whose hands were covered in blood, moving away from hovel back into the mass of combatants on the street. Breaking into a sprint, Edmund bowled through villager and City Watchman alike as he closed in on the murderer. His ears rang with the pumping of his blood, drowning out the chaos that surrounded him. Never before in all of his years at his post had ever felt such rage. Edmund caught the man by the nape of the neck, swinging him about in the way he would pick up a kitten from the ground. His sword thrust through the man's stomach before he even had a chance to meet the man's gaze.

The villager looked confused as he fell off the blade, his hands covered in even more blood now. "The inner city bitch," he mumbled as he collapsed onto the street.

"She was one of you," Edmund spat.

*She was one of us.*

Behind him, a woman started to scream, louder than any of the others in the melee. This voice he did not recognize, but something about it drew his attention. When Edmund finally looked from the dead man on the street to source of the screams he saw a blood-covered Ajax in the strange woman's arms. The woman herself was near collapse, a dozen wounds covering her neck and face. Delirium played across her slack features. As she fell, Edmund was there, pulling Ajax from her arms. The babe's breathing was shallow, but the child was alive. The City Watchman moved away from the killing-ground to the safety of another doorway. The clash of steel echoed from behind.

He kicked open the door and forced his way into the house. A man rushed down the steps from above, screaming and waving his arms wildly. Edmund ignored whatever the man was saying and thrust Ajax upon him. The confused man stopped yelling and reflexively cradled the child close. He didn't even seem to notice the blade of Edmund's crimson sword leveled at his face.

"Keep this child safe on the floor above. I will return for him when this is done. If you live, and he does not, gods help me I will nail you to the gates of this city and let their opening tear you apart."

Without another word Edmund went back into the street, flinging his way into the mass of people. It wasn't in his nature to threaten people like that. His claim of allowing the gates to tear the man in half hadn't even been original, anyone who knew their history would know that was the fate that befell the Seraph Arkos when Arendt overthrew him. Still, Edmund was no longer himself. He was something else entirely in that moment.

His first assessment of the carnage told him all he needed to know. It was clear that the Watch would soon lose this engagement. The villagers were too many, and they fought with the cruelest master whipping at their heels: hunger. He shouldered into the crowd again, kicking and punching his way to where he last saw Redrick. Even with the bloodlust upon him, he refused to kill unnecessarily, choosing instead to maim and disable where he could. Other Watchmen soon saw him and began to gather around, cutting a swath through the crowd.

"Don't kill them!" Edmund cried out. "The Gods of Darkness wish to divide us. Do not kill them!"

Images of Willa and the dying man flashed through his mind. His hand tightened on his sword.

Soon they had pushed through to Redrick who was surrounded by a pile of corpses. The captain was covered in blood from wrist to shoulder. Almost as suddenly as they had swarmed, the villagers began to flood in other directions, leaving the barricade free of obstruction. Edmund approached Redrick, shouting orders to the men and women that had followed him.

"Restore the barricade!" Edmund barked.

Redrick snarled like an animal, looking about for another villager to lash out at. It was then that the stone struck him in the head, sending him to his knees. By the time Edmund was there to catch him, he was gone. A solitary stream of blood flowed between his eyes and down the front of his face. Edmund kneeled there, cradling the body of the dead commander of the City Watch, surveying the carnage around them. One of the nearby buildings had caught fire, and now some of his Watchmen were rushing to put it out. Injured and dead villagers and Watchmen were strewn about the street, but it seemed that the bulk of rioters had dispersed.

"What do we do know, Captain?" a man asked.

Edmund stared at him blankly.

# Chapter III

*He was falling. Tumbling end over end. The world spiraled around him so much that he couldn't tell up from down. He faded in and out of the light, darkness overtaking him again and again, but never freeing him from the madness of falling. He could hear nothing but the wind whipping in his ears. It deafened him. Soon his senses were so numbed that he might as well have been in total silence. He didn't know how high up he was, nor how far he was to fall before splattering on the earth.*

*-Trent-*

*The voice whipped past him, like the wind in his ears, yet he heard it clearly. It whispered to him, something that had once been his name.*

*Now he had no name. Nothing but the fall.*

*Faces fluttered past him in the air as he tumbled, faces of those he had lost. Terric. His mother. Devin. They opened their mouths to speak to him but no sounds came out. The wind in his ears drowned out whatever words they wished to impart. Each of them looked longingly at him, sadness filling their eyes. He looked through the faces for Gil, but never saw him. Neither did he see Ren, nor his father…*

*-Trent-*

*The spinning continued. The faces vanished. He tried to right himself, tried to gain some orientation to the earth and sky. He failed. A new face appeared, this one remaining in the center of his vision no matter which way he turned. The woman was plain, yet unnaturally beautiful. She looked familiar, yet he couldn't recognize where he had seen her before. She looked like his mother. She looked like Ren. She looked like the goddess.*

*Arra. The goddess who had torn the sky asunder and smote their enemies into the earth. He couldn't remember why thoughts of her gave him pause. She had done something to him. She had killed the Herald and broken the army of the enemy. Then she had...*

*He couldn't remember.*

*-Trent-*

*He looked at the face of the woman again, floating before him. She was mouthing something to him. He could almost hear her, not over the wind, but whispering in his mind. She was trying to comfort him. And to warn him. Then she vanished. With her disappearance the spinning stopped. He could finally tell up from down.*

*He wasn't falling. He was rising.*

Trent opened his eyes.

Before him, everything had a hazy glow, as if he was looking at it from underwater. Slowly, he tried to sit upright. His head ached, which he expected after the dream he had just awoken from. What he didn't expect was for his back to ache too. If a sword was being pounded flat on an anvil behind his temple, then the heat of the forge was between his shoulders. The pain was stronger than it had ever been in his life. He tried to reach back to feel what was wrong, but that only made matters worse.

His memories of what had transpired to bring him to this point were murky to say the least. The battle had been lost, that much he knew for certain. Ren had fallen. Then Arra had split the sky and routed the host of the enemy. What had happened after that was nothing but a broken dream of rising through the air. Though it hadn't been pleasant, he was thankful that he no longer dreamt of the dove and the vulture, not now he had lived it.

*Where is Arra? Where is Ren? Where am I?*

As if his mind had been read, a voice softly spoke to him. "Trent? You are finally awake."

Trent started in shock. That voice was one he had almost given up on hearing ever again. His head swiveled to the left where he saw Ren rising to a seated position. Her once shining armor was dented and blackened, cracked in multiple places, and covered in blood. It was a miracle that anyone wearing that armor could still draw breath. The woman herself looked groggy, but otherwise seemed stronger than Trent had seen her since the battle had begun. Her eyes regarded him coolly. He had never seen her look at him like that before. There was a curiosity behind those dark orbs, and something else he couldn't place. The glow of the room bathed her ebony skin with a halo of gold. It was then he paid attention to the room in which they sat, if one could call it a room, for it seemed to have no windows or doors, and looked as if it was made of glowing tree branches.

Realizing he had spent an inordinate amount of time before speaking to his lady, he dumbly opened his mouth. "My-my lady, I thought you were dead." He nearly choked as said the words.

He tried to stand but faltered at the last moment and landed on one knee. Trent gritted his teeth. Salvaging the embarrassing moment as best he could, Trent bowed his head in deference. It wasn't that he was weak—other than the pain in his head and back, he felt a strength he didn't know he possessed— No, his stumbling was due to a new lack of balance he couldn't account for.

"There is no need for formalities, Trent," Ren said. "Not anymore."

He looked up at her, standing over him now. The white of her wings hung unmoving at the edges of his vision, not moving. For some reason he felt that the wings were not attached to her. In that moment he felt a sense of vertigo, and nearly lost his balance again. The Seraph lowered her hands and pulled Trent to his feet. She must have noticed the confusion that was undoubtedly on his face. Her hand caressed his cheek, her soft fingers currently free from metal gauntlets.

"Where are we?" he asked.

"You still don't understand. Trent, look at your shoulders."

The tone of her voice was not stern or commanding, but almost motherly. Trent did as he was asked, looking over his shoulder on his right side. What he saw brought a mild cry to his lips. Sprouting from his back was a white wing, just like the ones attached to the woman before him. His mind raced, but he couldn't accept what he was seeing. His head snapped to look over his other shoulder, from which hung the wing's twin. Instinctively Trent ran his fingers through his long red hair, brushing the strands within his vision. Each had turned starkly white.

"I-I am a Seraph? How?" The strength in his voice was failing. "This cannot be."

"It can, and it is," Ren said matter-of-factly. "Ravim is dead. The Fallen One killed him. There is no Pact of the Gods any longer. That is why Arra broke through Aenna and saved us. As she cradled me, I don't know if she thought I was dying, or if she knew I could be saved and just didn't care. Either way, she chose to imbue you with her power and her blood. Since I survived there are now two of us, and no Grey God to say that there should not be."

"Then that means we are on the Divine Plane?" Trent asked.

"Yes. We are on the upper levels of Ayyslid, Fortress of Light. This is the sanctum of the gods whom you and I have spent our lives worshipping. The gods are below, waiting for Arra to pass on from the realms of creation."

"Pass on?"

"When she discovered the treachery of the Fallen One she was severely injured. The others do not believe she will last much longer. When she dies, she will not rejoin the High God as us mortals will.

She will simply cease to be."

Ren choked out that last part. Her eyes held the familiar glaze of an impending loss. She was certainly closer to the goddess than Trent ever could have been. Ren had been in communication with the Gods of Light since Trent was a boy. Trent had always favored the goddess since his induction to the ranks of the Paladins, due to some connection he couldn't quite explain. It wasn't uncommon for Paladins to have a patron god they favored more than the other two, though there wasn't usually any practical use for it. Even so, her impending loss didn't have the effect on him he would have expected. Even though Arra had been the one to turn him into a Seraph. He still couldn't believe it. It all felt like another of his dreams. One of the last true powers of the world was dying just feet from him, and yet he felt hollow.

*I have cried all of the tears I have left.*

With little thought or outward signs of what he was intending to do, Trent leaned into Ren, kissing her hard on the mouth. He didn't know why he did it, and somewhat expected to have his advance scorned. Before he had made contact he was already regretting following impulse. To his surprise, not only did Ren kiss him back, but she grabbed him and pulled him close, clutching him into her arms. In moments she was the one in complete control. They stood entwined like that for several minutes, neither choosing to break the embrace.

Like all good things, it did end, and when it did neither seemed to wish to speak of it. He had finally accomplished something he had hoped for nearly his entire adult life, and now he couldn't even find the words to speak of it. In what had seemed like only a matter of moments, Trent's entire world had been changed. As he silently followed the woman he loved out of the room, Trent mused it wasn't just his world that had changed, but all of creation. When Ren approached the wall the living wood split apart without a single word or touch. The branches that were so tightly entwined that they had been seamless, and now they unwound into a doorway that looked like it had always been present. They passed through the door and stepped out into the hall beyond. Within moments, branches were lowering them down to another floor, one Trent assumed was the ground level of the fortress.

Standing in the middle of the large open room were two glowing figures, armored in metal that scattered light in a myriad of colors. Both figures, a man and a woman, were gold of skin and white of hair. Reflexively, Trent brushed his own hair in front of his eyes again. Trent knew these to be Samson and Luna, the two remaining Gods of Light. Lying on the floor between them, propped up by several writhing branches, was the Goddess Arra. Arra was covered in silver blood, and it pooled on the floor underneath her. Resting across her lap was her giant greatsword. Behind the goddess a great white tiger padded back and forth, eyeing the newcomers cautiously.

Upon seeing the scene Trent was finally filled with the emotion that had eluded him before. His eyes grew hot as he gazed upon the dying form of the being he had prayed to all his life. She was his savior, and the savior of Ren. She had bestowed him with her blood, blood that now soaked into the earth below her. And soon she would be no more. The two Seraphs approached the side of their gods and kneeled.

Neither spoke, Ren due to respect, Trent simply being awestruck at being in the presence of such power. The air seemed to be electrified around him, as if he was in middle of channeling a blast of energy at a Demon. His skin prickled, and his body was wracked with faint shivers. There was no way that any of this could be real. Once more he was plagued with self-doubt. The power radiating off each of the gods was a palpable force that nearly made him ill. His eyes drifted toward the pool of silver blood, his mind jumping to the fact that this same liquid now flowed through his veins.

*Trent.*

The newly-made Seraph nearly jumped from his skin. He looked around from god to god, but they still seemed to be ignoring him. Their eyes were on Arra, as they had been. None were speaking, not to him, Ren, or each other. Where had he heard the voice? Was he going mad?

Trent. You can hear my voice because you carry my blood.

He finally looked at Arra. The dying goddess was staring directly at him. Her eyes were glossy, and her golden skin had lost much of its luster. Yet her lips had curled into a faint smile.

"Rise, my champions," she said weakly.

Samson snorted as Trent and Ren rose.

"Now we get to the heart of it," the god intoned. His voice was rough, like the rumbling of the earth. "You made this man a Seraph, knowing full well that it would not have been up to you to decide who would next bear the blood. And now, behold, both of our Seraphs were chosen by you, and this one doesn't even carry the blood of Luna or myself."

"My mistake—" Arra began.

"Will be our undoing. The rest of us will be challenged by the ramifications of your mistakes for the millennia to come, while you fade from this place," Luna chided.

"There is no Pact any longer," Arra sighed. "Desperate measures had to be taken."

Trent tried to follow the meaning of their words, but found himself getting lost. He had not been privy to all of the machinations of these three as Ren had. She surely understood what was happening better than he. Beside him, he could feel Ren bristle at the harsh words of their deities. Even in the face of such power she did not show fear. Perhaps, the length of time she had been exposed to such things had made them commonplace. Ren had been speaking with the gods since Trent was just as boy, after all.

"Now we have two failures of ours to lead our armies. Armies which have been smashed," Samson growled.

"Ren fought valiantly for you!" Trent heard himself say.

He felt Ren grab his arm tightly to bid him to be quiet. Samson and Luna glowered at him, but, surprisingly, neither of them spoke.

Trent suddenly felt flush and his eyes fell back to the wounded goddess. Arra was looking at him, smiling again. That was when he noticed that the tiger had come closer, its hackles slightly raised. The beast exuded power, just as the gods did. Trent was sure that this creature could hold its own in a battle even with the bearers of Divine Blood. The goddess must have seen him eyeing the great cat, for she mentioned it when next she spoke.

"This is Divinity. She has been my companion since the High God created this plane. It was her that saved me when the Gods of Darkness ambushed me. I wish you to take her with you when you return to the Mortal Plane."

Ren looked possibly more shocked than the two other gods. Samson clenched his fists and Luna gritted her teeth. Dumbstruck, both Seraphs simply nodded.

"You would introduce another creature to the Mortal Plane that does not belong?" Luna asked in shock. "Those things that you warped half of our army into were not enough tampering with creation for you? Do you have any idea what damage this will cause to the natural order of things? The High God did not create such abominations for a reason."

Arra ignored this comment when she responded, "I do not worry of the ramifications of my actions. Consider my part in this pantheon done. I appreciate your timely intervention to bring us back here, but my time is now at an end. Trent shall be my agent, even after my death, while Ren is still constrained by your foolishness."

*You will need a weapon, Trent. Come closer.*

Trent did as the goddess commanded, though he was still shaken by the sound of another's voice in his head. When he was beside her he kneeled, her silver blood sticking to the armor on his legs. She looked frail this close, not like she had when she had been on the Mortal Plane, sowing salvation and destruction in equal measure. Death affected all magnitudes of being in the same fashion.

Arra lifted her massive sword and placed the hilt in Trent's hands.

He gripped the blade tightly but remained silent.

"I fear this war will reach its final conclusion soon, whatever end that will be. It will not be decided by the actions of the gods alone, but by mortals as well. I intend to bridge the gap between the two and even those odds, Trent. With this blade you will be able to slay even a god."

Samson snorted again. "Has the blood loss made you delirious? In the hands of a mortal that will be nothing more than uncommon steel. Or have you forgotten when Nightbreaker first came?"

"He is right of course," Arra sighed. "But he will not be right for long. I name this blade Godtaker. I pray that more silver blood will join mine on its edge. The time of gods is done, so let it end."

Suddenly, she grabbed Trent by the hands. Her grip was iron. Trent tried to break away but it was no use. He felt akin to a child fighting against a parent.

*Don't struggle Trent. This will be over soon.*

Arra pulled the blade into her chest, filling the room with a blinding light as she did so. Trent squinted hard against the flash, but he was not quick enough. His eyes burned and colors danced before his vision. He could feel the goddess flooding him with energy while her weapon sunk deeper and deeper into her divine flesh. Heat radiated from the blade, burning the flesh of his hands through his gauntlets. Trent's scream mingled with Arra's until both were so intermixed that he couldn't tell his voice from hers. In moments, the light was gone, and with it the heat. Trent's hands stung and his throat was raw. Arra lay motionless on the ground.

The world around them suddenly grew slightly dimmer and less in focus. The effect was disorienting and made Trent slightly dizzy. It was as if he was looking at his surroundings through a thin layer of water. Numbly, he stared down at the blood-covered blade in his hands. He squeezed it tighter, something about it made his entire arm prickle like he was being stung by a swarm of insects.

Trent stood and tried to keep his chest from heaving. The dizziness from a moment before returned, and he retched out what little was in his stomach onto the floor of Ayyslid. Once he wiped his mouth, he tried to gather his thoughts. The Seraph was overcome with emotions he didn't know he was capable of feeling. He held power now. The power to kill a god. He looked over the blade, twisting it in his hands and studying its surface as if it was a foreign object. Trent couldn't help but notice that Samson and Luna seemed to be giving him more space now that he held what could potentially be a god-killing blade. They may have been wise to be cautious, but there was no way he would ever raise his weapon against the Gods of Light. They would have known that if they could listen to his heart as Arra had. It seemed they were right to chide her, for they had no mental link to him like they did to Ren.

"What now?" Trent asked, his voice shaking.

It was silent for several minutes, silent save for the sound of Ren's quiet sobs and the guttural noises made by the tigress. Divinity lightly pawing and nuzzling at Arra's corpse, the silver blood of the goddess staining her fur. Trent tried to ignore the immense sadness he felt by looking for a place to set the sword until he could fix it to his back between his wings. Ren must have noticed his searching for she took Godtaker from him and made it fit to the fastenings that once held his shield. When they were done, both Seraph's again looked expectantly at the two remaining gods.

"I wasn't lying when I said that our army was shattered due to your incompetence," Samson said, no longer as confident or condescending. "We have not gazed through Aenna since we rescued Arra and yourselves. Whether or not the survivors have begun heading toward the city we do not know. Regardless, they are an army no longer. Our best course of action is to send you two back to Illux to begin preparing the city for siege. Perhaps when that is done one or both of you can begin awakening Divine Beasts. The Guardian of Illux will be needed, of that I am sure. If only we still had Ash Company to disrupt the enemy while they regroup."

"It shall be done," Ren said.

"How do we return?" Trent asked.

"The same way you arrived," Luna replied. "The Basin of Aenna. Only through the opening can you be restored in Illux. It is unlikely that the Gods of Darkness will still be sulking about. Let us go now and see to it that this shall be done."

Without further pause the two gods walked to the edge of the room out of the opening that formed before them. Ren followed behind, with Trent bringing up the rear. When he reached the opening in the branches, he looked back at Arra one final time. The big cat still nuzzled at the goddess, right until the branches of Ayyslid wrapped about her and bore her body beneath the wood. It was a surreal sight that Trent imagined would be immortalized in stained glass in the Grand Cathedral one day. Then Divinity let out a cry of anguish Trent almost thought was human. Once she was finished the cat bounded after the small party and left the fortress behind.

The small group continued through the forest for what Trent thought must have been hours. It was slow going, for even with his new wings and the powers of the gods, none could fly on the Divine Plane. The massive trees towered over him, like great wooden gods themselves. At the edges of his vision Trent could see small creatures that passed under the shadows of the foliage, but never quite revealed themselves. Divinity continued to track them from some distance, never truly falling out of sight, but never getting close enough that she could be interacted with. Trent wondered at the wisdom of bringing such an animal with them, especially one that held as much strength as Arra claimed this one did, but he would not ignore the dying wishes of a god.

*A tiger and a blade and her blood. Arra has given me everything she had but godhood.*

Finally, they left the cover of the trees and stepped onto a plain of smooth grey stone. It seemed to stretch on for miles in every direction except for the one from which they came. The seeming infinity of the Divine Plane was enough to make Trent feel more insignificant than he ever had before in his life. Even as a boy in Illux, staring up at the Cathedral for the first time, he had never seen any so enormous. Over his shoulder he noticed the tigress stopping at the forest and looking behind her. After a brief moment, she continued after them again, apparently making up her mind once and for all.

It seemed again like they traveled for an incalculable amount of time. Trent had no way of knowing how much time had passed on the Mortal Plane below, for time here was of no consequence. The light in the sky hadn't changed since they started walking, and he was now sure that it never would. By the time Ren and he returned to the City of Light, the remnants of their army might have already returned before them. That thought brought him pause. If Castille heard of what had transpired on the battlefield before the Seraph's he surely would use the Seraph's disappearance to bring the city fully under his control.

After putting those fears to rest, he saw it. Rising from the plain in the distance was the outline of several objects. They seemed to shimmer at first, like a mirage taking shape. Quickly, he was able to discern what they were as clearly as if they were right in front of him. Farthest away, and off to his left, was a ring of pillars, which must have been at one time the home of the Grey God. Directly ahead of them was giant throne with something at its base. There were no signs of any other figures in the area. It seemed that Samson and Luna were correct, the Gods of Darkness were back in Infernaak, licking their wounds and biding their time.

When they approached the throne, Trent saw that the object at its base was a great basin filled to the brim with silver liquid. Although the surface of the liquid was serene, Trent could tell by looking at it that the substance was thick and viscous—like blood. Indeed, this must have been the Divine Blood of the High God himself, placed here to allow the gods of the Divine Plane to gaze down out of Aenna at the Mortal Plane below. At one time, it was thought the gods all gathered here together to watch the lives and actions of their warriors. Until the battle a few days ago, Trent naively thought they still did this, focused as they were on caring for mortal lives. Now, having met the gods himself, he knew otherwise. Without Ren, they would have no idea of what actually happened below.

*At least the Gods of Darkness are even blinder than they are for now.*

As if reading Trent's mind, Samson spoke. "It will not be long before they create another Herald. You must rally the people of the city quickly. Once you have done that, we will begin the process of awakening the Divine Beasts. Until that time, Luna and I will be waiting in Ayyslid. We cannot risk open battle with them, not yet."

Samson and Luna walked to the edge of the Basin, running their fingers along the edge of the stone. The surface of the liquid shimmered, bringing forth an image of Illux just below the surface. The city appeared in between the ripples, solidifying as they died out. From where Trent stood it almost looked like what he was seeing could be touched, if only he would stick his hand into the silver blood. The Grand Cathedral nearly stuck out of the surface of the blood, it was so near.

"Lean into the blood," Luna said. "Submerge yourself. The transfer will be instant. None of the flash or thunder of when Arra arrived. Your return to the Mortal Plane will not affect the world thus."

Trent looked to Ren, who nodded, still remaining silent. Together they walked up to the edge of the Basin and slowly lowered their heads into the surface of the liquid. Just as his head began to submerge, Trent saw Divinity rising onto her back paws and throwing her bulk over the edge. The blood was warm and cool at the same time. His face prickled in a way that was both painful and pleasurable at the same time. It pulled him down as if powerful hands gripped him. As soon as his head was all of the way under the surface, Trent felt the ground fall out from under him. He saw the image of the city, just as he had seen when he had looked into the Basin, but now it was directly under him. It seemed like he was falling into it, but more graceful.

Then the city melted.

The buildings and streets began to run like melted paint, dripping down the canvas of his vision toward the edges of his sight. Underneath the city was a blinding white light. He knew that this wasn't normal. Something had happened that wasn't supposed to. Moments later the paint streams reformed, but now they made mountains instead of buildings, streams instead of streets. He was no longer floating above Illux-now he was over the Rim.

Trent blacked out.

When he opened his eyes again he was looking up at the sky through a dense canopy of trees.

# CHAPTER IV

The By the time he had the strength to leave the rundown tower for good, the sun had risen overhead, almost to its apex. It now hung beside Aenna, and its heat beat down upon him. Gil had hidden in that grim place for several days, living off the foodstuffs that the bandits had left when they had fled in fear. It wasn't as good of food as he had gotten used to in Marna, but he was thankful for it. If they had thought to pack their belongings he might have had to resort to eating less savory things. As it was, he was able to bury the two dead men in shallow graves just outside the outpost. He hadn't spoken any words over them, but sparing their bodies from carrion creatures or a second life as an Accursed was more mercy than bandits like those deserved.

The days of hallucinations and waking dreams were finally behind him. What was left of his arm had healed, and with it, what was left of his mind. Healing would use more strength than he could spare, so he only amplified what his body would repair naturally. Gil now knew the direction in which Illux lay, just a few weeks walk to the northwest. But with the horse that been left behind however, it would take even less. A feeling a dread hung over him. Somehow he knew that worse things had happened than just the burning of Marna. It was his duty as a Paladin, no matter that he had only one hand, to return to Illux and stand beside Devin and Trent to face the coming darkness head on.

*Only Devin can make the loss of my hand fade.*

Clumsily, Gil gripped on the reins of the horse with his left hand and pulled himself into the saddle. The reins bit into his palm in a way he wasn't accustomed to. The sword he would normally have kept at his side was secured to the saddle bags on his steed so he could draw it forth easier. If the gods were good, he wouldn't need it. The maimed Paladin rubbed the side of the beast's head before turning it in the direction of Illux and urging it onward. The sun was just beginning to lower itself toward his left, leaving him just a few hours to begin his journey. He had wasted most of the day gathering enough strength to leave. It mattered not. The tower was receding behind him now, and he was finally moving forward.

Already his mind was trying to piece together what had really happened since the night Marna had burned. It was clear that the Forces of Darkness had finally decided to strike against Illux as they had in the days of old. Villages could expect the occasional raid, but Illux hadn't been in any real danger since Jerrok was assassinated. If this was truly happening, then that must have meant they no longer lived in fear of the Grey God. It must have been Ravim that died days before when Aenna had dimmed. That meant that there wasn't much time for him to reach Illux and bring them word of what was to come. Hopefully he wasn't too late.

The rest of the day seemed to drag on, no matter how quickly he urged his mount forward. When the sun finally set, he continued his journey for at least another two hours, stopping only to relive himself and allow his horse to drink. He cared little for his own fatigue, but he knew he wouldn't get to Illux in time if he pushed the horse too hard. It was when the moon began inching closer to Aenna, that he settled the horse down beside a rock in a small copse of trees and unrolled the bedding he had taken from the bandits. The sounds of the Wilderness were quiet here; crickets chirping over the sounds of the gentle breeze. For a moment, it was peaceful. Not long after he laid down Gil was asleep. His dreams were dark and restless.

The next day Gil awoke when the first amber rays touched his face. He saddled the horse, ate the last of his food and continued on his way. Wind tossed his braid across his shoulders as he left the trees, the angry sibling of the gentle breeze from the night before. Even the sky seemed more foreboding—dark clouds swirled above, blocking all but the gentle glow of Aenna. Gil swallowed hard. He had never been superstitious, but the weather today was not a good omen of things to come.

After a few hours of riding he found himself upon the road that led to the golden gates of the city. Based upon the general state of disrepair he estimated he was still at least two- or three-days ride away from Illux. Marna was the most southern village, but even it was not too far from Illux that aid could be sent in case of an emergency.

*Little good that did us.*

It seemed as if it had been years since he had ridden on this road. When he had left his assignment to the north in Rinwaithe he hadn't traveled much away from Marna. Indeed, he couldn't remember a time he had traveled at all since the death of their old commander Broderick. After Gil and his friends had dealt with the bandit cult that was plaguing Rinwaithe, he had decided to give up ranging and return to his roots. The plight of those villagers had spoken to him in a way that the others could never have understood. He most likely would have stayed and even died in that village to the north if Ren had not asked him to travel south along this very road. Devin had never forgiven him for choosing the village life over their love. Gil had considered stopping off at Illux on his way south to see Devin and Trent, but the pain of leaving them again would have been too great.

Instead, he had traveled around the City of Light and made his way directly to Marna. Now he headed straight for Illux. Now he would return a failure, and less whole than he had been before.

That evening, as the sun began to set again, Gil saw something in the distance that gave him pause. It seemed as though he could make out the forms of dozens of villagers making their way toward him. At first, he thought he was having a fever-dream again, their presence shocked him so. He hadn't seen any signs of travelers beyond those bandits. He waved his good arm in acknowledgement when they were close enough to see him.

*Why would they be headed this way? Perhaps, word of what happened at Marna has not yet spread.*

One of the villagers rode ahead to see who Gil was. As the outrider got closer, a young woman no older than twenty, she must have realized what Gil was from his size and armor. She wore the traditional tattered garb of a villager, though she kept her had tied tightly in a bun—a fashion of the inner city. The woman turned back to look over her shoulder and motion to those behind her that it was safe. It was only then that she addressed Gil.

"Who are you?" she asked, colder than he would have liked.

"My name is Gil, I am a Paladin of the Light," Gil replied. "I was stationed in Marna. The Herald of the enemy razed it to the ground. The creature took my arm and killed all of those in my charge."

At that last point he motioned with the stump of his right arm, drawing her eyes only for the briefest of moments. She continued to consider him in silence until another rider reached her side, this one an older man with a weather-lined face. His eyes looked Gil over even harsher than she had. The mistrust in his face cut Gil like a knife. The woman whispered to the newcomer before talking to Gil again.

"Word of what happened to Marna is what drew us to Illux," she said. "We were led to believe that none had survived the slaughter." There was an accusation there, thinly veiled behind her words.

"None did," Gil growled. "Why are you questioning me thus? For what reason are you fleeing Illux?"

The man spoke up then. "They closed the gates of the city. It seems that the Paladins left within did not want to share their precious streets with the likes of us, so you'll have to understand that seeing another Paladin doesn't fill us with respect anymore. We were told that this decree was made by a man called Castille. Most of us have family who were able to make it in before they shut the gates, but none of them were able to leave either."

"Or they chose not to," the woman muttered.

"Where are you headed now?" Gil asked. "Surely, you don't think south is safer than north?"

"We are headed as far away from the city as we can. If the army of the Seraph fails, then Illux will fall under siege. There is no safety for us if we are up there cowering outside the walls."

"Army? What army?" Gil asked.

By then most of the others had joined the first two, and the villagers had begun to grumble loudly that their hasty retreat had been halted by some Paladin in the middle of the road. They were right, it seemed that being a Paladin didn't mean even cursory respect from this lot. The man motioned for some of the others to follow him off the road to a suitable location nearby for them to make camp. The woman still sat her horse across from Gil. Her expression had hardly changed, and she would not answer his question while the others were still nearby. Finally, when enough of her companions had left the road she spoke again.

"How long have you been stuck to the south? Since the village burned?" she asked.

"Yes. I haven't seen anyone else until now," he lied.

"When word of what happened to Marna reached the city, it came not long after two rangers brought word of an army gathering near the Great Chasm. It seems that the High God placed events to happen all at the same time."

*Devin and Trent. They found something.*

"It was then that the villages were commanded by the Seraph to evacuate and come to the safety of Illux. The city itself had mostly been emptied out from the gathering of the Army of Light, just as in the stories of the days of old. The Lady Ren and her army marched into the Wilderness days ago, and they haven't been heard from since. We were some of the last to gather outside the walls, and we were turned away."

Gil nearly fell off his horse. His head swam from the revelations that this woman had just provided him with. It seemed that his premonition wasn't wrong about the enormity of events. It also seemed he had wandered about deliriously for far longer than he had realized. What was he to do now? Gil would not be content with finishing his journey to Illux only to hide behind its walls while the army returned victorious. Not while his friends were risking their lives in the battle for the fate of the world. His thoughts clouded suddenly. Once again, he could feel sweat break out upon his brow. He knew he wouldn't be able to reach the army before the inevitable battle was fought. What could he do?

"My name is Jaina," the woman said, finally.

"What?" Gil asked, shocked. "What name did you say?"

"Jaina."

Gil fell from his horse into darkness.

He awoke before the warmth of the fire, Jaina sitting beside him, wiping his forehead with a damp cloth. Her touch was firm but reassuring. Somehow, he knew that there was a hidden strength in this woman that she rarely shared with others. He sat up slowly, fighting back a wave of nausea. Jaina handed him a water skin he drained lustily. When it was emptied, he handed it back over to her, and tried to stand. She held him down, proving he was weaker than he thought.

"You shouldn't get up yet," she said, firmly. "You were dehydrated. It must have been days since you had the right amount of water. Some of the others think that you might have an infection from your injury.

You have been delirious—you've been mumbling my name in your sleep."

"I don't have an infection," Gil replied. "It must have been the water. I-I found some food to keep me going, but I didn't make an effort to get more water other than what the horse needed. And it wasn't your name I was saying. It was…somebody else."

Gil shifted into a more comfortable position, quietly cursing his luck. His weakness would prevent him from making any difference, just as he had made no difference that night in Marna. The Herald had toyed with him then, and the High God toyed with him now. This Jaina would die just like the last one did, and he would be able to do nothing to stop it.

"In the morning we plan to continue south, some even think that we should make for the ruins of Marna. It seems odd, but they think that we will be safe there, that none of the Demons or Accursed will go back to the ruins of a village they already razed. You are welcome to come with us."

"I thought that you didn't want another Paladin around," Gil said.

"We didn't, but I see something about you…It's hard to explain without sounding crazy, but I have the Gift."

Gil nodded. The Gift meant she was touched by the High God and could potentially see visions of the future. It was a rare power, but one that cropped up from time to time. It was said that the last Seraph, Jerrok, had had a Paladin he kept close, who had the Gift. Every child who knew the legends of Daniel Nightbreaker knew of his silent companion Springjack, who was likewise blessed. While some lied about having this power, Gil could tell that this woman spoke truth.

"What have you seen?" he asked.

"Fire. Water. Screams of pain and death. I see you standing before an inferno of your own making, Gil. I see no happiness for you if you continue on the path you have set yourself on."

"Where did the others go?" Gil asked, wishing now he hadn't asked about her visions. "The others from outside the gates. Surely they locked out more than just you all?"

"Some went north, but most made for Seatown. It seemed like the only fortified settlement that could withstand a potential siege besides Illux. My feeling was that south was the safest, so south is where we decided to go."

*Seatown. They must have dozens of Paladins there. Hundreds of men and women that could fight.*

It had been generations since the people of Seatown and the people of Illux had truly been united in anything more than name only but, perhaps, there was a chance they would answer the call of the Seraph to come to Illux's aid. Dark days such as this had a way of bringing people together, or so Gil had always believed. If Jaina was right, and the worst came to pass with Ren's army faltering in the field, then Illux would need more help than whatever paltry force had been left behind. It would take him another week to get there from here, but if he made straight there and ignored Illux altogether he had a chance at not being too late. If Gil could muster another small army in time to return to the city, he could help defend Illux before it was too late. That must have been why the High God had put these people in his path, why Jaina had been given the premonition to head to the south. It was from her lips that he had been presented with a chance at redemption.

"Where will you go?" she asked.

"Where I can make a difference."

# CHAPTER V

The traitor stood beneath the shimmering surface of the Basin, conversing with a Seraph on the Mortal Plane below. Under the silver blood the world seemed calm below in the small village tucked away in the Rim. It was impossible to tell that armies had clashed just days before, that gods had died. Vardic didn't recognize the place, nor the man who spoke to Lio as if they were old friends. The man was a Seraph, his white hair was kept short above his pale face. He certainly was not the woman who had commanded the Forces of Light in battle from the days before.

"Who is this Seraph?" Vardic muttered, more to himself than his companion.

"He must be one of the Forsaken Ones," Rhenaris replied. "Clearly they were not all hunted down as we were led to believe."

*The Forsaken Ones. Of course.*

He had not thought of those imbeciles for an age. The Forsaken Ones had been those few Seraphs who had been most loyal to Lio before the death of Xyxax. They had been the remnants of those who had served alongside Daniel in the Northern Campaign and other major battles around that time. When Ravim had been made the Grey God he instituted the Pact, which declared that only one bearer of Divine Blood in service to each of the pantheons could walk the Mortal Plane. This meant that hundreds of Seraphs and Heralds had to be put to the sword by their gods. Many of them submitted willingly, even among the Heralds. But not these. They had felt that their patron god had been wronged, and they would not submit to the will of the remaining Gods of Light. So, they fought and fled, wreaking havoc among the followers of Light and Darkness. The one Seraph who had been ordained to rule Illux spent the next decade hunting them to believed extinction. It seemed she had failed.

"If this is truly one of the Forsaken Ones then he shares blood with Lio," Vardic said. "If the Fallen One knew of this Seraph for all of this time, and did nothing to turn him over to Ravim…"

He trailed off, his anger rising to the surface. Never had he trusted this pretender, but neither had he believed that the Fallen One could have been capable of returning to his roots as a God of Light. He had been condemned to the Darkness, and that is where he was to stay. It was not possible he returned to the Light, but for what other reason would he still remain in contact with a Seraph, even one branded a heretic by the Fourth Spire?

As they shared no blood with the creatures below, nor were they engaged in a prayer, Vardic and Rhenaris had no way of hearing what was being said. It mattered not. The images in the Basin were damning enough. Clearly the Fallen One and this Seraph shared some kind of common goal.

"He plans to betray us, just as we feared," Rhenaris said, quietly. The spines that covered her head and neck bristled. "I do not know what he is playing at, but we cannot let our guard down. Now more than ever. For all we know Arra was in on this scheme and her wounds were never meant to be so grievous."

Vardic tensed at that name. He walked with a slight limp from the cat that had come to the goddess's rescue. The thing had surprised them all, injuring each of the Gods of Darkness before they had time to respond. It was inconceivable that such a simple creature could have done so much damage to a god. The tigress attacked, then Arra was gone, throwing herself into the Basin so she could interfere on the Mortal Plane below. The Gods of Darkness were forced to ignore the great cat and return to Infernaak, lest Samson and Luna appear having followed after Arra.

"Doubtful," he said. "We both felt her loss these days past. If she was working with him, he never would have sacrificed her so. The two had been much closer than that in the time before his condemnation. He would have made sure that neither of us has injured her."

*Perhaps, he was having her and that Seraph Daniel both.*

He looked up and down at his companion then, a familiar stirring brought forth by the sight of her. It was doubtful he would ever be able to enjoy her companionship the way he had in the days of old. Her grey skin called to him, and he imagined what she looked like with what little armor she wore removed. When Xyxax had lived the Gods of Darkness had engaged in debauchery of all kinds, but since the Pact the surviving two had spent less than a few passing moments together. Trust had grown frail between them, and with limited contact lust had lessened as well. Perhaps, when this was ended he would try again. For the end was coming, of that he was sure.

The Fallen One and his servant were standing before a great tree, with golden bark and scarlet leaves. It towered over all of the other trees throughout the village, a scion of greater forebears. The ground beneath the tree was smooth and cleared of all other life. It must have been one of Ravim's seals. Was it possible that the Fallen One planned to awaken his own army of Light now that their Herald and Akklor had been slain?

Vardic could no longer contain his rage. He fastened his great barbed spear to his back and gripped the end of the Basin, peering deeper into its surface. He could feel the energy of the High God's blood radiating off its surface. Hovering in front of Lio and the Forsaken

One he could see the vague outline of his own horned visage glowering back at him. He took a breath and began to plunge himself into the Divine Blood. At the last moment, just as his face began to touch the cool liquid, he felt Rhenaris grab him by the shoulder and yank him backward with such force that he collapsed into a heap on the smooth stone.

"What are you doing?" he spat, pulling himself up.

"Stopping you from making a fool of yourself. Lio has the blood of three of our number on his hands. You charging down there would only give him a fourth."

Vardic bristled again, but realized she was right. Rhenaris had always had a more calculating mind than he. Pride would be his downfall. He did not want to end up like Xyxax. The Fallen One was more of an adept fighter than any of them were willing to admit. Xyxax had possibly been the most powerful of all of the lesser gods, and he was smashed into the Mortal Plane like a rock falling from the stars. Vardic stood and turned his back on Rhenaris, making his way back toward Infernaak to better decide what was needed.

Then he heard it.

The Basin boiled and the Divine Blood surged upward in a fountain of silver. Before the droplets of liquid life rained back down the Fallen One was stepping out from the lip of the Basin onto the ground below. The surging and sizzling of the silver surface stopped almost as quickly as it had begun. Lio's face flashed an expression of rage before being replaced with an uneasy calm. It was obvious he knew why his new companions stood where they did.

*I must put him at ease.*

"How was the Mortal Plane, brother?" Vardic asked, innocently. "How do our forces rebuild without the Herald?"

"They do not," the fallen god replied harshly. "Some of the Demons attempt to gather what Accursed they can, but many have simply fled into the hills at the foot of the Rim, or even to the lands beyond the Great Chasm."

That almost surprised Vardic. The Great Chasm was the scar that marred the Mortal Plane where Xyxax had been struck down by the Fallen One over a thousand years before. That place was shunned even by Demons, the taint of that deed was so strong. Almost none dared to venture to the unknown lands beyond.

"What do you suggest we do then?" Rhenaris's voice was saccharine. Could she be trusted now?

"We cannot rush into choosing a new Herald," Vardic responded, before Lio was able to. "Lest we are left with the failure of the previous choice."

The jab was meant to rankle Lio enough to remove any doubts as to whether Vardic and Rhenaris were onto him. All three of them knew that the last Herald had only failed because he gone up against a goddess. Still, the insult against Lio would have been expected if all had been well.

"He was not my choice," Lio whispered. "Merely my tool. I agree with you, *brother*. We must wait to find a Herald who will adequately serve our needs in this new world that I have created. With Arra gone, we can expect the other two to wage war to the fullest extent they think themselves able. I fully expect them to begin awakening Divine Beasts of their own to defend their precious city with. We must be ready for that eventuality."

"Then what is your suggestion?" Vardic asked.

"I have candidates in mind for the next Herald. But before that, we must begin building our forces ourselves. We need to replenish the ranks of Accursed. Too many were lost in the battle, even if we could get the survivors to regroup."

"How will we accomplish this?" Rhenaris asked. "We cannot take any more villagers. They have all fled to the city. Seatown may be too fortified for our servants to take by force until more of them are gathered."

"Did you not wonder how I was able to amass such a large force before?" the Fallen One asked. "The slow war of attrition that our

Heralds had been losing since the Purge certainly did not help our numbers. Yet the two of you never considered how I could have gained such a large force so quickly?"

*Just get on with it.*

"It seems that I have more to owe Xyxax than this scar upon my face," he continued. "Shortly after having the last Seraph killed, I sent the Herald to explore the far south. I knew that something had driven Arendt and his forces on their march back to Illux after they had nearly wiped our troops from the Mortal Plane. Something scared them so much that they returned to hide behind the walls of Illux and await the slaughter. I was not wrong."

"So, it's true?" Rhenaris gasped.

"What?" Vardic was lost.

"Xyxax was nothing if not wise in the ways of war. He hid an entire army of Demons and Accursed after the Northern Campaign far to the south, farther than any other mortals had ever ventured before or since. Thousands of them had been standing in wait for one of us to command them to march north."

*That can't be. How is that even possible?*

"They have been waiting for a thousand years?" Vardic asked, incredulously. "I can believe that of the Accursed, but the Demons? Surely, they were driven mad."

Demons were possessed of the same cruel intelligence of any mortal man. A lack of purpose for any period of time, especially one as long as the Fallen One claimed they had been waiting should have forced them to madness, rendering them no better than the beasts they commanded.

"It seems they kept themselves entertained through infighting," Lio said. "They had created a hierarchy of their own, assuming that none of us would ever come for them, even though they didn't dare to venture north and face the wrath of Xyxax for disobeying him. I only took a small portion of their number back to the north, and most of those were Accursed. The Demons are still waiting there with the rest of their forces, for now they know that I will return to claim and use them as a second wave when the siege on Illux begins."

Vardic and Rhenaris were both dumbstruck. It was clear that Rhenaris had some inkling that Xyxax had done this thing, as incredible as it seemed. He must have mentioned something about it to her after the Northern Campaign had ended. Vardic was incensed that he had known nothing about it. Had Xyxax told Ravim as well? Either way, this was the advantage that their forces always had from the very beginning: the powers of Darkness brought immortality, something that the Light only tasted with Divine Blood. These Demons and Accursed were almost as old as the gods themselves. Many of them had fought alongside Divine Beasts. They remembered when Vardic had walked the Mortal Plane and sown death and destruction among the weak and unwilling. They remembered serving under real power.

"We must gather then," he blurted. "We cannot allow them to wait down there another moment. Perhaps, it is from these that we can create the next Herald. We have found real power here, and we must use it."

"I have found real power here," Lio said. "And like all of the other power I have at my disposal, I will use it to destroy my enemies. All of them will pay for what has been done to me."

Vardic cast a glance at Rhenaris. He saw that her spines had begun to bristle slightly. It seemed they were right, the Fallen One would turn on them very soon. He was no longer only a God of Darkness. It was only a matter of time before his madness turned its gaze in their direction.

*Unless we kill him first.*

"Yes," Vardic agreed. "The great injustice of your fall will be corrected very soon. We will make certain of that. All of the Gods of Light will perish."

# CHAPTER VI

The towering trees had a primal energy about them. It was as if they were as old as the world. Their canopies were dense with leaves, cutting out all but the most stubborn of the sunlight, and their gnarled trunks were three times as wide as his arm-span at least. Trent was reminded instantly of the forests of the Divine Plane above, where Ayyslid sat. There was something else about these trees, however, a feeling that was more sinister than their divine brethren. That feeling came from the mountains themselves, he guessed. It had been these mountains that held the majority of the evils of the world. It was beneath these towering sentinels that Ravim had chained the majority of the Divine Beasts, both of the Light and the Darkness.

*Chains of earth. Chains that are breaking.*

Ahead of the newly made Seraph walked the woman he loved. Her wings were folded back; Nightbreaker hung at her side, its black blade hidden in an ornate scabbard. He had to remind himself she was no longer the only Seraph who walked the Mortal Plane. The thought was still foreign to him, and he imagined that it would be for some time. It was easy to forget he had wings of his own, especially since they had decided to walk out of the mountains rather than fly over the treetops. Something had gone wrong when they had entered into the Basin—someone had prevented them from being transported back to Illux directly. Ren had suggested that it would be too dangerous to fly back when they could be spotted easily from the air. They couldn't risk it until they knew exactly who it was that had meddled with the gods' plans and set them on a different path.

Beside Trent, the great white cat known as Divinity padded along silently; the other reason that the two Seraph's were prevented from flying out of these mountains. Trent did not wish to scorn any gift from the late goddess, but he would have left the cat there if it meant they could have gotten to Illux faster. There was no time to waste on sentimentality. Even so, he marveled at the beast born not of this world. She sniffed and pawed at the ground here and there, taking in smells and sights that must have been as new to her as she was to these mountains. Trent expected that the differences to her between these woods and those in the Divine Plane were even more pronounced than they were to him. Tigers such as her were not found in the Rim, for example. Animals like that were only spoken of in stories, by those who claimed to have traveled beyond the Great Chasm. Her fur was snow-white, striped with coal. It was thickest on her jowls, which could pull back to reveal the largest teeth he had seen on any animal. Feral power radiated off Divinity, and Trent wondered at the wisdom of having such a creature as a traveling companion.

The air here was earthy, tinged with a scent of iron that Trent could only describe as bloody. Memories of the only other time he had traveled past the foothills of the Rim flooded back to him. It had been years ago now, a mission of his own choosing that was fraught with danger. He thought of the cult that had ensnared a small village to the north of Illux, a cult that had tried to fashion a god of their own. There had been blood that day as well. He often wondered if the other survivors still thought of what they had seen as he did.

*Other survivor. Only two of us remain.*

With Gil and Devin dead, Trent had few left he could share any common memories. His history was his own now, a fact which filled him with the utmost regret. Fewer still would be able to relate to him now that he was no longer merely a man. Silver blood flowed through his veins as much as red did. He was now one of the chosen few who could speak for the gods above to the men below. To make matters worse, no gods could actually speak to him any more than they could to any other mortal, not since the very sword he carried drank the lifeblood of the goddess who had made him. No, Trent was truly isolated from both the divine and the mundane.

Mercifully, there was still Ren. Ren, whom he had loved since he was barely older than a boy. Ren, whom he would have died for time and time again if she had let him. Ren, whom it seemed may have loved him back. Doubt still plagued him though. She had not spoken of the kiss since it had happened in the upper reaches of Ayyslid. Ren had most certainly kissed Trent back, but since that time she had shown no signs of affection out of the ordinary. He wondered if she regretted it? Did he do something wrong since then? Trent would wait for her to broach the subject. It was not his place to force the issue.

"What do you think caused us to end up here?" he asked, finally, hoping that the hours of walking might have given her new insight.

Ren stopped walking and turned to him, crouching to run her fingers through the white fur of Divinity. The big cat licked at her familiarly. Trent knew that the connection to Arra gave Ren some modicum of peace.

"I still do not know," she said. "I wonder if the Fallen One was lurking near the Basin and ambushed Samson and Luna. I haven't mentioned it until now, for I didn't want to alarm you, but I haven't been able to hear them since we arrived."

When she looked up from Divinity, Trent saw deep concern mirrored in her dark eyes.

"Aenna did not dim. They cannot have been killed," Trent said.

*Could they have?*

"You are right, they have not been killed. But they may have been incapacitated in some way. Why else would they remain silent, especially since we were not sent to the proper place?"

Trent's mind raced at the implications. If the last remaining Gods of Light had fallen, then what hope did any of them have? Even with Godtaker, he did not seriously believe he and Ren would have any means of doing battle with three dark gods. Not even in the time before the Pact could a Seraph hope to stand against the Gods of Darkness alone. What had happened to Daniel had been proof enough of that. It would only be a matter of time before Illux fell with no gods and no Seraphs to protect it. Indeed, they didn't even know the means of freeing the Divine Beasts yet. What would they do if they had to face another Akklor?

"Perhaps, we should forgo stealth and fly back to Illux as quickly as we can," Trent suggested.

"And what of Divinity?" she asked.

Trent looked at the great cat before answering. "I'm sure she will understand. I don't wish to leave any friend of Arra's behind, but I don't see us having any other choices, High God help us."

"There are always other choices, Trent," an unfamiliar voice said.

Trent and Ren both whirled in the direction that the voice came from, drawing their swords as they did so. Godtaker seemed to shiver in Trent's hands as if it anticipated drinking more silver blood. Divinity sprang before them, snarling at the figure stepping out of the shadows of the trees. The figure was wearing a loose shawl made of brown fabric not unlike what a farmer from one of the many villages would wear. It was tattered and had clearly seen better days. Clutched in a gloved hand was a large staff that the figure leaned upon.

"Who are you?" Ren asked firmly, pointing Nightbreaker at the being.

The hooded figure lifted its hands and removed the hood that obstructed its face. Instantly, Divinity stopping growling and bowed her head to the ground. Trent was nearly blinded from the glow radiating off the newcomer's face. As the glow started to fade he could see the details that seemed to form anew under the light. Before them stood a young woman, with a skin tone Trent couldn't quite decide upon. It was nearly golden like that of the gods, yet it seemed to never stay one shade longer than the span between blinks. Likewise, her hair was brilliantly white one moment, and red or black the next. Her face was familiar to him, but he couldn't place where he had seen it before.

"I am me," she responded. Her voice was beautiful and strong. It reminded him of his mother.

"We don't have time for riddles, nor do we have the patience! Tell us who you are!" Trent commanded.

"By what right do you command me?" the woman asked, a faint smile twisting her lips.

"You address Seraphs of the Light, woman," Ren said. "We are in a time of war, choose what you say next wisely."

"Divinity, dear," the woman said to the tigress. "There is no need for such formalities. Please show our mutual friends I mean no harm."

The white tiger stood and walked up to the woman, licking at her fingers affectionately. The woman stroked her behind the ears in return. When Divinity was finished, she turned and laid down in front of the figure, sleepily closing her eyes. Trent could feel his mouth hanging open as the sword he held before him became heavy in his hands. Slowly, he began to lower the blade, noticing out of the corner of his eye that Ren did the same. He wasn't sure if he wanted to do it or not, but he couldn't seem to help himself.

"Still, you wonder who I am?" she asked. "I have stood in the fires of Infernaak, walked the forest paths of Ayyslid. I swam through the depths of both the sea you know and the ones you don't. I have journeyed beyond the Rim. Nay, I have journeyed beyond this Realm, to all of the others. I have floated through the stars, I have run through the streets. I have held hands with those of rock and those of the wood, with those of the cherub and those of the pit. I have looked upon the twins before one was lost to smoke and the other to steam. I have slept between the spheres and seen those that claw at the very rim of the world. I knew you before you were flesh, I have known you since your spark was created in the Realms beyond this one, and it is to my side that you will one day journey again."

*I can even speak in your mind.*

Trent looked at Ren to see if she had heard the woman's voice within her head as he had. By her concerned express and the tightening of her lips, he could see that she had. It didn't seem possible. Nothing she was saying made any sense.

"I am the High God," she thundered. Her voice had taken on a supernatural volume, shaking the very earth beneath them.

In that instant, both Trent and Ren knew she spoke the truth. Trent couldn't explain how he knew, but this truth seemed to him to be immutable. It was as plain to him as Aenna above. He felt as if the silver in his blood sang her praises and yearned to return to the original veins from which it sprang. Instantly, both Seraph's fell to the ground and buried their faces in the dirt. Trent felt sweat bead up on his forehead, and his tongue began to stick to the roof of his mouth. Tears welled up in the corners of his eyes. They had drawn steel against the creator of the universe. What fools they had been!

"Forgive us!" Ren cried. "We did not know you!"

"There is nothing to forgive. Please, stand. Both of you," the High God said calmly. "As I told my friend Divinity here, there is no need for such formalities. I have known you longer than you have known yourselves. I wish to talk with you as old friends, not as God and mortal."

The two Seraph's slowly lifted themselves upright, neither wishing to be the first to stand. Trent still hesitated a moment, but once Ren was again on her feet he followed. They made sure to leave both of their swords lying in the dirt. When he finally cast his eyes on her again, Trent realized where he had seen this woman before. It had been she who had called out to him in his dream as he was rising to the Divine Plane. She had tried to comfort him while he was undergoing his transformation into a Seraph.

*Was it a dream?*

"I have brought you both here, rather than allowing you to travel straight to Illux, for I wished to have this conversation in the open air, far from the stenches of that place," she said. "There is much that you must do, and not much time with which you are to do it."

"Anything," Trent said. "We shall do anything you ask."

"Know this, you no longer fight simply for the Light, but for all of creation. Lio knows not what he does, but his madness threatens more than the people of Illux. If this world falls, then all of the Realms of Creation fall as well. There are greater evils that stir than just the Gods of Darkness. If I am the lock, then the Mortal Plane is the key. Those from beyond are trapped in the spaces between, but should the Mortal Plane destroy itself, they will be able to free themselves from the shackles I have placed upon them."

"Who?" Ren asked.

"I do not expect you to understand, child, nor should you. If you knew the details it would only bring madness. Just know that more than the fate of the Light hangs in the balance. The Empty Gods cannot gain entry to the Mortal Plane."

In the back of Trent's mind, some hint of recognition stirred at that name. He had heard it before, in the ramblings of a dying man who would have made himself a god.

"How do we stop them?" Trent asked, confused.

The High God smiled again.

"You simply do that which you were already going to do. Awaken the Divine Beasts and stop the Gods of Darkness from destroying the City of Light. There is no hope for you otherwise. An army will rise out of the sea, and it will not be enough to save Illux without the aid of the Divine Beasts who once served the Gods of Light in the time before the Pact."

"Then we shall awaken them all," Trent said. "Tell us how to find them."

"I am sending two of my servants to your side. You shall come across them by this time tomorrow. They will know the way to awaken the creatures, and the locations they are imprisoned. Respect their insight, and trust your own instincts. I gave them to you for a reason. Now, I expect that you have questions of your own. Rather, I should say I know that you do, and now would be an appropriate time to ask them."

Trent shot a glance at Ren. He had no idea what to say. Never in his wildest dreams had he ever thought he would be asking questions of the creator of the universe.

"Where have you been all of this time?" Ren finally blurted out.

Trent looked at her, shocked. Ren seemed embarrassed herself at the outburst.

"I have been all places, my dear," the High God answered. "Ignoring the time I have spent in other realms, I have simply been wandering the byways of the Mortal Plane. I created such a vast world, and you mortals haven't even seen a fraction of it. There are lands full of animals such as Divinity, islands where the animals would seem as fantastical as Divine Beasts. Mountain ranges that dwarf the Rim. After Lio slew Xyxax, I knew I could sit upon my throne no longer while I watched as my children killed each other. Instead, I found joy in traveling through that which I created. Where else could I have been?"

"Why do all of our teachings act as if you are a man?" Ren asked.

The High God laughed at this, her smile becoming broad.

"To the gods, I am father, to creation, I am mother. The very notion that I would be constrained by the binary gender system I designed for the sake of mortal procreation is ludicrous. I can become whatever I choose. I was there before there ever was man or woman, before there was ever mother or father, and I will be long after."

She turned directly to Trent then, her eyes looking through him. The Seraph could feel the weight of those eyes pressing down on him like a stone. The knowledge and strength of untold millennia cut through him no less than if it had been a physical blade. He nearly buckled under the strain, trying desperately to find an escape from her gaze. Ren would be no help, for she too averted her eyes while Divinity still snored between them.

"Speak your mind, Trent. I already know all that is within. It would be rude to not let Ren know the questions that I am inclined to answer."

"Did you send my dreams?" Trent quickly said, his words tumbling over themselves as if he had no control over them.

"I did not."

Trent looked at her confused. He didn't know how he should respond to that. If she hadn't sent them, who had? The dreams of the dove and the vulture had been an ever-present facet of his life, since even before Terric had been killed. The Gods of Light were said to influence dreams from time to time, but he never assumed it was more than a slight nudge to the sleeper's mind. These visions had been a figurative push, keeping him from ever knowing a truly good sleep other than from exhaustion.

"I did not send them to you," she reiterated. "I have never influenced the Gift that some mortals have experienced throughout history. The Gift is a byproduct of the spark within you having a closer connection to me than the spark of other mortals. It gives you a glimpse of the foresight that I myself possess, but I do not directly interfere. That would go against what I hoped to accomplish by injecting choice into this world. Whether or not a mortal receives the Gift is truly random.

"But that wasn't your big question, Trent. I want you to speak the question you have wanted to ask me since you were a boy."

"I-I can't," he stammered.

"You can. Ask about Terric."

"Why did you let him die?" Trent whispered.

"The single greatest power in this universe is choice, Trent. It was choice that led to the creation of the Gods of Light and the Gods of Darkness. It was choice that brought you to this very point. Choice is the greatest gift I have given to mankind, and I would never take that from them. I would not even be interfering now if I did not think that all of which I have strived to create was in danger. Even the gods have choice, although they have forgotten this. Terric made his choice, and that choice put events into motion far greater than he could have ever realized.

"Death is part of life, Trent. Whether it comes from a disease, a storm, or another man matters not. If death was always under your control, it would not hold the same weight it does. That doesn't mean it is supposed to be the specter you have made it, hanging over every action. No, life is supposed to be enjoyed and cherished. Death simply brings meaning to life, to what little time you have been given. And choice gives you power over that time. Some have their choices made for them, and some don't live long enough to even have that chance. That is part of being human. Terric's choice isn't something that you should blame yourself for. He doesn't blame you. I promise he would do it again."

Trent felt overcome with emotion. Hot tears welled up behind his eyes, tears he tried to hide from Ren and the High God alike. Finally, he couldn't hide them any longer. Within moments he found himself clutched tightly to Ren's breast, her hands stroking his hair as he sobbed. For those few moments, he was a child again, lying in the snow. The scent of Terric's blood clung to him, and his tears froze on his cheeks. He loathed himself in those moments, for his weakness, for being overcome with such emotion. But then something changed within him. He thought he could feel a presence replace the High God. It felt almost as if Terric was there, whispering to him that he needed to be strong again.

*I will, brother. I promise. Just as you were.*

When he looked up, the High God was nowhere to be seen.

# CHAPTER VII

It had been several days since the voice had last spoken to him, but Teo still hadn't let Rella in on his secret. As far as she knew, he had come up with a plan for them all on his own. Most of his vanity had vanished over his years as a Balance Monk. Hiding the truth of his new epiphany had not been to seem wiser or more grounded after what had happened to them, but to keep Rella from becoming alarmed. Voices weren't something one often heard, even when the gods were involved.

Over a week had passed since Grey Temple had fallen; over a week since the Grey God had fallen with it. Teo's whole world had shattered in an instant, and he had almost lost himself in the process. For a few hours he had stood on a precipice, with madness howling at him from below, drawing him down. If he hadn't been grounded by Rella, if he hadn't been guided by the voice, then he would have died by now.

*Both of us would have.*

At one point, his life had been dedicated to maintaining the balance of the world, ensuring that neither the Light nor the Darkness would overcome and overpower the other. Following that charge mostly entailed meditating and practicing for what potential violence could arise—it involved little actual action. Now, he was energized with a new purpose, led by the voice to discover something in the Rim that they would be able to use to restore balance to the world. If not for that, he didn't know what they would be doing. He wasn't sure he would have been able to lead a new life in the villages of the world south of the mountains. He didn't have the stomach for such mundane living. Besides, anyone who knew him there wouldn't have fond memories of the once-bandit captain. Anyone who would have cared to see his return was long dead, some by his hand.

*Jin.*

He shook his head, trying to rid himself of the dying woman straddled beneath him. It had been more difficult to kill her than anyone who he ever crossed blades with. Her life faded between his fingers, and he hated himself for it. Teo had been commanded once, to never again say her name until he was ready to meet the High God. When he had been at peace within the Grey Temple, under the tutelage of Ravim, he had been able to forget the woman he had loved and killed. Now, even with his center restored, his fortitude of mind was not what it once was. Her bones cracked as he stepped on loose twigs on the ground. Hopefully, they would end up where the voice was leading them soon—before he lost his mind.

"How much longer?" Teo whispered to himself.

*Midday.*

There it was again. The voice that called to him in the temple. The voice that saved him from giving in to the loss that had overtaken them. With the death of the Grey God the Balance Monks had lost the source of their strength and they were easily overrun. It had been easy to give up hope, liberating even.

At first, he hadn't known who the voice was, thinking it was maybe some part of himself, or even the Grey God somehow communicating with Teo after his death. A few hours after their escape from Gaxxog, however, he realized that it was the High God himself talking in Teo's mind. That realization was frightening at first, but once he came to terms with it, he finally found it comforting. The Creator of the universe thought him important enough to save. It was both humbling and empowering. Ever since he had joined the Balance Monks, he had the voice of a god to rely upon, what difference did the magnitude of the speaker make?

The two monks stopped to rest by a small brook that flowed between the roots of the trees. It trickled quietly, added a comforting layer to the sounds of the forest. Rella ran her fingers through the water, splashing some on her face before she sat in a meditative position and closed her eyes. Teo watched her for a time, letting his mind drift through the sea of emotions he was feeling. He wanted to tell her the truth about what was leading them, but he feared she wouldn't believe him. He feared she would turn on him like Jin did. The thought of losing her was too painful to seriously consider it. What would he do if that happened?

Overhead, small birds chirped and darted through the foliage, a reminder that not all of the world was in shambles. Teo chose not to close his eyes as his companion had, rather, he decided to take in all of their surroundings as his form of meditation. The cool waters of the brook were cool to the touch, yet the liquid almost burned as he cupped it in his hands and sent it running down his cracked throat. His stomach rumbled, disturbing the relative stillness. Running from the collapsing temple as they had, hadn't left much time to gather supplies beyond the few books they had been able to save. No supplies meant no food and no water skins. Thankfully, running water wasn't hard to find in the Rim, but food was harder to come by without the means to hunt for it. It was good then, that the ascetic lifestyle of the Balance Monks had prepared their bodies to persist with so little to consume.

After several minutes of contemplation, Teo reached over and grabbed one of the heavy tomes they had been able to save from the assault. The first he found was a leather-bound copy of the *Canticle of the Forsaken Ones*, a series of hymns and sermons chronicling and decrying those Seraphs who refused to die when their master Lio was cast down. He set the book aside and grabbed another. The book he now held in his hand was one of the *Bestiaries*; thick volumes that had tried to catalog all of the Divine Beasts from before they were sealed by the Grey God. Its cover was wooden, inlaid with thick clasps of iron. This was an older volume, most likely due to be rewritten soon. As all of the Divine Beasts had been locked away before Ravim had created his order of servants, the information that filled these pages had been imparted by the god himself. The images that accompanied them had been painted or drawn from that same divine inspiration. A sudden flight of curiosity struck Teo, and he found himself flipping through the brittle pages to a specific entry: *Gaxxog the Incorrigible.*

There it was, a painting of the vile thing plastered across two pages, its name scratched above it in spidery script. Teo almost smiled in spite of himself as he looked at the black and green and purple paints that swirled to make of the six-legged lizard. It seemed to him that the artist's rendition was nearly perfect, the strokes making up its bulk gave the creature a life-like quality. It was hard to believe that the artist had never actually seen Gaxxog. The Grey God had surely inspired his folk with a variety of skills to maintain the balance of the world, not all of which required violence.

Teo continued to see familiar names as he flipped through the book: Akklor, Tyr, Rexin, Kryx. Some of the creatures inspired dread, but others looked to be hopeful reminders of what chance they still had to overcome their enemies. If the Divine Beasts that had served Xyxax and Rhenaris and even Ravim could be awakened, then surely so to could those that once fought for Lio or Arra. Looking over the Divine Beasts that had once served the Light, Teo wondered for what may have been the first time, at the true wisdom of the Grey God's Pact. What good was served the world by imprisoning champions of justice? Even if their existence upset the balance?

*An injustice that you will soon fix.*

Teo nearly jumped as the voice spoke to him, breaking the near perfect silence he had encapsulated himself in. It was then he noticed Rella was now watching him.

"Are you alright?" she asked, gently.

"I am fine."

Teo quickly closed the book and put it back into the knapsack from which it had come. The grey fabric was stained with dark spots, he noticed. Spots he didn't want to think on too long.

"Are you ready to tell me where we are headed?" Rella asked.

"I—" Teo began. "I need you to trust me. I have found a new purpose for us, one that will help us to restore the balance that has been taken from this world."

She looked at him in silence for a few moments, looking for the truth in his face, he imagined. He had spent a lifetime lying. She would find nothing there that he didn't want her to see.

"I trust you Teo," she said, finally. "If you say we shall have a purpose, then I shall follow you whichever way that purpose leads. Tell me, though, does your new plan somehow involve beginning the order again?"

"No. Even I don't see how we could do that, not while the war is continuing, at least. Not without the Grey God."

"We don't need Ravim to follow his teachings," Rella said. "I am confident we can find likeminded souls who wish to rid themselves of the conflict of the Light and the Darkness, who wish to dedicate themselves to the space between. The power for that is within us, even without Ravim's guidance."

Teo sighed and pulled himself to his feet. He hoped she was right, and that hopefully one day they could reclaim the Grey Temple and restart the order, but there was much to be done before then. He wasn't sure they would live long enough for that. It seemed they were being faced with an insurmountable task.

*There is always hope.*

"There is always hope," Teo parroted.

Rella nodded and smiled, pulling herself up as well. She scooped up the knapsack of books and threw them over her shoulder, falling into step behind Teo. He tried to flash a smile at her in return, but for some reason he failed. Guilt still ate at him in the pit of his stomach, and he still ignored it. Gripping his staff in his hand, Teo continued forward on the path the High God set for them.

It was finally midday when they decided to stop again, this time in a clearing where no trees or plants of any kind grew. Rella nearly stumbled over Teo as he came to a complete stop at the edge of the clearing, looking over the smooth earth in awe. There was something unnatural about the way that the ground was perfectly flattened here, and the place felt almost hostile to even stand in. Not even a pebble was out of place here. Animals seemed to have avoided this area as well, as if they knew something mortals did not.

Suddenly, there was movement on the far end of the clearing. Out of the shadows three shapes pushed into view. Two of the figures were white-haired and armored head-to-toe in bright plate mail. Upon their backs were affixed white wings. Teo instantly knew them for what they were: Seraphs. Beside the Seraphs stood a snow-colored cat, nearly as large as a horse. It padded along silently, which was surprising for a creature of its immense size. As soon as the Seraphs saw the Balance Monks they had steel drawn. The woman held a sword with a black blade in one hand, while the man clutched a giant two-handed sword that was bright silver. Both grimaced as if they faced death.

Teo tightened his grip on his staff, waiting for the voice to guide him on what he should do next. No answer came. For what almost felt like hours, the two groups stared each other down, neither side taking a single step into the clearing. Teo sized up these two servants of the Light. He doubted that Rella and himself would stand a chance against these two if it came to violence. Not without Ravim lending them his strength. The moments dragged on until Rella broke the silence.

"Trent?" she called.

"Rella?" he responded.

Instantly the hostility was broken and the two were walking into the center of the clearing to meet one another in person. Trent must have been the male Seraph, who somehow Rella had recognized. That must have meant that the woman was Ren, the thirteenth reigning Seraph who commanded Illux. But how were there now two Seraphs in the world? There had not been more than one since the Pact had been created.

*What is going on here?*

When Rella and the man called Trent met, they embraced as if they were old friends. Teo quickly followed behind, eyeing the pair with confusion on his face. A pang of jealousy flashed through him, but he cast it away just as quickly as it appeared. Opposite him was the woman he imagined to be the Lady Ren, and, she too, looked bewildered. The great white tigress loped up behind them, cautiously pawing at the earth. She sensed something wrong with this clearing.

"You know this Seraph?" Teo asked.

"Yes," Rella said, excitedly. "I knew Trent long ago, along with his friends Devin and Gil. I was sent by Ravim to investigate a cult that had formed among some bandits in the Rim. I joined with three Paladins who were on a quest to put a stop to the same evil I was. We found some terrible things in these mountains…"

She trailed off, her voice losing some of her excitement.

"So, you were the Balance Monk who helped my champions bring down that cult," the other woman said. "I am the Lady Ren." She bowed slightly toward Rella. "The people of Illux owe you a debt."

"This cannot be a coincidence," Trent said. "W-we were told we would meet someone here. I couldn't have possibly imagined it would have been you, Rella. Gods, it's been over five years."

"Six," she responded. "It was the first time I had ever been sent into combat on behalf of the Grey God."

"Who told you that you would be meeting someone?" Teo asked, his stomach knotting in anticipation.

Trent looked as if he was about to speak when Ren stepped in front of him.

"It was the High God. She met us in the forest some miles back. She claimed that servants of hers would meet us by this time today. Given your status with the Grey Temple that must be you."

The confidence with which she spoke such madness made it clear to Teo that she told the truth. This must have been what he himself had been told would happen by midday. Indeed, his own experience would have sounded just as mad if he had been the first to utter it aloud. The only detail that gave him pause was the gender of the High God. In all of the texts passed down by Ravim the great being had been styled as he. How could the Grey God have gotten such an important detail wrong?

"You are who we have been seeking as well," he said at last.

Rella looked over at him, confused. He smiled as the butterflies left his stomach. The truth was coming out.

"We fled the Grey Temple, as it has fallen to the Forces of Darkness," Teo said. "While inside, a voice spoke to me, urging me to push on and make sure that at least some of us escaped. The Grey God had fallen by this point, so I knew that it wasn't him who spoke, but it wasn't until we were safely below the temple that I knew it was the High God speaking." Teo turned to Rella then. "It has been the High God leading us along ever since. I didn't tell you because I was afraid that you would think me mad."

She smiled and nodded. The two Seraphs seemed to be no less understanding than she.

"Well, we were told to awaken the Divine Beasts, and that only then could we hope to save Illux and prevent the Fallen One from conquering all of creation. She said that you would know what to do next," Ren said. "Do you?"

"I do," Teo replied. "We must find the seals that imprison the Divine Beasts. We are standing upon one now."

The other three looked at the ground and let out mild cries of disbelief. He had known exactly what this clearing had been from the moment he had laid eyes on it. Apparently, he had been the only one. The seals of Ravim were strong enough that nothing could take root over them, but they could not hide the power that emanated from within. That was what kept the animals away.

"How do we release the creature?" Trent asked.

"We don't," Teo said. "This seal holds one of the agents of the enemy. The High God has told me which, it is one that we do not want to face. With any luck, the Gods of Darkness will not send a Herald here to awaken it. We must head for a village far to the west. It is there that...she says we will find the first Divine Beast that shall be loyal to our cause."

"Which village is this?" Ren asked. "There are none of our people in these mountains beyond Rinwaithe in the foothills."

"These aren't your people," Teo replied.

# CHAPTER VIII

The hill crested, and then gradually sloped downward toward the settlement. In the distance, as far as Gil could see, was a shimmering blue expanse that slowly rose up to meet the sky. White crests bobbed up here and there. Seatown was still a mile or so off, yet it seemed close by comparison. The crisp breeze brought with it the scent of fish and salt. Gulls screeched as they flew overhead. The white and grey birds circled like a carrion flock, looking for morsels to devour. The air here was more humid than anything he had ever felt before, as if the moisture from the great body of water before him was wafting up the hill and clinging to his flesh.

The stump of his right arm continued to produce a dull ache that colored all of his other senses. He knew the phantom itches and pains of his missing hand would fade in time, but the nerves in what remained of his flesh would never fully recover. He had known amputees before. In the beginning they would face their mutilation with shock and horror, but many of them came to live with a quiet dignity. They learned to cope. He was not sure he would be such a person. Gil tightened his grip on the horse and moved to the side of the road where he couldn't be seen as easily by prying eyes from below.

Dismounting, he removed the satchel that contained his armor and his sword, hiding them in a gathering of scrub brush. He was clothed in a villager's garb he had been given by Jaina. It was loose fitting—the only clothing that would fit him had belonged to a very large, heavy-set man. Wrapped about him was a great brown cloak he hoped would hide his immense size. If the rumors of Seatown were to be believed, a Paladin, even one who wasn't directly from Illux, would be as unwelcome as a Demon. Few Paladins were ever sent there on assignment. The one's there already had been there for years—some since the city was burned back when Gil's old mentor Broderick was in his prime. Sometime before he parted with the villagers fleeing from Illux, he had decided it would be much wiser to enter the settlement disguised as a refugee. Once he had learned all that there was to learn about the power structure of Seatown, and he knew it was safe, he would reveal himself and ask for their aid. It was a gamble to be sure, but he did not want to alienate them by making them think he was some stooge of Castille's, coming to demand their allegiance.

*Although they have sworn themselves to Ren as the voice of the gods, they have grown bolder in their desire for independence as of late.*

The settlement spread out along the coastline below him, brown against the blue of the sea. It was not even half the size of Illux, and yet it had a rambling sprawl to it that made it seem larger than it actually was. Seatown looked like it had been cobbled together by the leftovers of Illux's slums, each building haphazardly slapped here and there by some drunken architect. While it was mostly flat, some of the buildings rose higher than others, not due to their own height, but from small hills that had not been leveled during the city's construction. The wharfs and docks at the far end of the city were mostly obscured by a light haze, but even through the mist of the mid-morning, Gil could make out what must have been nearly a hundred ships, some larger than any of the buildings that made up the city-proper. From this distance it was hard to tell, but some of them looked to be in various levels of construction. Was the fishing fleet that fed the people of Illux during the months between harvests really that large? Absentmindedly, Gil reached up to scratch his chin with the stump of his arm. He cursed when he noticed his mistake and urged his horse down the hill.

A small wall encircled the city, mostly made of timber and outbuildings. The walls were weathered from brown to grey in several places, while others seemed of fresh construction. Here and there, a tower rose which was made of actual masonry, cut from the darker stone that made up the coastline. By the look of it, these towers may have been the only structures that had survived from when the city had been initially founded some five hundred years before, a far cry from the ancient structures that populated the inner city of Illux. It had been the Seraph Arendt, the very man who was responsible for the Purge of Illux, that had created Seatown. Prior to Arendt's forays into the wilderness, when he slaughtered the Forces of Darkness, there had only been a few small fishing villages that dotted the coast. Each of those would periodically fall to the enemy and have their citizens butchered. In order to prevent the continued disruption of any fish from reaching Illux, Arendt had begun his campaign to make the wilderness outside the city safe, just as he had cleansed the city itself during his rebellion against the Seraph Arkos. The crowning achievement of his mission to clear the wilderness, before his fateful march into the south, was the construction of Seatown. With the death of their patron Seraph sometime later, the citizens of Seatown started to despise Illux and all that it stood for. A sentiment that Gil could certainly empathize with.

The marsh-like dirt and mud from the past several miles gave way to a gritty sand that blew across the road in small wisps that were carried on the wind. Gil eyed the landscape in awe, for he had never seen such sand before. It was very different from the dusty consistency of the lands to the south, or the rich dark soil of the Rim. His mind raced as he drew nearer to the town, second thoughts creeping out of his subconscious like worms wriggling out of the dirt during a spring rain. He knew he was doing what the High God had set him to do, for why else would Jaina have been put in his path? And yet, he worried he was on a fool's errand that would only end in disappointment.

*What if I can't muster them to help? What will become of Illux then?*

Ahead, the road widened and flattened out, terminating at a large wooden gate that led into the town. The gate was open, but guards were posted at either side of it, and men peaked at him from above through murder-holes over the opening. None of the guards appeared to be Paladins, which brought him some relief. It would be much harder for him to hide who he was from fellow Paladins, even if they were of Seatown. The faces of the guards showed him they were a grimy lot, closer to bandits that the City Watch he was accustomed to. Gil slowly made his way toward the opening, stopping his horse when the guards motioned for him to do so.

"What is your business?" a gruff woman asked, spittle visible leaving her bulbous lips.

"I—" Gil began weakly, "I am a survivor of Marna. I was headed for Illux when they turned me away. I was hoping that, perhaps, the good people of Seatown would take in a pious farmer."

"He's awfully big to be a farmer," the other guard said, a small man with wicked eyes. "What'd you think Shae? Shall we fetch the Paladins? I heard the Ten wanted more muscle to finish the fleet."

Instinctively, Gil held up the stump of his arm. Both the man and the woman took a step backward when they saw it.

"I would love to be of service," Gil mumbled, "but the bastards took my arm when they razed the village. Only the High God above knows what use I can be now."

"We don't have any need for cripples here," the woman spat. "Give us your horse and we will let you through. The city will find uses for such a beast. You, on the other hand, may be allowed to beg in the streets, though I doubt you will be permitted to come with the rest of us when we leave."

"Leave?" Gil asked.

The man shot his companion a dark look and gripped onto the reins of Gil's horse forcefully. He pulled downward with a fierce tug. The animal began to rear, bucking Gil off onto the ground with an audible *thud*. Acting more dazed than he really was, Gil dumbly fumbled for a way to pull himself up. He felt around for a moment before looking up. A boot planted itself right between his eyes, sending him spiraling back into the sand. He blinked away the white spots in his vision, trying desperately to keep his calm. Already, he could feel the energy of his magic swirling in his good hand, an instinctual defensive response. When his vision returned, he saw the woman standing over him with her short-sword drawn. Her face was twisted into a snarl.

"What'd you do that for?" the man asked.

"I still don't trust this big brute," she replied. "Maybe we should fetch the Paladins. He doesn't seem like the other refugees that have been filtering in the last few days. Something is off about him. He's more solid than he seems."

Her sword point found its way to his throat. Gil's mind raced. He needed to come up with something, and quickly, or else he would find himself in more trouble than if he had simply ridden into town proclaiming himself a Paladin. Now they would definitely think of him as one of Castille's spies.

"Please," he whimpered, looking at the ground again and letting his words tumble out. "Don't cast me out. Those bastards in Illux never cared for the people of the villages. They always treated us like we were scum. I hoped that here would be different. I was told that Seatown held the last true believers on the Mortal Plane. That bitch that rules in Illux doesn't speak for me. I—"

"Let him pass," a new voice said.

Gil looked up and saw another woman standing before them, this one garbed in a deep blue cloak that was highlighted with swirls of sea green. Her hair was a deep black, and her skin a nutmeg brown.

The woman bore a scowl that sent the other two guards scurrying back. The quickly bowed their heads and lowered their weapons.

"Admiral!" the female guard said. "We were only doing our job as the Paladins ordered."

"I am aware," the woman replied. "No one is to enter our gates without learning who they are and where they come from, that is true. The Ten are very cautious. Spies of the enemy come in all shapes and sizes. Spies from Illux have no doubt infiltrated our home with the influx of refugees. Even so, we are servants of the Light. We will not dishonor our name or our gods by abusing the wretched among us. You, what is your name, traveler?"

"Gil," he muttered, avoiding her gaze.

"No family name, Gil?" the Admiral asked, her voice firm but not cruel.

"None, my lady. Most of us farmers don't have family names."

"I am Admiral Wyn Thacker, commander of the fleet of Seatown and protector of her people," she said.

Gil prostrated himself at her feet, muttering his thanks. Admiral Wyn firmly gripped him by the shoulder and pulled him to his feet. While she stood so close to him, he could smell that she was wearing a fragrant perfume. Gil tried to hunch his back so as not to seem so much taller than the woman. If any in the city could guess his true nature, he knew it would be this woman. Even so, he wanted to learn more about who she was, so he took a chance.

"I mean no disrespect, my lady," he said, "but I didn't know that Seatown had a fleet. I thought that only Paladins could give orders, just like in Marna."

Wyn eyed him for a moment before answering. "If you are truly a pious man, you will learn many things as a citizen of Seatown. We are not like Illux or Marna. I suggest you do as you are bid and don't ask any further questions. Now, enter the city or leave, though either way, we will be keeping your horse."

With that, she turned and made her way back through the gate and up a set of stairs cut into its backside.

*I haven't seen the last of you, I expect.*

Gil acted outwardly confused for a moment before gathering his cloak about himself and stumbling past the gate into the city itself. The two guards let him pass, the woman spitting at his back and the man leading the horse off to the side. Instantly, he was greeted with the stench of fish and unnaturally loud screeching of gulls. The streets twisted and turned in wicked angles, some seemingly leading nowhere. The streets were covered in so many potholes that they appeared pockmarked. Gil made his way toward the sounds of the sea, hoping to get a better look at the fleet of ships he had seen from the hill behind him. Never had he expected to get such a cold welcome to a place, Paladin or no. Something was off about Seatown that even Illux had been blind to. Something was festering here that Ren had missed.

As he made his way through the town, he noticed a marked difference between what he supposed were older residents of Seatown, and those who must have been refugees from the villages. The refugees seemed altogether dirtier and tried to avoid eye contact with everyone they could. The residents of Seatown didn't appear much more outgoing, although they didn't act as if looking the wrong way would get them killed. At least the refugees didn't smell of fish.

After several minutes of navigating the crooked byways of the settlement, Gil found himself in a large central square. Here, the ground was covered in paving stones, loosely cobbled together over various years, it seemed. Some were a pale white, while others were the dark shale of the coastline. All were covered in accumulated grime. Off to one side of the square was a large building that looked like a poor imitation of the Grand Cathedral in Illux. Every village had some chapel of sorts for the worship of the Gods of Light, but none tried to imitate Illux directly. Beside the cathedral was a statue of a man holding a sword out before him. It looked as if he had wings at one point, though those had been broken off over the years.

*Arendt.*

Gil nearly gasped when he saw the scaffolding to either side of the statue. They had constructed a gallows. Dozens of men and women hung from nooses throughout the square, with gulls picking at their bloated flesh. The breeze twisted the corpses as they gently swayed. Gil nearly staggered into another person trying to walk past him. When the man noticed how shocked Gil looked, he pulled him aside, into the shadows of a building. Somewhere in the distance, a man was screaming for someone to help him. His voice cracked and broke into choked sobs.

"I don't know where you come from, friend," the stranger said, "but it isn't wise to stare at the gallows for too long. You must be new to Seatown, I take it?"

"Yes, I am," Gil replied, distantly.

"I have only been here a few days myself," the stranger continued. "I was from Amel originally. Moved around a bit since then, got caught up in the refugees making their way here. My name is Lin. And you?"

"Gil."

"Well, Gil, like so many others before you, you are probably wishing you had gone to Illux instead."

Gil saw two large men, who could have been Paladins, armored in the same mix of blues and greens that the Admiral was, drag a screaming man to another section of the gallows and wrap a noose about his neck. The screaming stopped as they strung him up, but he continued to flail for several minutes in silence, his face slowly turning a shade of purple.

"Who are they?" Gil asked. "Why are the Paladins doing this?"

"They could be anyone," Lin responded. "Some are refugees, some are locals. All had the poor judgment to openly admit they still consider the Lady Ren to be the voice of the gods, or some variation of that sentiment. It doesn't matter really. They spoke up or were heard by the wrong ears, and now they are dead."

"What do you mean?"

"I mean exactly that. The Paladins of Seatown have declared that Ren and the people of Illux are apostates who have perverted the teaching of the Gods of Light. It is no secret that this idea has been brewing for a while, and Ren did nothing to stop it. It seems that given the current chaos that has engulfed the countryside they saw the opportunity to openly voice that opinion. The people you see strung up refused to go along with that."

*This can't be possible.*

Gil felt his stomach knot up. He had never assumed the situation here could be so dire. It was maddening to think Seatown could really be so lost. How could anyone hope to rally these people to come to the aid of Illux? Had he made a mistake?

"On the bright side, they won't be here for long," Lin said.

"What do you mean?"

"Didn't you see all of the ships?" Lin asked. "They have turned all of the fishing boats into passenger ships, and constructed dozens more. The Paladins plan to flee the Mortal Plane in search of lands beyond, far from the reach of Illux or the Forces of Darkness. With any luck they will drown in the attempt."

"Do they really expect that to work?" Gil asked. "What of all of the rest of us?"

"The rumor is that the Admiral has pleaded for our lives, should we decide to not accompany them, but no one knows what the Ten wish."

"The Ten?" Gil asked.

"The Paladins," Lin said. "Look, I don't mind filling you in, but we can't do it out here, not now at any rate. They are looking for reasons to string people up, and I don't want to get any taller. There is an inn that you can stay at. I have a room there. It's owned by a woman who is more receptive to refugees. I don't think she is a native. Came from Rinwaithe or something."

*The High God is watching.*

Gil nodded and followed Lin away from the square and sounds

of the hungry gulls. They made their way through the city farther from the sea toward the landlocked side of Seatown. As they wandered the streets, Gil caught sight of a blacksmith hammering out the blade of a sword. He made a mental note of the place, realizing he had left his weapon outside of the city. The stump of his right arm began to itch again.

After what seemed to be hours of navigating the winding streets, they arrived at a lopsided building with a faded sign that read: THE DRUNKEN OX. The namesake creature was painted on the wall with a faded mug of ale between its hooves. Lin entered the doorway, motioning Gil to follow behind him. The burly man behind the counter nodded in recognition but said nothing. Lin sat Gil down by the hearth and disappeared for a moment. While he was gone, Gil looked to the man behind the bar, catching his eye. The man was large enough to be a Paladin himself. A man that looked strangely familiar tried to walk into the common room. Gil thought for a moment that he resembled Trent. The barman came out from around the corner, grabbing the man by the neck and throwing him back into the street yelling about his lack of payment. After a few moments, Lin returned with two glasses of ale. It was when he handed one to Gil that it seemed he noticed Gil's missing hand for the first time.

"How'd that happen?" he asked, sipping his ale.

"I was in Marna when it fell," Gil whispered. "I don't particularly want to discuss it."

"Nor would I," Lin said. "Now, let's finish this ale, and I will see about getting you a room."

"No need," a distantly familiar voice said. "We don't serve his kind."

Gil looked up to see a woman standing over them, who he instantly recognized from his time in Rinwaithe. Her name was Alyssa. She had been a good friend of his while he had been stationed there, all of those years ago. It was her friendship that helped him be away from Devin for so long. The broad smile on her face removed some of the uneasiness that her words had brought just a moment before. Gil quickly got to his feet and reached out his arms. Without missing a beat, she had embraced him. He felt a tear run down his cheek.

"Gil!" Alyssa exclaimed. "I never thought I'd see you in Seatown. Especially when word came of what happened at Marna. Your arm?"

"The same," he said.

"How did you get into the city?" she asked, quieter this time. "I didn't expect them to allow any Paladins in. Not with their heresy in full swing."

Gil cast a wary glance at Lin, who seemed to be hiding his shock at the revelation relatively well. Alyssa nodded her head at the man, again putting Gil at ease.

"I pretended to simply be a large farmer. When you act weak, people don't tend to question you much. I did have a close call when I met Admiral Wyn, however."

"A close call indeed," Alyssa said. "Wyn is the highest ranked non-Paladin in the city. If anything happens to the Ten, gods willing it will, she would be the one in charge. Perhaps, then they would give up this fool's errand with the ships. It matters not. What brings you here, old friend?"

"Illux is in danger. I came here to muster an army and go to their aid."

The laughter of Alyssa and Lin drew the attention of the rest of the room. The barman looked their way through bushy eyebrows. Once he noticed Alyssa he quickly looked away, suddenly finding some glassware to clean. When Lin and Alyssa finally stopped, seeing the discomfort on Gil's face, they resumed conversation at an even lower whisper than they had been speaking before.

"I appreciate the sentiment, friend," Lin said, "and, perhaps, you could bring some of us with you, but you would never be able to change the minds of the Paladins. Not while they have ships to carry them to safety."

"What if we remove the Paladins then?" Gil asked.

Lin and Alyssa looked at each other in silence.

Later that night, after the rest of the inn had been asleep for several hours, Gil slipped out of his room and made his way into the street. He pulled his cloak tight about himself and darted from shadow to shadow, making his way back toward the blacksmith shop he had seen on his way to The Drunken Ox. He wasn't sure when he had decided what action was needed to save Seatown, but he had decided it all the same. War or not, the Paladins here had to be punished for what they had to be come. Evil came in many forms, and all of them needed to be destroyed. Speaking out against Illux was one thing, something that many village Paladins had done over the years when they had drunk too much ale, but executions of people loyal to the Lady Ren? There was only one answer to crimes such as that.

Two guards on some kind of night patrol sauntered past him, barely taking notice of the large beggar that moaned in the gutter, clutching the stump of his arm. He tried not to overdo it. Once they were past, he was back on his feet and on his way toward the blacksmith. Upon arriving at the building, Gil climbed through an open window and looked about the room. In the darkness, he could just barely make out the shapes of the forge and the bellows, with various arms and armaments hanging from the walls. It seemed the smith held his quarters somewhere else, perhaps in an adjoining building, for this room was empty. He wasn't sure what gave him the idea in the darkness, but he knew that simply grabbing a fresh sword was not enough. Gil quietly lit a lamp and began looking for what was required.

After several minutes of searching, he found what it was he had been searching for: a sword blade with no pommel or crossguard. The unfinished weapon was sharp to the touch, but had not yet been finished for normal use. Gil picked up the blade and set it on an anvil. Next, he began working the bellows to reignite the forge, getting it as hot as he was able in such a short amount of time. The combination of the exertion and heat made him begin to sweat profusely. Once the forge was hot enough, Gil removed his cloak and set the stump of his arm on the anvil just below the blade of the sword. He took a swig of wine from the skin he carried at his side and removed the cleaver he had stolen from the inn for protection on the walk here.

A moment later, he had cut off the end of the stump.

Gil bit down into a piece of shoe leather to prevent himself from crying out. The pain was agonizing. It almost seemed that it hurt worse now than it had when the Herald had taken the rest of his arm in Marna. Blood flowed from the end of his arm in a torrent, and every fiber of his being cried out for him to heal himself and stop the pain. Already, he could feel the warmth of the magic traveling down his arm.

*Not yet.*

Gil gripped the blade with his hand and jammed it into the bloody stump, grinding metal against bone. Then he willed the magic to life, knitting the flesh around the base of the blade. Even that would not be enough to hold it in place in a battle, however. For that, he needed the weapon to truly become a part of him. Before he gave himself enough time to have second thoughts, Gil shoved the blade into the forge, the heat igniting the skin of his arm. The smell of burning hair and flesh filled his nostrils. While his arm was in the flames, he forced all of his energy into the magic, healing what was being melted. Joining metal to bone. When it was done, he pulled free his new arm and stumbled back into the night, barely conscious.

# CHAPTER IX

The Divine Blood washed over him. He felt the cool presence of the silver liquid brush up against his flesh, tingling and prickling at the parts of him even beneath the skin. The feeling warmed him, an odd sensation he had almost forgotten. What had once been the most common feeling in the world was now strange and foreign. It had been nearly a millennium since he had stepped into the Basin and onto the Mortal Plane below. The Pact had prevented this journey for so long that he nearly given up on feeling the solid ground and cool air of the Mortal Plane again. There had been temptation, of course. More than once he had stared at the world below that Ravim had denied him. Now, he traveled there like nothing had changed since the creation of the world.

*Everything has changed. I am following a madman.*

Vardic hadn't shed a tear for Ravim. The real Ravim had died the day that the High God had changed his station, the day that Ravim had been *elevated.* Vardic had chafed under the Pact that the Grey God had installed upon them. Not only had the world below been barred from them, but their most powerful servants had been chained away, as had their ability to seek revenge for the death of Xyxax. Vardic had discussed with Rhenaris how best they could dispose of their one-time companion more than once, but both of them feared he was as powerful as he had claimed to be. What fools they had been. If it had been their hand that had slain the Grey God, then Lio would have fallen soon after. Instead, they were left licking his boots like they had been reduced to mere Heralds.

Finding a replacement for their most competent servant was what brought each of the three Gods of Darkness onto the Mortal Plane. Lio had tried to make the creature alone, but they had not allowed it. Even a madman such as Lio could be pressured into ignoring his own plans from time to time. Now, they simply followed him to some distant place near the Great Chasm, not truly any better off than they had been. Lio had conceded and allowed them to join him, but he had made it very clear he was still going to be the one creating the creature. Vardic couldn't allow Lio to control yet another Herald, not by himself at any rate. The crazed fool still controlled a Seraph as well. They couldn't leave him with their forces under his thumb.

The grey and black stones rose to meet them, slowly filling Vardic's vision. The lifeless landscape that marked the immediate area surrounding the place where Xyxax had died was as good a place as any to make their return to the Mortal Plane. He missed this feeling. It was one of the most exhilarating sensations of godhood. Vardic turned and looked at his companions. Lio looked grimmer than usual, while Rhenaris looked more at peace than he had ever seen her. The spines on her head hung limp, gently lifting from the resistance of the wind. Her exposed midsection heaved in anticipation. Below them, a cluster of black shapes milled about. As he got closer, they could see they were all Demons.

*When did he command them to arrive? Is he communicating with them some way we're unaware of?*

Reading his mind, Rhenaris spoke. "What is this?"

"The candidates to replace the Herald, of course," Lio answered, calmly. "These are the few Demons who had begun gathering together again after Arra scattered the others. I figured it would make for the best pool to choose from."

It was then that Vardic noticed the other things running about the clearing of stone. It seemed that the Demons had formed a ring around several creatures with the bodies of goats or dogs and the faces of men. These were the remnants of the soldiers who had turned their back on Arra. Lio had mentioned them earlier. They looked as if they had retained little of their former selves inside their now-twisted forms. The beasts ripped and tore at each other, spitting and mewling unintelligible sounds not quite animal or human. They each bled from a variety of wounds along their faces and shoulders. One or two walked with pronounced limps and cradled their clawed limbs close to their bodies. The Demons were keeping them confined and forcing them to fight each other. Whenever one of the creatures tried to escape the circle, the Demons cackled and threw the wretched thing back into the ring, where it was promptly eviscerated by its fellows. Entrails and dark fluids were scattered about, providing some sustenance for the victors.

When the Demons noticed the three gods descending from above, they quickly fell to their knees, ignoring the sport of the dying man-things. As good as it felt to see the Demons developing their own brand of cruelty, it felt ever better to see they still knew respect. Lio landed first, then Rhenaris, with Vardic grudgingly stepping onto the earth last. None of the Demons looked up from stone. In the background, the creatures continued to howl and tear at each other. Vardic began to think of their cries as an annoyance.

Before any of them could speak, Rhenaris walked through the kneeling Demons to the monsters within the circle. She swung her flails, swiftly crushing each in turn, leaving only one alive. As they crumpled beneath her, they yelped and cried out, sounding more human than animal in their dying fear. The last creature cowered in the presence of the goddess, howling, and mewling in equal measure.

As Rhenaris got close, it tried to lick at her hand with its long tongue. She bent and gripped the thing by the nape of the neck, lifting it up to eye-level. Wild slather dripped from the corners of its bloodied mouth as its teeth snapped wildly at her. No longer did the monstrosity seem to fear her as it should have. With a flick of the wrist, she threw the thing on its back and bathed its sides with red flame from her outstretched hand. It howled and cowered again, prostrating itself before her and away from the searing flames.

"It seems they retain some intellect, then," she said, matter-of-factly. "I want these creatures rounded up and joined with our forces. They can be used to replace some of what we have lost."

Rhenaris kicked the creature in the face, caving in its head. It collapsed onto the ground in a twitching heap. The goddess turned and walked back through the Demons to the side of her companions. All the while not a single of the dark-armored sentinels stirred. When she returned, Lio nodded slightly in her direction.

"Which of these shall we choose?" Vardic asked. "Shall we pit them against each other?"

"I don't think that to be necessary," Lio replied. "Why waste our time? I have already chosen the one to bear my blood."

"Your blood?" Rhenaris asked. "Why would we only give it your blood? Do you think we would allow you to have all of the power? Do you take us for fools?"

The sound of a metal gauntlet striking flesh rung out through the clearing. Lio had hit Rhenaris across the face, sending her spinning backward. She landed with her flails raised and her spines sticking up and quivering angrily.

"I take you as weak!" Lio spat. "You two live because I permit it. You followed Xyxax once, now you shall follow me."

Vardic gripped his spear and prepared to strike the traitor down once and for all. The very air about him seemed to crackle with energy. He cast a wary glance at Rhenaris to be sure that she was prepared as well. He was sure he could overpower Lio alone, but he didn't want to be proved wrong. The goddess shook her head at him and fell to one knee.

"As you command," she muttered.

Lio locked eyes with Vardic.

*I will never kneel to you.*

When the Fallen One saw that Vardic wasn't going to give in as easily as their female companion, he turned back to address the Demons. None of the dozen or so Demons had moved at all during the argument. They no doubt knew that doing so would have ended in death.

"Which among you is my champion?" Lio rasped. "Who was it that slew Jerrok, the last Seraph? I know he is among you."

A Demon from the back of the circle slowly stood and walked forward. Its helm molded to the shape of a skull, but it had no holes for eyes. The blood-red cape swirled behind it in the breeze as it lumbered up to stand directly before the Gods of Darkness. Even Vardic couldn't help but be in awe at the confidence exuded by this creature. When it finally stood before them, the Demon removed the giant black blade from its back and tossed it onto the ground. As it fell to its knees, it unclasped its cape and let it flutter away.

"You shall be my eyes upon this plane," Lio intoned, "when I am above, so shall you be below. You will gather our disparate forces and augment them with Demons and Accursed that I have stored to the south. Once you have reformed our army you will march on Illux and deal it the deathblow."

Lio pulled free his sword and slid the blade along his newly exposed forearm, bringing silver blood welling forth. Even from where he stood, Vardic could feel the change in the atmosphere as such raw energy was exposed. Lio's hands began to glow with black energy, draining the light from the area. After a few moments, the blood began to poor out of the Fallen One in a torrent, pooling on the ground at his feet in a small puddle that dimly reflected the black orbs surrounding his hands.

The energy hammered into the Demon, crushing its armor in several places, opening holes to the flesh beneath. The Demon howled in pain as it collapsed onto the ground. The Divine Blood began to flow across the rocky earth into the newly made rends in the Demon's armor. Silver splashed over black. The creature began to seize as the blood and magic filled its body. Finally, when all of the Divine Blood had vanished into the armor of the creature, the light returned to the sky. The chosen warrior of the Gods of Darkness lay motionless on the ground like a corpse. The intervening seconds drug on in silence, with the other Demons remaining still as statues.

Then a wing ripped from the fallen Demon's back.

The first wing was quickly followed by another. Both were leathery and blood-red, not unlike the color of the cape that had once adorned the back of the creature. Light from the sun shone through the membrane of the wings, illuminating the dark veins that cut across them. The Demon began howling again as it sat bolt upright, clawing at the helm upon its head. In moments, the steel of the helm was torn to shreds, revealing the horned visage beneath. Flinty black eyes scanned the three Gods of Darkness. Its head was covered in coarse black hair, which flowed down to its long beard. Using its claws, the creature tore every scrap of metal from its body, revealing its muscular, red physique.

A Herald was born.

The Herald fell to its knees, breathing heavily but saying nothing. Steam rose from its shivering body.

"Rise, my Herald," Lio said. "What will you call yourself?"

"Xyx," he said. "After Xyxax."

Vardic could see Lio bristle at the name, but the Fallen One did not show the creature any open disdain. He simply nodded and motioned for the Herald to make its way back toward the Great Chasm. Xyx bowed and took to the sky, winging his way, still naked, to where their army had been broken some days before. With any luck, the creature would gather the remaining Demons and Accursed to their cause. Fear was a good motivator for the Forces of Darkness, but strength was as well, and this Herald was nothing if not strong. Then, with no warning, Lio was again in the sky and returning toward Aenna, his work finished. Once he had gone, Vardic and Rhenaris were left alone on the Mortal Plane.

"Why didn't you fight him?" Vardic asked through gritted teeth. "Now that the traitor has control over the Herald, we look weak. We have no voice over our army, and now Lio thinks we are his servants."

"You don't think, do you?" Rhenaris chided. "Why would we stop with one Herald only? Do you not remember that Ravim lies dead? And what if Lio thinks we are weak? We cannot fight him on his terms, Vardic. We must make him think he has won, and then we strike."

"If we are making more Heralds, then we cannot allow him to know," Vardic said, looking at the still kneeling Demons.

"You read my mind, brother," she said, coldly.

Vardic gripped his spear and threw it through the first of the Demons. The barbed weapon punched through the creature's breastplate and impaled the next Demon behind it. Those kneeling to the left and right of the two that were impaled, exploded from the outpouring of red lightning that erupted from the spear as it made contact. In the blink of an eye, Rhenaris was in the middle of the Demons, swinging her flails this way and that, crushing helms and chests with animalistic ferocity. Some of the Demons tried to resist, but their attempts were futile. Vardic pulled free his spear and pointed the tip at another Demon, melting the creature with a blast of black flame. When they had finished, there were only two Demons left. The two Demons fell to their faces before the Gods of Darkness.

Rhenaris held out her arm toward Vardic. He slit it open with the point of his spear, before doing the same to himself. Each god initiated the same ritual Lio had done minutes before. Within moments, there were two more Heralds upon the Mortal Plane. Each of the Heralds now stood side by side, naked and shivering with power. Rhenaris's creation was a sickly, pale creature, with skin that was translucent and covered in black veins. Her Herald was female, as evident by her exposed breasts. Vardic's Herald had larger than average horns, and his skin was a shade of green similar to the color of corrupted flesh in an untreated wound.

"You will not carry out the wishes of the Fallen One," Vardic said. "Is that clear? You are only to listen to our will."

The Heralds each nodded in turn.

*Good.*

# CHAPTER X

Edmund scowled at the men before him. The two Paladins, Yon and Hunt, were handpicked by Castille to be a pain in his ass. He studied the two miscreants while trying to hold back the bile that their presence brought forth. Yon was tall and dark, while Hunt was short and fair. Their armor had become more ornate than it had ever been under Ren. Where these new pieces of plate mail had come from, Edmund didn't know, but they were covered in more intricate details and garnishments than was fitting for actual warfare. It was as if they no longer expected to face the Forces of Darkness, but merely to rule over the people of Illux. They were accompanied by the heads of several important inner city families. Those men and women were robed in even more superfluous fineries than Edmund thought possible. Crisp white and blue fabric inlaid with gold stitching and embroidery glinted in the early morning sun.

The group stood upon a newly constructed fortification that separated the inner city from the slums, one of the many barricades that Castille had ordered to be built and fortified since Redrick's death some days before. While they had blocked off the inner city during the initial influx of refugees, now they had completely cordoned it off from any undesirables. Lumber and masonry had been combined into a short wall connecting the two large buildings on either side of the street. A door, just large enough for one man at a time to duck through, was closed and secured in the center of the wall. The door was heavily reinforced from the inner city side, with an overhang that could be collapsed to block it from opening at all if need be. Throughout the city, in a crude ring, were many lesser versions of this wall, some with no doors at all, separating the slums and gathered masses beyond from the niceties of the inner city of Illux.

"Our progress would move more rapidly if you would give us more men," Yon said in his soft voice.

"Yes," Arkon, patriarch of the Lighthammer family, agreed, "Lord Castille has promised us that the inner city barricades will be done within the week. We need your assurances that this will be so! The sanctity of the holy city cannot be lost to your unwillingness to—"

"That's enough," Edmund said, calmly. "Don't pretend to care about the sanctity of Illux as a whole. Speak the truth. Illux could be burning around you, and none of you would bat an eye so long as the enemy was kept beyond these barricades. I doubt even if you care for the safety of the Grand Cathedral above your own homes. If it had been built closer to the walls, none of you would ever have even seen inside of it."

"You would dare—" Arkon began.

"I would," Edmund said, cutting him off again. "You might think yourselves the most powerful in the city now that the Seraph is gone, but you don't hold sway over the Watch, just as you never held sway over the Lady. I know Castille respects your bloodlines, but I couldn't care less if you were sired from the loins of the High God himself. I have sworn to protect the people of the city, no matter which part of the city they call home. Build the walls your damn selves. We won't be your slaves."

*I wouldn't tell a single man to save you if you lot were the last in the city, oath or no oath.*

The Paladins eyed him coolly, but said nothing further. Arkon and the other family leaders could barely keep their mouths from hanging open. It wasn't often that men such as these were spoken to in this way, especially not by some wretch from the slums. The enmity between the people of the slums and those of the inner city was an old feud that stretched back half an age. These families held real power once, back before the Lady Ren had become Seraph. Her predecessor, Jerrok, had been a scion of one such house. As was Castille. Even Trent's friend, Devin, was a lesser son of the Lighthammer family.

Edmund shouldered past them and made his way down toward the small staircase on the backside of the fortification. He was almost jittery with adrenaline. He had never felt so confident or spoken so plainly before in his life. The choices made by Castille and his lackeys had filled him with rage at first, before he had come into his own power. Now, he spat in their faces and laughed about it. Now he—

"Guardsman," Hunt rasped, the first words he had spoken in the meeting. Edmund turned back to look at him. "Do not think you can ignore the will of Castille forever. The Seraph hasn't been heard from. Her army has vanished. There is no power on the Mortal Plane that ranks above him now. Those who show weakness in the face of the coming darkness will be…dealt with, accordingly."

Edmund locked eyes with the smaller Paladin. It was then that the hairs on the back of his neck began to stand on end. All of the men gathered before him had hands upon their blades, even the pampered heads of the inner city families. He doubted Arkon and the others even truly knew how to use their weapons, but there was no way he could last against Yon and Hunt. Edmund quickly glanced about at the men and women on the streets below. The members of the City Watch stationed at the fortification were not ones he was sure he could count on, especially in the face of opposition from the Paladins. The Captain of the City Watch nodded and made his way down the steps in a hurry, pushing through the gate to the slums beyond, sweat beading on his brow.

It was the early hours of the morning, and much of the city still slept. The sun had only just begun creeping over the edge of the great walls that surrounded and protected the city. Though Edmund felt more comfortable here, in the slums, he missed the cleaner smelling air of the inner city already. In the days since his promotion, Edmund had taken it upon himself to find ways to placate the people of the slums and the refugees camped there, all while preparing the city for the possibility of a siege. No one wanted to admit it, but it seemed very likely some evil had befallen Ren and her troops. It had been far too long since the last word of their whereabouts had made it back to Illux. If the worst was true, then it was only a matter of time before the army of the enemy was at the gates. This meant that Trent and Devin were gone as well. He was more saddened by this than he wanted to admit.

*It's Trent's fault that I'm in this damn mess. Though the alternative...*

If Trent was truly gone, then Edmund would be the only person left to care for Elise. He still hadn't gone to see her himself, though he still had guards watching her home day and night. At first, they had been sent there in secret but, recently, they told Edmund that she was catching on to their presence. From what Trent had said, the woman could have taken complete care of herself without the help of him or his men. If a siege was imminent, however, he would once again try and evacuate her to the inner city. Edmund took his word very seriously, and he would not allow the last wish of one of Illux's greatest heroes to be ignored.

Edmund turned down the main thoroughfare and started toward the merchant's home he had commandeered as a central headquarters for the Watch. Once the barricades around the inner city had started to go up, he had decided to move the main operations of the City Watch to a location that was more accessible by the people. Everyone had liked the idea save for the merchant. After all, it was the people

Edmund fought to save, and most of them knew it. The rioting had died down after Redrick's death, though the retaliation for that death had been fierce in the first few hours. Edmund had spent the rest of the day reining in his men, who sought vengeance for the death of their previous captain. It had taken several days of work for the people to trust the Watch again.

Back in his headquarters, Edmund knew he would find Ajax in the care of some of some of his closest guardsmen. The child had barely survived the rioting that had killed his mother, and Edmund had still not decided what was to be done with the boy. He couldn't stay with the guards forever, certainly not if the city was to fall under siege. Then, every member of the Watch would be called upon to defend the walls. What then would he do with the child? He thought of the boy's mother, her head smashed with a rock. For some reason, his mind returned to the Paladin who had engendered such respect in him several weeks before.

*What would Trent have done?*

As he was mulling this over, he entered the dilapidated shop that was now one of the most important structures in the city. Inside, the shop was a bustling hub of activity, with Edmund's most senior Watchmen issuing orders and sending couriers to all parts of Illux. Edmund had chosen this building because of its immense size. It was, after all, one of the largest buildings not inside the inner city. The merchant who had run this store lived fairly lavishly above, though the lower floor where they now stood had fallen somewhat into disrepair.

They had tried to find ways to occupy the many refugees and members of the slums by getting the people to begin fortifying their homes and communal living areas. This was in case the worst happened and the enemy made it inside. Soon they would begin weaponizing the wall as well. Edmund had several plans for ways they could make the first line of defense for Illux stronger. He didn't wish for there to be any chance that the people of the slums would be forced to fight.

If that happened, thousands would die, even if the city somehow eked out a victory.

"What word, Captain?" Roark asked, silencing all of the others. Those around him quickly stood at attention.

"At ease," Edmund mumbled. "The inner city is to be defended at all costs." He spat. "But not by any of our men. I told them to build walls their damn selves. I will waste no lives to keep them safe while they do nothing to help the rest of us."

His voice was gaining confidence as he spoke. Those around him began to crack grins and beam at him in admiration. He looked from face to face, seeing all of his most trusted men and women looking back at him. The guardsmen in this room would stand and die with him if he asked it of them. They would fortify and secure the inner city before their own homes if that was what he commanded, and they would do it exactly because he would never command them to do it. What he was proposing was mutinous, and some would even say blasphemous, but he didn't care, and neither did they. This city would stand or fall as a whole, just as the City Watch would.

"For the Lady Ren!" Edmund shouted.

"For the Lady!" they answered.

*For Trent.*

"I don't care who commands you to help fortify the inner city. Ignore them, send them to me, but under no circumstances are you to aid them. We are to prepare the slums for a siege. I want any building that isn't currently housing more than one family to be taken apart and used to fortify doors and windows on the others. I want every smith in the city making blades and shields. Every man, woman, and child in this city is to be armed and prepared for the inevitable. We also need to send a team to search out every entrance to the catacombs. If need be, we will use them to get around the city after the walls are breached. They may break through the wall, but they will not take Illux."

A few quick nods later and his senior officers were running back and forth, barking orders, and preparing to carry out his commands. When Castille heard of Edmund's rejection of his orders, he would seethe, but once Edmund's men openly ignored the commands of his Paladins, the old man's very blood would boil. Edmund hoped that his directives wouldn't end in violence, but he was open to taking full control of the city if needed. He was no ruler, but he was a man of conviction. The children of the slums would not die just so that the inner city families could live.

"Ajax," he muttered.

Edmund quickly made his way up the steps at the back of the room to the landing above. He suddenly knew what to do with the boy, a suggestion he had presented to his mother before her death, in fact. It was as if the momentum of the moment was building in such a way that it gave his mind added clarity. Every action felt right to him, and he knew exactly what the High God required of him. The Captain of the Guard made his way into one of the small rooms at the back of the upper floor. The rooms here were somewhat luxurious, and he allowed the members of the Watch to use them to gain some respite from their duties. In the back of the room he found the small boy being cradled by Liara, his second-in-command. The female guard was gently cooing to the fussy child. She looked at Edmund and nodded in acknowledgement, handing Ajax over to Edmund as she did so.

"Have you decided?" she asked.

"Yes," Edmund replied absentmindedly. "He cannot stay here."

"Where will you take him?"

"To the safest place in this city."

"I'm going to miss him, actually," Liara said, wistfully.

"I can tell," Edmund said. "You hardly leave him alone. You missed my speech even."

"I've heard windbags like you before," she snickered. "I sure I can guess the gist of it. Castille wants our help defending the inner city, and you told him to fuck off."

Edmund laughed. He nodded at Liara and took the child out of the room. He had devised a way he could hold himself to oaths this day. Perhaps, the High God smiled on him. Or perhaps his bad luck hadn't found where he was hiding.

Once he was out on the street, Ajax began to wail even more obnoxiously than he had been before. The poor child hadn't been truly calm since the riot when his mother had been killed. Edmund wasn't sure how much the child knew about what had happened to her, but he was certain it was more than he was giving him credit for. Edmund patted Ajax on the head awkwardly while he squeezed the boy tight against his chest. He nodded to a few of his guardsmen while he passed, mentioning his destination to one of them in case some emergency required them to locate him. The smells of the slums wafted to his nostrils and reminded him of the irony of what he was setting out to do.

*No one would believe that this is the safest place in the coming siege. I must be going mad.*

It wasn't long before the winding side streets brought him to the small, dilapidated hut that was his final destination. The house was leaning to one side, and light seemed to filter through its roof in several places, but something about it reminded Edmund of home. His mother and father had made such a rundown shack into a place of love and hope. Whether or not Trent had been able to admit it, Elise had most likely tried to do the same. Or so he hoped. Edmund looked down at the crying boy and gave him a weak smile. This was no start to a life.

His hand visibly shook while he rapped on the door. The silence that followed was only occasionally broken by the wining cries of Ajax. Somewhere behind them, the sound of a bucket full of unmentionable liquid sloshed into the street. Finally, the door was slowly opened by a frail old woman, who looked like she had been ancient when Edmund had been no older than the boy he now held in his hands. She looked the Captain of the City Watch up and down with squinty eyes and a vague look of disapproval.

"What do you want?" she asked coldly. "I won't be leaving this house. Not for any of the Creatures of Darkness or pompous idiots in white armor."

Edmund nearly choked on his response. "Are you Elise?"

"I am. And who are you?" She squinted even harder.

"My-my name is Edmund, my lady. I am the commander of the City Watch, and a good friend of Trent."

"Are you now?" she said flatly. "I've never heard of you. The only friends Trent has are Gil and Darren."

"Devin," Edmund corrected, biting his lip after he spoke.

Surprisingly, the old crone's expression softened some. It seemed she would respect him more if he was going to stand up for himself rather than if he whimpered like the boy in his arms. Perhaps she would have been more amenable to his offers to move her if he had come in person earlier. Steeling himself, Edmund tried to improve his posture and engage her like he had engaged the family heads from the inner city earlier that day.

"Well," she said at last, "spit it out. Why are you standing on my doorstep? I have washing to do. Is there news of my s—Of Trent?"

"Not yet, I am afraid," Edmund replied. "However, I did swear to him I would keep you safe if the city came under siege. I know that you won't move to safer quarters, you told my envoys as much. Instead, I will be making your house one of the most guarded places in Illux."

He could see her expression sour again, but he raised a hand to cut her off before she could argue with him.

"I won't take no for an answer. I made a promise to Trent, and I intend to keep it with my dying breath if need be. As we have not heard from the Lady or her troops in some time, we are assuming the worst and preparing for the enemy to attack the city. I have already begun preparations for fortifications and an armed guard to come to your home. I will make sure they do not get underfoot. Now, the real reason for this visit is—"

Ajax started crying again, cutting Edmund off. The guard captain fumbled with the child, trying to coo him into silence. When she realized he wasn't going to succeed, Elise took the babe from his arms without asking and began to sing quietly in her shaky voice. Edmund recognized the song as one his own mother had sung to him once, a song about the beauty of the world on the day it was created. After a few moments, Ajax began to grow less restless.

"His name is Ajax," Edmund said. "His mother died in the rioting. I was hoping you would be able to take care of him, like you did for Trent. The boy has no one else."

"Do I look like I am the right age for children?" she snapped. "I might have hoped for grandchildren by now, even great-grandchildren, but the gods never blessed me with my own, and Trent is too...occupied to help that department either. Too busy running off on fool's errands and fighting in foolish battles. I don't need to take another orphan in. Not at my age. Can't your guards be tasked with caring for the boy?"

"They are too busy making sure the city is ready. I can see if some of the refugees will take him in," Edmund said, defeat creeping into his voice.

The old woman began to sing to the boy again, looking him over. His small clothes and swaddling were badly soiled. She sniffed at the child in disgust, and then pointed an accusatory finger at Edmund.

"You haven't been giving the child the care he deserves!" she snapped. "You must be a friend of Trent's. You have no manners and you expect help from total strangers. Gods have mercy, I will save the boy from your care."

"Thank you," Edmund said, relieved.

"And I don't want to see any of your guards," she added. "Not a single one, or I will make them wash these clothes. The ones you have out there now are an eyesore!"

Just then, an exasperated guardsman run up to the small house, nearly keeling over when he came to a stop. Sweat had plastered his once curly hair to his head. Between gasps, the man tried to speak, but he had to wait and catch his breath before he was able to get anything out.

"Captain," he wheezed. "At the western gate, some of the army has returned!"

"Trent!" Elise yelled.

"Yes," Edmund said. "Is the Lady with them? Her generals?"

"I do not-I don't know, Captain," the man said. "They are demanding entry, but the gate has not been opened. Castille's orders to keep anyone else from the city are still being followed. The others sent me to—"

"Enough!" Edmund snapped. "I will not stand by while that fool allows this city's heroes to die beyond its walls. Come, we will be opening that gate. My lady."

Elise nodded and slammed her door in the face of the two men. Edmund began a brisk jog toward the direction of the western gate, which was far from the house he had ventured to. The streets seemed empty now, as if the citizens of Illux were gathering somewhere else.

*No doubt they are trying to see what is left of our army.*

Finally, after what felt like an hour of running, Edmund found himself shouldering through a crowd of people choking the streets near the western gate of the city. The din of the crowd was nearly deafening.

"Make way!" he called. "Make way for the Watch!"

He pushed his way through the crowd to the opening near the gate where dozens of guards and three Paladins stood, including Yon and Hunt, keeping the people back from the gate. They held sour looks on their faces, and held blades aloft, as if the crowd was going to turn on them at any moment. Dozens more guards lined the ramparts far above, looking down and pointing at what lie gathered beyond the city.

"What is the meaning of this?" Edmund asked the Paladins. "Are those not our troops beyond the walls of the city?"

"They might be," a female Paladin said. "Castille's orders were clear. No one is allowed in the city. It appears the Lady Ren hasn't come with them, so none outside may overrule the orders of the Regent. And none inside, either."

Edmund ignored the venom in the woman's voice and motioned for the men and women under his command to move aside.

"I want these gates opened!" he barked. "Give me enough room to go outside and speak with them."

The woman who had challenged him started to speak, but when she saw that hateful glances of the City Watch that had begun gathering around, she backed down. Even a Paladin could be overwhelmed. The crowd seemed to grow restless as well. Several shouts of, "Ren!" and, "Open the gate!" erupted from behind Edmund. The gates began to creak as the giant doors slowly swung inwards, permitting just enough space for a single man to squeeze through. Edmund started to walk through the opening when a woman pushed her way through into the city from the outside. She was a lithe figure, well-armored, with a bow slung across her back. Most striking was the white streak that colored her dark hair. Edmund was instantly smitten by her dusky skin and dark eyes.

"What is the meaning of this?" the woman shouted. "We did not climb through the pits of Infernaak itself to be turned away at the gates of our own home. Who is in charge here?"

"I am," Hunt said, stepping forward. "In the name of Castille, Commander of the Paladin Order, Champion of the Fourth Spire, and Regent of Illux, you are denied entry to the City of Light. None are allowed entry until the Lady returns or this crisis is averted. As you are not the Lady Ren, you cannot demand entry."

"I don't care who you speak for," the woman said. "My soldiers are tired, and some are still wounded, even with the healing we have provided for them. The Lady Ren isn't coming back. Not from this plane anyway. Now open these gates and allow my people through or I will splatter you upon them and tear the fucking things down."

Gasps rose from the crowd as the woman spoke, but the Paladins didn't back down.

"Who are you?" Hunt asked.

"I am Tess of the Divine Blood," she answered.

Suddenly, her hands began to turn blueish-white, as if they had iced over. The frost moved from her fingertips, up to her elbows. Swirls of blue and white shimmers danced around her arms like a small winter storm. Her eyes had gone icy blue as well. From where he was standing, Edmund felt a chill. Tess flung a hand in Hunt's direction, sending him flying backward, awash with an icy blast. The other two Paladins tried to unsheath weapons, but Tess had already dispatched them both before they could even think, freezing their hands to their blades. The City Watch swarmed her then, while cries of fear rose up from the crowd. One man put a hand on her, which she quickly grabbed and snapped sideways before tossing the man aside like a ragdoll into the gathered mass of his fellows.

"Enough!" Edmund shouted. "All of you, stand down."

The guards stepped back from the woman, who now looked as if frost was about to cover her entire body. Once the others backed away, Tess began to return to normal, looking more human than she had before. The air seemed to warm up as well.

"Open the gate!" Edmund commanded.

*Castille be damned.*

Tess looked at him with curious eyes before nodding in thanks. Over his shoulder, Edmund could see that Hunt had been freed from the block of ice he had been planted in. Hunt and the other Paladins made their way through the crowd and away from the opening of the gates. No doubt they ran to warn Castille that some new power threatened his hold on the city.

"How do you have such power? Edmund asked. "You are no Paladin."

"No," she said, "but I have tasted the blood of a god."

# CHAPTER XI

"Somewhere up ahead is the first of the Divine Beasts that we are to awaken," Teo said solemnly.

It had seemed that the forest had been thinning as they traveled over the last several hours. A surprising number of tree stumps dotted the landscape around the little band. It was clear that whatever people lived near here were being selective in what part of the forest they cut down. It was enough that they could get by, but not so much that they alerted those below the mountains to their presence. Trent and the others had been hiking through the Rim for several days now, finally beginning the gradual descent into a shallow valley nestled between two of the smaller peaks. Though the sun was nearing its apex, much of the valley was still touched by shadow. Trent noticed a river ran through the valley that must have fed the grazing grounds in the foothills below.

*How is it possible that none of us knew that this place existed?*

Teo had remained relatively tight lipped about they should expect to find in this valley. They knew that there was a secret village here of some sort, but what manner of people populated it they did not know. The High God had stopped talking to the cryptic Balance Monk the day before, or so he said. It seemed she had wished to take her declaration that she didn't want to interfere more than absolutely necessary rather seriously. Setting them on the path was enough. Though what they were to do after awakening the Divine Beasts with no instruction was anyone's guess. Hopefully, by then their path would present itself.

"Do you suppose she will speak to you again once we arrive?" Trent asked, looking at the man to his left. "Or after, possibly?"

"I do not suppose anything with the High God. He—she—doesn't respond when I inquire. The communication isn't two-way like what you have with your gods."

Trent wasn't sure he liked Teo, and responses like that were a large reason why. The man only really seemed to engage with Rella and Divinity. To him the Seraphs were, at best, a burden, and at worst, an annoyance. It wasn't as if Balance Monks and the people of Illux had an outstanding relationship since the Purge, or more recently, when one disappeared during the assassination of Ren's predecessor Jerrok. Even so, Trent was grateful they now numbered five counting the tigress. That gave them better odds than the enemy currently held on the Mortal Plane, at least.

The sounds of bird calls had begun to lessen as the day continued on, signaling they were getting close to a human settlement. Even the scent of the Rim was different here, less earthy and pungent than it had been in the center of the mountains. Humans had their own stench that slowly took over anywhere they lived for too long. Any boy from the slums could tell you that. Trent looked past Teo to Rella, the female Balance Monk he had never expected to see again. Something about her presence here brought him comfort, but it also reminded him of what he had lost. Rella seemed more confident now than she had been all of those years before, though something intangible was missing from her as well. The last time he had seen her Devin and Gil had been alive. Now, he marched by her side into a village that would once again certainly not be what they expected, in the shadows of the Rim of Paradise no less. Rinwaithe was far from here, as was the time they had spent there, yet Trent couldn't help but shiver as he remembered that accursed place.

*Life certainly has its own sense of humor.*

Ren was walking to his right, alongside Divinity. The great cat had taken to them both, but something about Trent's scent kept her closer to him than she was to Ren. Trent found it odd, for he figured Ren would remind the tigress of Arra more than he would. The other Seraph had taken on a newfound apprehension as they neared this mysterious place in the mountains. The ominous feeling that they had all been feeling seemed greater in her. Whenever her hands absently brushed Nightbreaker, she seemed to tense. Trent decided it must be because this would be the first time she had ever encountered any humans who didn't swear fealty to her beside the Balance Monks. Perhaps, that lent an extra air of anticipation to this place for her. It wasn't often one that held so much power, even someone as humble as Ren, entered a situation where rank was meaningless.

The first signs of life were glimpsed between a break in the tress, just ahead. Two large oaks seemed to part and form a gateway to a true clearing beyond. Somehow, they had not been able to see this place from the mountains above in the days before. Birds flitted about overhead, drawing Trent's attention for the briefest moment. He looked back at the distant structures he could somewhat make out through the foliage. This valley had been chosen wisely by someone who did not wish to be found.

Suddenly, several hushed whispers were heard from just beyond the trees, and dark shapes darted away. The birds Trent had been watching seemed to have vanished as well.

"We have been seen," Teo said. "We must take caution, but do not unsheathe your blades just yet. We do not know the character of those who have been guarding this seal. Perhaps, they follow Ravim, just as Rella and I did."

Trent could tell that not even Teo was convinced by his remarks, but he kept Godtaker hidden, in any case. It did them no good to start a fight before they knew that they would need to. Allies were growing thin in this war so, perhaps, the High God sent them here to gain more than just a Divine Beast. Taking a deep breath, Trent plunged through the two oaks into the light beyond, leading his companions to their ultimate destination.

Stepping past those trees took the five companions into another world. They stood on the outskirts of a village, larger than they ever would have assumed possible. Several great trees, clearly as ancient as the mountains themselves, shaded the village from prying eyes that could gaze at it from above. The clearing had few enough trees that it was filled with the light of the midday sun, yet Trent now could see why they had not noticed any of the houses from farther up the mountainside. The small homes of the village people clung to the bases of the giant wooden sentinels like children clutching at their mother's skirts. It seemed that the homes stretched on for some distance, clearly sheltering several hundred people at least.

"Gods," Ren whispered. "Some of our villages aren't even this large. Where did all of these people come from?"

Then they saw them. The first of the villagers to make themselves known approached the small band from the center of the community. They were unarmed, an unarmored, wearing nothing but white shawls. Each of them bore a similar scar across their faces, and all of them seemed to have lost the use of their left eye. Looking at them, Trent could notice no discernible difference between them and the people of the lands below beside that unique disfigurement. Something about it was familiar to Trent, but he couldn't remember why. The leader of the people, a woman of some years, stepped forward and bowed slightly in acknowledgement. Her long dark hair remained unbraided and unadorned.

"Welcome," she said in a thickly accented voice. "Have you come to shirk off the trappings of the deceivers and the defilers to worship the Light?"

Trent started to open his mouth when he was cut off by Rella. "We have," she said. "My companion Teo and I have come for this purpose." She motioned next at Trent and Ren. "These two are Seraph's of the Light. They have already attained purity. We wish the same."

Confusion washed over several of the villagers, and they whispered to the woman. A drop of crimson formed in the duct of her damaged eye, but she quickly wiped it away, smudging some red onto her white shawl. She looked concerned at first, but then she regained her original stoicism.

"We only recognize one Seraph here," she said, slowly. "Yet you have brought two, bearing the blood of false gods. It is not up to us to judge you, but only for he above. Perhaps, you will be allowed to be purified of your sinful blood."

"We serve the High God," Ren said, harshly. "We do not serve the false gods. He sent us here for a reason."

"Yes," said Teo. "We have come to attain purity, at the behest of the High God. We were told that it could be done at a great seal. It would look like a smooth circle upon the ground. Nothing may grow there. Do you know of such a place?"

"You have spoken to the High God?" the woman asked. "The one true God of Light does not often speak with mortals! We shall show you the seal of which you speak. Though something has grown there. Now come."

The woman turned and began walking further into the village, though none of the other villagers followed her. Trent swallowed hard before he and the others fell into line behind the woman, keeping a watchful eye on the rest of village. None of them appeared to have any weapons, but their unflinching stares from their good and bad eyes alike gave Trent pause. They did not seem at all surprised to see a Seraph, let alone two.

"Who are these people?" he whispered to Ren. "What do they mean by 'one true God of Light?'"

"I am not sure," Ren answered. "We must tread carefully. I almost crossed a line back there. They clearly do not worship the same gods you and I do, or at least not in the same way. If we make one mistake, I feel that this village will turn on us."

Trent glanced down at Divinity. The great tigress had the hackles on her shoulders and spine standing on end. The group followed the woman between the large trees and small homes toward the center of the village. The pathway underneath their feet didn't look like it had been constructed, so much as it had been worn from so much traffic. Adults and children alike stopped their walks and peaked out at them from inside homes, each with the vaguely familiar scarring. All of them bore the same intense stares. When Trent made eye contact with some of them, they refused to look away.

*Why are you not afraid?*

Near what must have been the central point of the village they came upon a giant tree, larger than all of the others they had seen until now. This tree was even stranger, for it resembled nothing else upon this plane. It had bark that seemed to glow a golden color, and its leaves were amber. It didn't appear that any of the leaves had fallen on the ground, so this must have been their natural color year-round. In fact, nothing covered the ground around the tree at all. The earth here was smoothed over, and nothing had ever broken its surface. Trent was immediately struck by the immense power of the place. Trent could feel it radiating from the ground up into his feet.

"This is it," Teo proclaimed. "The first seal. This tree should not be here, though. I do not know how it grows on the Grey God's hallowed ground."

"This tree was grown from a branch of Ayyslid," the woman said softly. "It marks the betrayal of the God of Light by the deceivers."

"Betrayal?" Ren asked, her words measured. "What is the name of this place?"

"Liorus," the woman said. "The last vestige of purity in this world."

Trent's stomach began to twist into knots. He suddenly realized why the scarring of the villagers looked familiar to him. The people of this village worshipped the Fallen One as he was when he was still a God of Light. They had stumbled into a den of the enemy without even realizing it. How had they been so blind?

"I will tell lord Merek you await him at the tree," the woman said, turning away and leaving the group at its base.

"Why does that name sound familiar?" Ren mumbled to Trent.

"I don't know," he said, tensing.

"Because Merek was the last of the Forsaken Ones," Teo replied. "He was killed by the Seraph Fiora in the early years of the Pact. Or that is what history recorded."

Trent's mind reeled at the implication. The Forsaken Ones was the name that had been given to those Seraphs loyal to the Fallen One who had not given themselves up to execution when he had been cast down. The Gods of Light and Gods of Darkness had butchered their own servants in those first hours after the Pact had been created, and the Forsaken Ones had fled rather than suffer that fate. Then they had led a guerrilla war against the people of Illux, the Forces of Darkness, and the early Balance Monks of the Grey Temple. Using their knowledge of warfare and their Divine Blood, they wreaked havoc. The first reigning Seraph, a woman named Fiora, had been tasked with hunting down and killing the Forsaken Ones, many of whom she had once called friend. She and Merek finally killed each other over the sea where Seatown would eventually be founded by Arendt several hundred years later. It wasn't a story that many in Illux told anymore, though it was sometimes referenced in religious services when the Canticle of the Forsaken Ones was recited.

"We must hurry then," Ren said, pulling free Nightbreaker. "If this is the same Merek that the woman fetches right now, then we not only risk open battle with a powerful enemy, but we risk alerting the Fallen One to our cause."

Teo nodded and walked about the circle, seemingly counting his steps. When he returned to the others, he flashed his hand out, gripping Nightbreaker by the blade. The black steel cut him deeply across the palm, sending blood flowing down its surface. A grimace twisted his features for a moment. The others quickly tried to see if he was hurt, but he waved them off, returning to walk around the seal. Every few steps he shook some of his blood onto the smooth surface of the earth. The smooth ground absorbed the scarlet liquid hungrily. When he was back in front of the tree, he placed a bloody handprint on its surface and walked back to the side of his companions.

"Would you mind?" he asked Trent, holding out his bloody palm.

Trent quickly obliged by gripping the Balance Monk by the arm and filling him with healing energy.

"Only mortal blood can break the seal. Mortal blood and Divine Energy. Ren, Trent, place your swords at opposite ends of the seal."

The two Seraph's did as the Balance Monk bid them, sinking Nightbreaker and Godtaker deep into the earth at the edges of the great circle. Once they were done, Teo spoke again.

"Now, one of you fly above the tree and channel as much raw power into the swords as you can. This energy will be channeled into the Divine Beast itself, giving it the strength to break its chains and shatter the seal that I weakened with my blood."

Ren nodded and took to the air, hovering just over the top of the tree. Her wingbeats became rhythmic as she held herself aloft, closing her eyes to concentrate on the task at hand. The sunlight glinted off her armor as she began. Her hands began to crackle and glow with white hot energy, seemingly draining the light from the sky above her. Within moments, she was blasting that energy into the two swords in the earth beneath her. Trent squinted, trying to make out the details of the woman he loved as she channeled the power of a god. There was a loud rumble as the ground began to shake. Leaves finally fell off the golden tree as its branches shook furiously, cracking and popping as they did so.

"It is not yet time!" a voice boomed over the thunder.

Light returned to the world, and the rumbling stopped as Ren was knocked from the sky by a blast of blue energy. The magical attack had come from the ground at the other end of the seal, just where

Trent couldn't see its source. He ran to Ren's side, cradling the dazed woman in his arms. She wasn't badly hurt, but the attack had caught her off guard. She shook her head as she tried to sit up.

Divinity growled and rushed around the great tree, only to be thrown back where she landed with a thump. The cat was up again in an instant, shaking off her injuries. She howled with a fury that shocked even Trent. Rella and Teo took defensive stances, preparing themselves for whatever came at them now.

A winged figure flew over the tree, glaring down at them with dark, hateful eyes. His white hair was cut short, and his pale skin had been rarely browned by the sun. In each hand, the winged warrior held a sword. There was no doubt that another Seraph now hung in the sky above them.

"You dare defile this sacred place?" he boomed. His voice may have once been sweet, but years of solitude in this place had made it bitter and rancid. "You would dare to try and awaken *his* chosen?"

"We meant no disrespect," Rella said, gambling. "The High God sent us here. We need this Divine Beast to battle the Gods of Darkness."

Trent gritted his teeth as he scanned the area, noticing that the previously unarmed villagers now had surrounded the clearing with weapons of all kinds. They carried swords and cudgels and axes as naturally as a farmer held a hoe. Trent pulled Ren to her feet and tried to judge the distance to Godtaker. If he flew, he could reach the sword in seconds, but that would surely bring the attack upon him from the other Seraph. He would have to let Ren try her plan first…

Merek laughed for a moment. "Do you think me a fool? I know why you wish to free Tyr. You think you could use him against his own creator. You are fools. All in the village, both above and below the earth, have sworn an oath of fealty to Lio, the last true God of Light. None of us would turn on him, not for you or your pretenders."

"The High God herself sent us!" Trent barked, noticing that Teo had seemingly closed his eyes to meditate. "It is you who is a fool, following the Fallen One after he betrayed his oath and his people!"

"Enough talk," Teo said. "If you are going to come, then come."

Merek nodded his head, and the villagers raced across the clearing, swinging their weapons in a mad frenzy. It took only a moment for them to fall upon the companions, tearing at them with swords and axes. Trent had never seen such crude weaponry wielded so ferociously. Divinity growled, and men cried out as she raked their bellies, sending their bowels spilling onto the ground. Trent sent a burst of blue magic into his nearest attackers, completely incinerating some and catching those around them on fire. He lifted into the air to make his way toward his sword when an arrow took him in the wing and sent him back into the crowd. As he fell, he saw Merek and Ren blasting each other with spouts of white and blue energy near where Nightbreaker was lodged in the ground.

"You are not fit to carry this blade!" The male Seraph shouted. "I shall reclaim this for Daniel!"

Teo and Rella deftly split skulls and broke arms as they made their way to where Trent had fallen. While it seemed that this rabble had been prepared to attack Seraphs, they were taken aback by the speed of the Balance Monks. One of the villagers sank their hatchet into Trent's arm at the shoulder. He threw the man away, but not before the damage had been done. It seemed they would be overwhelmed by sheer numbers alone. Momentary fear overtook him, causing Trent to blindly send lighting lancing from his fingers into the crowd. The attack tore through the nearest villager and ignited the house behind them. The villager collapsed in a smoldering heap. Beside the man a little boy dropped his cudgel and began sobbing, cradling his dead father. Trent nearly retched, he had almost killed a child no older than Terric had been.

"No!" he cried out, his voice sounding foreign.

The next villager to reach him had tears in her eyes as she swung an axe at the Seraph. Trent had pulled himself to his knees by then, but didn't see the blow in time to stop it. Thankfully, Rella was there to divert the weapon with her deft fingers. The Balance Monk grabbed the haft of the axe and tossed it away. The village woman collapsed under a flurry of strikes that shattered bones in her chest and face. When she landed in the dirt, she dumbly clutched at the smoking ruin that had been her husband or brother just moments before. The small boy wailed louder now, grabbing at the blood-covered woman.

*What have I done?*

Rella grabbed Trent and shook him back to reality. "Trent," she gasped. "You must complete the ritual. That is the only way we can get out of here alive! Now go!"

The Balance Monk pulled him to his feet and motioned for him to take to the air. He did so, dumbly at first, but he eventually gained enough height to stay suspended above the tree at the center of the battle. Below he could see that the carnage had made more than one child an orphan. Some children even lay dead on ground. Steeling himself against the tide of anguish that washed over him and threatened to overwhelm him, Trent focused as much of his strength as he could into channeling Divine Energy into his fingertips. He could feel the power in his blood crackling to life with excitement. Heat radiated from his arms down to the ends of his hands where he released it into the two swords far below him.

Distantly he could hear a voice yell, "No! Stop him! Stop the defiler!"

Then Divinity let out a yowl, and the same voice cried out in pain. The great tigress had silenced the leader of the village, at least for a moment. Trent didn't open his eyes to see if his companions were keeping the arrows or the attacks of the rogue Seraph from reaching him. It didn't matter. With this much power coursing through him, nothing seemed to matter. He could hear what he thought was the ground below heaving and cracking, the branches of the tree collapsing onto the fighters below it. Still Trent kept on, until there was almost nothing of him left. Something in the air changed then, and he knew it was done.

The Seraph opened his eyes to see that the entire seal was covered with fissures that seemed to be continuously spreading. At the edge of the clearing several of the villagers tried to flee just as the ground gave way, and the earth collapsed into a great pit, taking most of them with it. Trent didn't see if the now-orphaned boy had escaped. The tree that had grown from a branch of Ayyslid fell into the darkness where even its glow could bring no light.

Trent struck the earth just beyond Godtaker, dragging himself to his sword and pulling it free. When he sat up he saw no sign of over half of those that had been fighting. In the distance, he realized that much of the village and the trees that sheltered it were ablaze. Divinity and the two Balance Monks ran to his side.

"Where is Ren?" he choked.

Then he saw her, throwing Merek aside like a doll. The other Seraph tumbled into the pit as she pulled free her sword from the ground and flew to where the group stood. The surviving villagers had begun to flee into the burning chaos of the village. Their entire world had been shattered, and Trent had done the shattering. Although his group had proven victorious, he felt hollow.

"The creature?" Ren snapped as she landed beside them, instantly placing her hand on Trent to heal him.

Suddenly, the earth shook even more violently than it had before. A great shape shot out of the pit and unfurled its wings, blocking out the light of the sun and the faint glow of Aenna for the briefest of moments before the Divine Beast landed on the lip of the pit and stared at the Seraphs and Balance Monks with inquisitive eyes.

Tyr was said to have been one of the greatest and wisest of the Divine Beasts. Looking into his sad eyes, Trent knew that it was so. The creature was nearly as large as Akklor had been, and for every bit that monster resembled a twisted bat, Tyr held the majesty of an owl. His rounded head and body were covered in blue and white feathers, giving him the coloring of the icy peaks of the upper Rim. Rather than talons upon the creature's legs, it bore great claws covered in white fur, not unlike that of Divinity herself.

"Tyr the Enlightened," Ren said deferentially, bowing as she did so.

The others, including the tigress, bowed as well. Tyr looked at them still, cocking his head one way and then another. After a moment, he closed his eyes in deep thought.

*He shares the blood of Lio...*

Then the owl opened his eyes again and regarded those below him with intense grief. When he finally spoke, it was like the sound of waves crashing upon the rocks near the sea.

"I have just spoken with Lio," he said slowly. "Do not be alarmed. He could not hide his true self from me, though he wished to. I remember the Grey God cast him down, and seeing that two of Ravim's servants stand before me, I doubt much has changed in that regard. Lio is no longer a God of Light, so I will do what I can to close my mind to him. Now, tell me, Seraphs, why have you awakened me and violated the Pact?"

Trent could feel himself sigh in relief after the Divine Beast had finished speaking. It seemed something this day had finally gone their way.

"We were sent by the High God herself," Ren said. "Lio, the Fallen One, has killed Ravim and Arra. He wages war upon all of creation, turning on those he once watched over. We have been tasked with freeing as many of your brethren as we can, or else Lio and his forces will cast the world into darkness."

Smoke began to choke the air as the fires of the village raged around them.

The great owl sighed. "It is worse than I feared. You will never know how much Lio's betrayal saddens my very spark. I see the truth of your words, Seraph. Arra's passing saddens me as well, for she was a friend to me even in the darkest of times. As for Ravim, and I mean no disrespect to his servants, I feel only the regret I was not freed sooner."

Teo and Rella nodded but said nothing.

"Now," Tyr continued, "I am at your command, Seraphs. You may tell all that has transpired while I slumbered at a later time. Where do we go from here? How best may I serve Illux?"

It was Ren and Trent's turn to look at Teo. The Balance Monk closed his eyes to see if the High God would give him any further instruction on where to find the next seal. As usually, Teo's face was impenetrable. Suddenly Tyr screeched in pain, drawing back the gaze of the five companions. A black shape hung from a blade stuck in the creature's neck. Hovering over Tyr's shoulder was the winged form of Merek.

"No!" Merek cried. "Brother! Spare him! He is not responsible for what has happened to us."

Trent and Ren took to the air, flying for the dark form that pierced the great creature. Tyr screeched again and shook his body violently, sending the dark shape careening to the earth. The owl took to the air then, the gusts of wind from the beats of his wings knocking the Seraphs earthward.

The dark figure returned to its feet and stared at the group from across the chasm. Just looking at it made Trent involuntarily shiver. It was a hulking thing, not unlike the shape of a Demon. A black cloak billowed from its neckline, cutting the ashen gray armor that it wore with a dark shadow. Its fingertips ended in talons, and various gaps in its armor showed swollen and bulbous flesh that was covered in putrescent boils and lesions. Only the bottom half of the things head was helmed, leaving thinning white hair to billow freeing in the wind above its copper skin. The creature pointed at Ren, hissing as it did so.

"That blade isss mine," it said, its voice a thin whisper.

Ren looked down at Nightbreaker, and then back at the creature.

"I know not who you are, but this blade only belongs to the ruling Seraph of Illux! Not the likes of you!" she cried out.

The creature raised its hand and sent black energy flying across the chasm into the group, slamming each of them backward in an explosion of sparks and loose stones. Suddenly, the thing stood over them, unsheathing a thin, curved blade. Trent looked up and saw pure hatred burning in the being's eyes.

"You do not know pain," it whispered. "You do not know loss. You do not know death. I will teach you."

Its blade swung down at Ren, who just barely kept it at bay with Nightbreaker. She struggled against the force of the creature while the others tried to stand. Merek joined then, hammering them with his own magic again. Ren faltered and the blade cut deep into her shoulder and sliced open her cheek. She cried out as the creature reached down to take Nightbreaker from her grasp.

Suddenly, white fire knocked the creature and the rogue Seraph away from the group. Tyr was there, raking the ground with his claws. The Divine Beast caught Merek by the wing and shredded his means of flight before casting him away. Tyr's beak opened, and white flames issued forth, pressing the other dark shape deep into the ground. Smoke and steam wafted from the crater the thing had been hammered into, bringing with it the smell of decay. The heat of the barrage should have melted even the sturdiest of metals, let alone mortal flesh.

"Quickly!" Tyr thundered. "We haven't much time. Daniel did me great injury. We must go before they have the chance to recover. We still don't know if Lio himself will attempt to face us."

The owl lowered himself and outstretched a wing so the companions could climb upon his massive back, finding purchase between his feathers. Even Divinity clawed her way upon him and nestled in.

It wasn't until the Divine Beast was flying away from the smoldering village and deeper into the Rim that Trent finally realized who it was that Tyr had named the new enemy.

*Daniel. The greatest hero the Light has ever known.*

# CHAPTER XII

How long had they been at this? His motions had become mechanical, passionless. He hadn't ever noticed his own lack of enthusiasm for bedding her before, but upon reflection, he supposed he hadn't truly enjoyed this activity for several hundred years at least. Why then did they continue? Something about the idea repulsed him in a way he didn't even think was possible. Sex was for the mortals whose lives were fleeting and already limited in pleasure. Was this the problem? Or was it something more sinister? Her golden skin and white hair reminded him too much of Arra perhaps, and the noises she made irritated him. Even so, he decided he needed to carry on, out of habit more than anything.

When he was finished, Samson shuddered and rolled off Luna, dressing himself in his armor—this ritual followed the first almost immediately, there was no warm embrace after this deed. The branches of Ayyslid rose to his every need, lifting his pauldrons and greaves to a level that made them easy to place upon himself. His armor was too clean, he realized, far too clean considering its intended purpose.

Beside him, Luna still lay upon her back, the rising and falling of her chest returning to its normal rhythm. She seemed to be ignoring him, which he honestly didn't mind.

*When did I start to hate them all?*

Arra had turned on him first, no matter how many chances he had given her. Once the wedge had been so firmly driven between them that there could be no chance of reconciliation, he had focused all of his energies on Luna. She had only interested him in passing before that, but once she had become his only option, he found her far more agreeable. Something about Luna had never seemed to sit right with him though, and now he couldn't keep that uneasiness out of his mind. Not since Arra had died, truly leaving him alone with her.

"What bothers you?" she asked, sitting upright.

"Nothing," he muttered to himself.

In his mind's eye, Arra thrust her blade into herself, the inexperienced mortal clutching at the hilt like some awestruck fool. The image filled him with rage. They were now outnumbered by the enemy due to her foolishness, and now there was even a new Seraph on the Mortal Plane with no connection to either Luna or himself. That left them with only the failure Ren to stand against the forces of the Fallen One. She had already proven herself inadequate once, and he had no doubt she would do so again before long.

"Are you thinking about the Seraphs again?" Luna asked.

"Ren has been ignoring us since we sent them back," he said. "How are we to know the progress they have made? We should punish her for this disrespect. Perhaps, it is time to elevate Castille."

They knew something had gone wrong when the mortals had stepped into the Basin, but what or how, they did not know. Tyr had been awakened sometime after. Of that they were sure because they could feel his presence in the world again like a familiar smell on the breeze. His mind had reached out to theirs, but he had not had much to say. Though he had once been Lio's creature, Divine Beasts could communicate with all of their gods, no matter whose blood they shared. It seemed that even after a thousand years to contemplate his existence, Tyr had not quite come around to respecting Samson and Luna in the way he had Lio and Arra in the days before the Pact.

Fear of attack from the Gods of Darkness had forced Samson and Luna away from the window to the Mortal Plane and back to the safety of Ayyslid. Samson didn't like to admit to himself that he was afraid of what Lio could do to him, but deep down he knew he always had been. The onetime God of Light had been a shining example, greater than any of his peers could ever have hoped to be. He was braver, stronger, and more loved by the people. And when he fell, it was as if the strongest branch of Ayyslid had withered to nothing.

"Ignore them," Luna cooed. "We have no need of their weakness. Let the last vestige of Arra's folly fade with her. Castille will make sure that the city doesn't fall. As a reward for his service, you and I will journey to the Mortal Plane to give him the gift he has sought for so long. Then he will lead our armies and crush the enemy upon the Mortal Plane, once and for all."

*How could she possibly think it will be that easy?*

Samson walked to the wall opposite where he had been sitting. An alcove formed, producing two goblets of clear liquid. The ambrosia was sweet and full-bodied; it warmed the body without dulling the senses like the wine that the morals craved. He tilted the smooth wooden goblet to his lips and let the drink fill his mouth and run down his chin. It tingled where it touched, even through his armor. This was possibly his favorite of the many gifts of the High God to make their fortress feel like a home.

He hoped the pause would give him time to think. Luna eyed him silently, awaiting his response, tapping her fingers on her hip. When he spoke again, his mouth was surprisingly dry.

"Do you really think Illux can stand alone?" he asked. "What of the Divine Beasts? Those cretins in Infernaak haven't been sitting idly by, waiting for us to bring the fight to them. They have been rebuilding.

They have most likely already created a new Herald, and have begun awakening Divine Beasts, just as we should be doing. Castille will not be prepared for the powers of Divine Blood to rage against his walls. We need to take direct action, we need to intervene."

"On the Mortal Plane? Luna asked, a quiver in her voice.

"Or the Divine."

He turned his back to her and let that final pronouncement sink in. No matter how much he secretly feared Lio, he had been contemplating an attack on their enemies since before the Pact had even been broken.

*I have been weak, hiding in this place.*

Samson took the second goblet, normally reserved for Luna, and drained it as well. When he was finished, he casually cast the thing aside. It was swallowed up by the wall of the room before it should clatter onto the floor. He leaned into the alcove that the ambrosia had come from, gripping the bottom of the ledge so tightly he thought the branches recoiled some. Even Ayyslid could know fear.

Attacking Infernaak directly was the only way. They had stayed hidden for so long that none of the Gods of Darkness would ever think that Samson or Luna even had such bravery in them anymore. If they could get close enough for Samson to kill Lio with his bow, the contest would suddenly become much more even. He did not fear facing Vardic or Rhenaris.

*Perhaps, with that lunatic gone, the other two can be reasoned with?*

Luna still hadn't spoken, though Samson could feel her eyes burning a hole in his back. He hadn't been sure what her response to his suggestion would have been. After all of this time together, after every instance of their physical encounters, and he still wasn't sure what was going to happen next. He knew every inch of her body, but he didn't know her mind. Arra's reaction he would have been able to guess, but Luna? Her moods swung wildly from playful ambivalence to outright scorn so often that he found himself not really caring what she was thinking. After another few moments of ignoring the goddess, Samson finally turned to face her. Luna's face was even more unreadable than usual, though now she had crossed her arms to cover her chest, hiding her nakedness from him.

"You really think that direct assault is the right idea?" she asked flatly. "Have I finally drained enough of you that you are as idiotic as Arra was?"

Samson slammed his fist into the wall behind him. The entire fortress seemed to shudder, and the glow of the branches thrummed in and out of existence for a moment. His anger was not with her directly, but with himself for allowing them to fall so far from what they once were. In some ways he was more pitiable than even Lio.

"I am not confused," he said through gritted teeth. "Perhaps, you are. We have gotten soft, Luna. Passive."

Samson began pacing the room, no longer making eye contact with his companion. He couldn't afford to let her get into his head. He couldn't allow her to pull him back into the routine. Too much was at stake now. Too many gods lay dead to waste time with passions of the flesh, no matter how much he might crave it. He swore silently to himself that he would never enter her body again. He had not enjoyed her for hundreds of years—it would be no loss.

"We must attack Infernaak directly. If we move quickly, we can catch them off guard," Samson mused. "One arrow is all that it will take to end Lio. Then we can deal with Vardic and Rhenaris. If they will not heed our whims, then we will crush them. What happens on the Mortal Plane doesn't matter if we can win the war here. Illux itself could fall and the Light would still be victorious."

She seemed to be considering his words carefully. Finally, she uncovered herself and began to climb across the bed toward where he stood.

"I will trust you," she cooed, lifting herself up to eye level. "Now come back to me."

Ignoring his previous protestations, Samson leaned in to the open-mouthed kiss of the goddess. Within moments, he was again unclothed and falling upon her. For the first time in longer than he could remember, the action excited him.

# CHAPTER XIII

The air here was thick with sand and dust. Swirls of brown and white drifted over the hills, nipping at each other like the fighting of wild dogs. Nowhere else on all of the Mortal Plane was as dry and lifeless as the sprawl before him, a shallow husk of the world to the north. He despised this arid landscape almost as much as he had despised Infernaak. That fire-filled prison would be the first place he was going to destroy once he had become the lone God of Light. The towers would topple into the magma, the isle of the meeting place would be obliterated, and only then would he turn his sight east. All of the Divine Plane would be cleansed, leaving nothing but his throne.

The Fallen One stood atop a gradual slope, overlooking a broad valley several miles across. A dust storm obscured the bottom, but he could imagine what lay below: a sea of bodies, some made of ever-rotting flesh, and others shelled with slick black plate. Beside him stood his red-skinned servant Xyx. The Herald had chosen to only wear a small cloth to cover his loins, disdaining the flowing cloak that his predecessor had taken a liking to. This was a good sign. The previous

Herald had grown decadent, confident not just in the power of his gods, but in his own intelligence. This arrogance had been his undoing. If only he had slain the Seraph when he had the chance, then Arra's last interference would have had no lasting impact.

Once more he sized up Xyx, taking in the rippling musculature and coarse black beard with reserved admiration. Although the name of the creature had filled Lio with rage, he had somehow kept the emotion bottled away. It wasn't meant to slight him, though it was meant to revere his greatest foe. Even so, he couldn't lash out over something as simple as a name. The other Gods of Darkness would realize how desperately he clutched at his sanity, and then they would surely strike.

*I would simply be forced to kill them sooner.*

It was the hardest thing he had ever done, leaving Vardic and Rhenaris still breathing for this long. For the moment they were useful, just like the unfortunately named Herald. Lio knew he was the strongest of the gods that still lived, but he was no fool. Once the balance of power shifted, and his enemies outnumbered his allies, he could be crushed just as easy as any of them. Even Xyxax had fallen.

Maintaining his numerical advantage is what had brought Lio to this forsaken corner of the Mortal Plane. Xyx had had more trouble rounding up the scattered remnant of their army that Arra had routed than Lio had anticipated. Once Merek had warned him that the Seraphs had found Liorus and awakened Tyr, he knew he could waste no further time. It seemed that Arra had once again disrupted his plans—it had to have been her for the other two were too cowardly to even think of creating a second Seraph. That still didn't explain how they had found the hidden village. No one had known of its existence, not even the previous Herald. There was too great a prize tucked away in that place, and now it had been loosed upon the world.

*Forgive me.*

Lio tried to shut the guilt from his mind as he looked back across the plane below. The previous Herald had only taken a third of the forces gathered here, using those to augment the various bands of Demons and Accursed they had been able to gather together over the years following the death of the last Seraph. A death that Xyx had carried out. It was fitting that this champion would lead the remainder of these forces back to the city. It was fitting that Xyxax had hidden them here some thousand years before, and now his namesake would lead them out. Sometimes the High God smiled upon even his most wretched of creations.

The Fallen One spat and then began his descent into the valley. He could have journeyed directly to them from Aenna, or even flown down from the rise above, but something told him that this needed a more subtle approach. His previous army had formed under the guidance of the Herald, thinking that all of the Gods of Darkness were commanding them, a ruse that was fitting at the time. They had not known that it had been their one-time enemy alone that commanded them to come forth. Indeed, these he hoped to gather today had walked the Mortal Plane even when he had fought against them. It was too late to deceive them as to who really ruled in Infernaak. If Akklor the Unbidden, most loyal of all of Xyxax's servants, could be forced to submit, then so could these Demons.

The gradual slope finally gave way to level ground, though exactly what lie ahead of him was still masked by the swirling dust. After another few steps, giant structures loomed ahead of him, silhouettes behind a curtain of silt. The previous Herald had not told him what to expect when he journeyed to these long-forgotten reaches. All that the Fallen One had been told was that these Demons were tribal, and often fought amongst themselves. It wasn't natural for these creatures to remain leaderless for so long. They were crafted with the intent of being ruled by an iron will, and it was long past time for that will to be imposed on them.

Lio had overinflated the willingness of these Demons to join their cause and journey north to join the siege when he had told Vardic and Rhenaris of their existence. The third of their number that the

Herald had brought north had been all they could convince to leave the confines of their valley. The rest had spat in his face. Too long it had been since they had felt the yoke of the gods.

The first structures appeared out of the wall of dust, a black tower made of spikes and barbs, jutting haphazardly from the earth like a thorn from a branch. Even coated in a thick layer of silt it still glistened unnaturally. Corpses hung from the many points, the familiar bodies of Accursed hanging limply, impaled through the chest or the posterior. Near the top of the tower, a dark shape gripped one of the spikes, a red cape billowing from its neck. The Demon quickly leapt away, disappearing into the dust.

*Tell them the destroyer has come, for none of them shall survive in my new world.*

More and more of the spiked towers rose to greet them, appearing and fading into the wall of brown miasma that encircled them. They didn't spot another Demon among the towers though, for it seemed they had been warned by the first. Beside him, Xyx looked unafraid, foolish considering the situation. Even though he walked with a god, the Herald was not safe here. What had the previous Herald told him they had called this place? *Godsend*?

Lio knew they must have been getting close to the central location where he could call upon the Demons to treat with him, for the grouping of the strange structures seemed to be tightening. After another few minutes the pair found themselves standing in a giant circle of spine covered towers. Hanging from various heights around them were the familiar shapes of Demons, with smears of blood fluttering behind them.

"Xyx," Lio murmured.

"Yes, master?" the creature hissed.

"Leave me," Lio said. "Fly back north to the seal that I showed you, wait there for me. I won't be long."

The Herald looked confused but nodded and took to the air anyway, flying through the swirling dust back the way they had come. The nearly impenetrable wall swallowed the winged figure up without a trace. Lio had a feeling that the next part of this gambit wouldn't go as smoothly, and decided he did not need the Herald to bear witness to any potential questioning of his power.

*Soon, none of this will matter. Soon all of you will fall before me. Merek will stand by my side. Daniel...*

He shook his head to clear the thoughts, drawing free his sword as he did so. The Fallen One cast about warily, looking for any signs of attack from the gathering Demons. He could sense more of them than he could see in the haze. There had yet to be any signs of still living Accursed. Hopefully they had not depleted their numbers since the last time he had called upon this colony.

"Who among you leads here?" Lio shouted.

Silence answered him.

Then a cruel laugh rang out. It was a hollow sound, and it echoed off the spires and filled Lio's mind. He was being mocked, and he knew it. He gritted his teeth and spat on the ground before him. These creatures were no better than beasts to him. He would remind them of such. Using the back of his hand, Lio brushed his stringy hair from the front of his bad eye, making sure they could see the wound his enemy had given him.

"Are you Demons or cowards?" the Fallen One asked. "Who among you will speak to me?"

Dozens of the dark shapes dropped to the ground, slowly encircling him from the edges of the dust storm. Still, none of them dared to get within range of his blade. As if he needed steel to wipe them from the face of the Mortal Plane. Even in a place called Godsend, gods were to be feared.

It was when the Demons neared that he noticed something different about them. Each had a different pattern of red and ashen colored markings painted on their eyeless helms and spike breastplates. Few Demons had ever taken the time to adorn themselves in such a way before. The Herald had not been wrong. These creatures had changed in the millennium they had been isolated in the south. They had developed a culture of some kind.

"Who leads among you?" he shouted again.

A lone figure stepped out of the haze, a great brute even among Demon-kind. Its helm was made to resemble many branching horns, not unlike the antlers that adorned several of the beasts which roamed the Rim. From its belt hung the severed heads of five Accursed, many with little or no flesh left upon them. The Demon held a double-edged battle axe in each hand as it strode forward to meet Lio's challenge. When the creature was no more than a few feet from the fallen god, it spoke to him in a voice that sounded like iron dragging across stone.

"I lead those gathered before you."

The Fallen One smiled.

"No, I do," he hissed.

In a flash, moving faster than any mortal eye could hope to follow, Lio's now glowing sword had struck the head from the Demon's body. The hulking brute shuddered and fell to its knees. The dark god outstretched his hand and hammered the creature's corpse with a blast of grey and black flame, crumpling the armor into a smoking crater in the middle of the clearing. When he was finished the valley was once again as silent as the grave. This time the laugh that broke the silence was his own.

"Who's next?" Lio shouted.

Dozens of the dark shapes launched at him from all angles. They swarmed him like ants to a dying beetle. Fire lanced into him, knocking him this way and that. Black swords flashed to life at the edges of his vision; each he dodged with an inhuman swiftness. Even so, it only took moments for him to be covered by the creatures. Belatedly, he thought they really would have looked like ants to one watching them from above. How deceiving that would have been.

Cackling wildly, Lio threw out his arms, sending the Demons flying in all directions. The burst of raw energy that exploded out of him caused several of the Demons to be impaled by the spikes on their towers, while others tumbled out of sight into the swirling dust. The Fallen One followed up with a magic assault, sending glowing energy down the length of his blade into the Demons that were still standing. They melted before him as if they were nothing.

Once he was tired of seeing smoldering corpses collapse into the dirt, he gripped his sword with two hands and ran at those who were left. The Demons had begun to flee in terror, but none would escape his wrath. He had not seen Demons run like this since the Northern Campaign when Daniel or the members of Ash Company chomped at their heels.

Lio cleaved a Demon in two, then deftly leapt away, arcing through the air before landing on one of the towers where a Demon hung, watching. He grabbed it by the helm and crushed its head in his hand. Then he was on the ground again, slicing here and there, laughing all the while. The Demons screeched as they ran from him, their cries echoing from tower to tower. The spine-covered edifices began to collapse as godly magic split them in half, sending up a shower of sparks and dust. He leapt again, this time landing on a creature directly, creating a crater where it had been running. The earth shook so fiercely that several more of the towers fell.

It had been a long time since he had killed the Forces of Darkness. Too long.

It was several hours later when the Fallen One walked out of the valley with a host of Demons and Accursed at his back. He had continued to hunt and kill the twisted creatures for longer than he had intended. The feeling had been euphoric, addictive even. Blotting out evil was what he had been created to do. Once he had decimated perhaps a quarter of their number, the others kneeled to him in submission. They took him to the fighting pits where they had done battle with one another for dominance of the tribes. Apparently, their leader, whom he had killed had been undefeated for decades.

*They called it Godsend. Well, a god has ended it.*

Behind the pits was where they kept what was left of the Accursed. Many had been killed for sport over the years, while a good number of them had been given as tribute to the last Herald. The Demons had hoped that if they had provided him with a large enough force they continue to live here undisturbed for the rest of time. What fools they had been. Ravim was right in one thing, creation often righted itself when its balance was disturbed. Injustice would be met with justice in time. Now, Lio had an army at his back that nearly matched what they had lost near the Great Chasm.

He found Xyx where he had instructed him to wait, several miles to the north near a large smooth circle. This clearing was a seal that held one of the Divine Beasts. The shackled creature sensed his presence and stirred underground, calling to him to free it. When Ravim had sealed all of the creatures away, Lio had watched from the Basin, along with each of the other gods, making mental note of where each was chained. It was, perhaps, the only time that all of them had stood so close to each other without any violence. They had been too dumbstruck by the rapidly changing world around them to even think of raising a hand against the others. Not with the recent departure of the High God and Ravim forcing them under the Pact.

It was watching from the Basin that day that allowed him to know which seals to command the previous Herald to break. Now he would bid Xyx to do the same, starting with this one. Many more would be needed after this creature crawled forth. If Tyr was free and fighting alongside the traitors then they would need more than just a handful of Divine Beasts to ensure the destruction of Illux.

When Lio approached the seal, Xyx stared at the army gathering behind them in awe. This amount of Demons would not have been seen in one place in this wretch's lifetime, of that the Fallen One was sure. Xyx quickly kneeled before his master, nearly prostrating himself on the ground. Lio ignored him, quickly motioning for several of the Demons to gather around the area. They dragged between them an Accursed. The mindless creature did not struggle, but neither did it walk between them of its own accord. The Fallen One nodded and the Demons each grabbed a limb and pulled the thing into several pieces, spilling its black and red blood upon the earth. They dipped their swords in the blood and sank them at the edges of the circle. Mortal Blood was required to break the Grey God's seals, and any Mortal Blood would do. The previous Herald enjoyed hunting down prey to use for these rituals, when he had a limitless supply of Accursed he could have easily used. His penchant for theatrics and game-playing had been his downfall, Lio mused.

The Fallen One rose into the air, floating over the center of seal, high above it. He held out his hands as they began to glow with energy. Moments later the ritual was done and seal was cracking across its surface and bulging upward the Divine Beast struggled to break free.

The carapace of multi-armed creature shined in the glow of the midday sun, splitting the rays of light, and bouncing them into the god's eyes in a myriad of colors. Its chitinous armor was harder than any plate mail and twice as thick. It had two long tails, each terminating in barbed stinger long enough to skewer three men. Its front legs curled back in on themselves into scythe-like claws. The front of its body bulged upward to form a crude head that looked akin to a Demon's helm. Its mandibles dripped black venom and slather that sizzled when it hit the ground. Even from where he hung in the ground Lio could smell the poison on this beast.

"Guod the Venomous," Lio said, softly. "Tear down the stones of Illux, and bring me the head of their Seraph."

The hiss of the creature was answered by the cries of the Demons at his back.

# CHAPTER XIV

It had been over a day since they had last flown on Tyr. The Divine Beast was just too large to not be spotted by their enemies who were surely hot on their trail by now. The owl-like creature had been the one to suggest the change, and although it meant more work for them, no one had particularly argued with him. Trent knew that he, at least, wasn't comfortable flying on the back of the Divine Beast, no matter how convenient it was. He had to keep reminding himself he had wings now, which meant that if for some reason he was to fall off Tyr he would have been fine, but he still couldn't shake the feeling of discomfort.

The group was nestled in a small alcove under an overhanging rock that jutted out of the mountainside like broken glass from a tavern floor. Tyr was crowded at the back of the alcove, trying his best not to burst upward and burry his companions in an avalanche of rubble. The two Seraphs sat beside each other on one side of the small cook-fire, while the two Balance monks sat on the other. Outside, Divinity stalked through the woods looking for her breakfast. The others had to settle for cooked mushrooms that Teo claimed were safe. The Divine Beast went without a meal altogether. Trent had no idea what something so large could possibly eat in any case.

He had spent the night pressed against Ren, and he enjoyed every moment of it. It had been the first time they had done so since they had shared their kiss in Ayyslid. Whether it had taken her this long to admit her feelings that had burst out in the god's refuge, or whether she had just needed time to grow comfortable viewing Trent in the capacity he wasn't sure. Even with as much contact as they shared now, Ren refused to let Nightbreaker leave her side. The sheathed blade sat between them, one final barrier Trent couldn't overcome.

The appearance of the creature Tyr had named Daniel had shaken all of them, but Ren had been affected the most. She wouldn't talk about what they had encountered in that village two days ago, choosing instead to only really discuss what lie ahead. Even with her silence on the matter, Trent could tell that something about Daniel nagged at her even still.

The High God hadn't spoken directly to Teo again, but he did have a newfound confidence he knew the location of the next seal. He couldn't say why exactly, but he said he had an overwhelming feeling that they were headed in the right direction. It seemed the High God was content with feeding him premonitions rather than directly speaking to him now.

*I just hope the next one isn't buried under another enemy outpost.*

"Do you think we will find it today?" Ren asked, rubbing the last vestige of sleep from her eyes.

They had all just awakened a few minutes before. Teo wasted no time starting the small fire to cook the last of the food he had foraged for them the night before. The small fungi sizzled on a flat rock that Teo laid on the bed of coals. He promised that the taste would be adequate, but Trent had his doubts. The roots they had eaten last night had tasted bad enough that Trent had considered going without food of any kind.

"Yes," the monk said sternly. "I can feel it. We are close to another great power. In fact, within a few days, we will have freed four or five more Divine Beasts. The majority of them sleep beneath these mountains, after all."

"And then what do we do with them?" Trent asked, eyeing the mushrooms.

"Then we restore the balance," Teo said.

Tyr snorted. The sound was a loud rumble that reverberated through the stone and put everyone on edge for a moment.

"The very same balance that locked me away for a thousand years?" he thundered. "I appreciate that you are helping the Seraphs, but I do not serve the Grey God, nor the memory of him. I serve the Light."

The Divine Beast hadn't been very talkative since they had rescued him. He had come to terms with the changes that had occurred in the world since his imprisonment, and he knew the stakes in what they now set out to do, but he hadn't provided much in the way of his opinion until now. All they knew was that he was no friend to Lio any longer, and from what little they had gathered, he wasn't pleased with Samson or Luna either.

"We are serving the wishes of the High God," Rella interjected.

"I do not doubt that you believe that to be true," Tyr rumbled, "but your interpretation of her wishes is colored by your own philosophy. Just as ours is. I believe that the High God has intervened because she has always taken the side of the Light. Why else would she even have made you mortals if not to get you to strive for goodness and purity? The Gods of Darkness were only even created to give the Light purpose."

"To create balance," Teo said.

"As you say," Tyr said.

He shifted about, clearly feeling the confines of their shelter.

"Balance monks have always followed the wishes of the High God through her servant Ravim. That is what we did when we purged Illux, or helped the Broderick bring down the rogue Paladin Cecilia. Balance is the will of the High God, a balance that is now so damaged that we have been tasked with aiding the Light in restoring it."

The name of Trent's old mentor set him edge.

*I'm not letting this go.*

"Tyr makes a valid point," Trent said. "Why do you still follow the teachings of Ravim? Why not fully commit to the Light now that he is gone? Surely, that doesn't fly in the face of the High God's wishes, or else she would have tried to turn Ren and I toward your path, rather than keeping us on our own."

"Would you stop following the Light if your gods died?" Teo asked. "Would you simply fall to Darkness?"

Trent looked back at him over the flames, trying to read his face. Rella had earned his trust in Rinwaithe, and Broderick had even spoken of a time when he had given up his worship of the Gods of Light and taken up with the Balance Monks for a time after Cecilia. Still, something about Teo's commitment to Balance unnerved Trent.

"No," he conceded, "I suppose not."

Teo finished the mushrooms and pulled them off the stone, handing two to each companion. They nibbled on the fungi in silence, no one wanting to continue the discussion of what they would do if more gods died. Trent decided that the mushrooms were better than the roots had been, and in better circumstances he might have even enjoyed them. After some time, Divinity stalked back into the area, carrying a fox in her mouth. As she lay beside them and tore at the creature's haunch, Trent eyed her jealously. He found he didn't enjoy the mushrooms after all.

"Tell us of Daniel," Ren said, suddenly. The sounds of eating stopped, and the alcove fell silent.

"I wish I could, my Lady," Tyr said. "But it pains me to speak of such a friend. I knew what Xyxax had done to him, for I was present at the battle when Lio slew that foul being. While the gods fought, I did battle with Akklor and Glyyk. All the while, Daniel was left lying on the ground as a twisted wretch. His mind was gone."

The Divine Beast turned his great head so he was no longer looking at the group.

"I did not know he had survived to this age," he continued. "I never would have imagined he was imprisoned above me. After Ravim chained me beneath his seal I lost all connection to the world beyond. I could sense some of the goings on, but I had no idea Daniel was so close. Upon Ravim's death, I could feel my chains weakening and I grew restless, but even then, I never would have thought that one of my closest friends was going to sink his blade into me upon my awakening. If I could strike down Xyxax again, I would. I wish to devour his entrails and gorge myself on his silver blood."

The Divine Beast had begun to expand himself, his chest puffing out and his wings pressing against the walls of the overhang. When he realized how much he pushing the rest of the group around he shrank back to his previous confined size and returned to a sullen silence.

"Our histories say he was killed by Xyxax," Ren muttered. "They mercifully left out the truth."

"As do the chronicles set down by Ravim," Rella said. "Nor did we know that Merek had survived his duel with Fiora. Much, it seems, was swallowed up by the ages."

"What of the other Divine Beasts?" Tyr growled. "Who else has been freed by the enemy? You mentioned yesterday that I am not the first to return."

"Akklor," Trent said.

*That monster that killed Devin.*

"And Gaxxog," Teo added.

"Akklor?" Tyr bristled, rising again. "I am sorry, mortals, but I cannot stay here while that creature yet lives. I may not be able to rid the world of Xyxax, but I can slay his greatest servant! I will find you again when the deed is done."

"There is no need, Tyr," Ren said, firmly. "Trent killed that awful thing just before Arra died."

Tyr laughed then. It was the sound of crashing waves and summer thunder that echoed through the chamber.

"Is there no justice?" the Divine Beast asked. "I am robbed twice then. Next, you will tell me that Rexin the Blasted has returned from the dead and darkens the skies to the south once more. I am surprised, mortal. You killed him even before you bore the blood? Well done. Arra chose wisely."

Trent simply nodded.

"And Gaxxog?" Tyr asked.

"It was that beast that overtook the Grey Temple," Teo said. "It is because of that creature that we two are the last of Ravim's servants. As far as we know, it is still there."

"We will avenge your brothers and sisters, of that I am sure," the Divine Beast said. "Now, let us go and awaken mine."

With that pronouncement, the companions finished their food and cleaned up what little they had left behind, making their way into the forest beyond the clearing surrounding their shelter. From what they could guess, they were currently near the center of the Rim, several days, if not weeks, from the Grey Temple. Beyond that another few day's journey would be the coast. Even the Balance Monks rarely traveled this far through the mountains. The pathways were often steep and dangerous, but beyond that there didn't seem to be any monsters beyond those that were sleeping beneath them. The childhood stories that Elise, and his mother before her, had told him of the Rim had been overblown. Although, they had no idea what lurked beyond the village behind them, or further north in the mountain range for that matter. The Rim of Paradise continued to the north for as far as they could see, even from the air. Teo said he couldn't feel any Divine Beasts in that direction, and they knew that it wasn't safe to go back, so they continued east.

Trent felt he saw far fewer animals than he would have expected, though he imagined that this was due to Tyr roughly clambering through the trees at the rear of the party. The great boughs bent or broke as he slid between them, making enough noise that they could have very well been heard for miles around. When they encountered a section of forest he couldn't fit through, Tyr would choose to go around, preferring to stay out of the sky if at all possible. Trent tried not to laugh at the sight of the giant owl-shaped being as it lamely tried to squeeze between the firs and pines. Divine Beasts were not created with subtlety or stealth in mind.

*The trail Tyr is leaving could be tracked by a blind man.*

Looking over, Trent saw Ren's scowl had finally softened. He had finally pieced together what he thought had been bothering her. It seemed likely she had been so badly shaken by the appearance of Daniel because of what he represented. If a hero such as Daniel could fall, what hope did either of them have? She had never held the pride or faith in herself that her forebears had. Arrogance was a trait common to most of the ruling Seraphs, born out of their uniqueness as much as their position as the leader of Illux. Although his wicked words were meant to unsettle her, the Herald hadn't helped matters. Neither had the Gods of Light with the way they had called her a failure. Trent wished she could shrug them all off as he had. He knew her worth, and it was twice what any of theirs was. She was far stronger than he had even been or ever would be. Terric and Devin both had died on his watch, while Ren had kept Trent alive while his life had been in her hands. Arra had chosen well. He just hoped the goddess had chosen well twice.

"Are you all right?" he whispered to her.

"I will be," she responded, distantly. "I don't mean to take it out on you, but I have never felt so lost. Even when we were fighting Lio's army I at least had the victory of a glorious death to look toward. Now I ask myself why I was chosen, when others were not? Why I am holding this sword when its rightful owner was turned into a wretched ghoul?"

"I can't answer that. But I know you will see us through this," Trent said.

"That's just it, Trent," she snapped. "You follow me, still. Arra made us equals. Yet you still look to me. I might still command in Illux, and you may see me as your superior because I was made Seraph first, but I can't keep making every decision, especially when the ramifications end in so much death. I don't want you to protect me anymore, Trent. I know you love me, but it was love between Lio and Daniel that ruined the Mortal Plane. If I die, then I die. Don't put my life first, not anymore."

Ren skulked off, taking Divinity with her to walk closer to Teo and Rella. She pushed on ahead, shouldering through the leafy fronds of a large fern. Trent tried to blink away the burning he felt behind his eyes and keep the bile from rising any further in his throat. He had lost everyone he had ever cared about besides Elise and Ren. He would not stand by and let anything take Ren's life, no matter how much she protested.

*You may hate me for it, but I will die for you.*

He continued to stare after her as she wandered ahead, his mind playing back over the death of his brother and Devin. "Choice," the High God had told him, "everyone has a choice."

It was several hours later when they finally stumbled across the next seal. Some of the trees here leaned over the clearing, but once again, nothing actually grew within it. Birds and other animals did seem to gather at the edges of the seal in unusually large numbers, however. They were drawn to the essence of whatever was chained beneath. Trent tried to rack his brain for any such place he might have seen when he was on one of the various ranging missions he and Devin had taken over the years. He seemed to recall having seen places like this once or twice, but nothing stuck out in his mind. Had he known what they had been at the time? His memory of those adventures had started to bleed into what he knew of the world now. Broderick must have known. The old Paladin commander had told Trent once that he had been places and seen things that even the gods would balk at.

Teo undertook the same ritual as he had before, cutting himself on Nightbreaker's edge and sprinkling his blood upon the soil. When he was finished, Trent walked over to heal him, but Ren cut him off and did it first. Her back was to him while she placed her hands on the monk, sparing Trent from the embarrassment of her seeing his expression. When she was done, she took to the air and filled both swords with magic, until the ground crumbled and dropped away, leaving another great chasm in its wake. Some of the trees that had leaned over the clearing the farthest fell into the void. The gathering of woodland creatures peered over the edge in awe.

Then a great silver hand reached out of the pit, followed by another. A golden-haired creature pulled itself up onto the lip of the clearing. It was large and muscular, with a shaggy mane of fur the color of honey that covered everything but its face and hands, which were as silver as the liquid that filled the Basin. It sniffed at the air and beat its chest with its human-like limbs, howling and barring sharp fangs. Without warning, it gripped a nearby tree and ripped it from the ground, tossing it high over the tree line. The animals scattered into the forest.

"Finally!" it boomed. "I was days away from going mad! Tyr? Is that you? Gods be praised!"

"My friends," Tyr said, "this is Aion the Just. Greatest of the Divine Beasts who cannot take to the skies."

"Certainly on land, and even sea," Aion thundered. "Tell me, Tyr, what has changed in the world while we slept?"

"More than you could ever guess at," Tyr said. "Walk with me a while."

The Divine Beasts turned and ignored the group, pushing through the trees. Trent and the others watched them go, unsure whether or not they should follow. Finally, Teo turned and started in the opposite direction, heading for the next seal.

"They will find us," he said. "We don't have time to wait for them."

The rest of the day continued on the same as before. The trees and ferns and shrubs that covered the side of the mountain looked just as they had for the last several miles. If it hadn't been for the guidance of the monk, Trent would have thought they were headed in circles. Eventually, the two Divine Beasts rejoined them, with Aion helping Tyr make it through trees and over boulders that the owl couldn't have done on his own without flying. Before the day was over, they had awakened one more Divine Beast and, according to Teo, had made it half of the way to a fourth.

# Chapter XV

Lythe the Untainted flew just above the ground past Trent, undulating through the air like it was moving through water. Small ice crystals shimmered in a haze around the creature. The silver snake was the smallest of the three Divine Beasts they had yet awakened, but it was still large enough to swallow a man whole. Lythe resembled a silver adder, but with large membranous wings to carry it across the winds. When its mouth opened, it could blow a wind so cold that it could freeze a Demon solid. Lythe had been the least talkative of the three, but she often hissed her disapproval when the rest of the group decided what they needed to do next. Trent guessed it was due to the fact that she was now fighting on the opposite side of Merek. They had both fought together in the legendary Ash Company during the Northern Campaign over a thousand years before.

Aion and Tyr argued that all of the Divine Beasts should be heading directly to Illux, while Ren and Trent thought they should stay together until the time was right. Even now, they were gathered in a clearing arguing about what to do next.

"We don't even know if the enemy has regrouped yet," Ren said, firmly. "We cannot risk dividing our greatest asset."

*Or give them over to Castille.*

Lythe circled back again, hissing in distaste. Tyr stretched his great wings and rocked back and forth on his claws uneasily. Aion leaned forward onto his knuckles, eyeing Ren harshly. While the Divine Beasts were often under the command of the Seraphs in the days of old, they were certainly equally powerful, and it seemed they didn't want to take orders from two Seraphs their junior by more than a thousand years. Not when they were yearning for vengeance for a millennium of imprisonment.

"And what if they have?" Aion growled. "What if the city lies in ruin when we arrive? I have enough that I feel the need to avenge, I don't need to wait for more."

"I agree with the SSSeraph," Lythe hissed, coiling beside Trent and Ren. "How many of usss are left? We cannot risssk losssing three more. If the city fallsss, then ssso be it. The Light mussst live on."

"The city will not fall!" Trent exclaimed. "The High God herself set us on this task. We cannot falter, not now."

He cast a glance at Ren, but she refused to meet his gaze. It didn't seem that she would help him here. They had hardly spoken since the previous day, and last night she had slept beside Divinity rather than him. Feeling defeated, Trent started to move away from the group when Tyr finally spoke.

"We are all in this together, even you two." The great owl motioned toward Teo and Rella. "What say you, servants of Ravim?"

"We stay the course," Rella piped up, looking at Teo.

"I agree," Teo said. "We are nearly at a fourth of your kind to release, and after that I expect to find at least two more before the Grey Temple."

"The Grey Temple?" Tyr asked.

"Yes," Teo replied. "We cannot leave Gaxxog unaccounted for."

"We shouldn't even be wasting this much time!" Aion shouted, hammering his chest. "Let alone wasting even more avenging a God of Darkness. This is foolish!"

"The monk is right. What if Gaxxog leaves the Temple and attacks Illux or Seatown? What then?" Trent asked.

"Enough!" Ren shouted. "We have decided. We are going to continue to awaken more of the Divine Beasts. The issue of Gaxxog can be discussed again once our primary mission is accomplished. There is no telling how many other Divine Beasts Lio is awakening, we cannot allow their numbers to outpace our own."

*There is the woman I love.*

Ren turned and stormed past Trent, barely looking at him. Begrudgingly the others fell into line behind her. Teo made his way to the front of the group, leading them out of the clearing and through the tight clusters of trees toward the next seal. Amber light cut between the leaves, making a green and gold quilt beneath their feet. Rella fell behind to keep step with Trent. She gave him a reassuring smile he tried to weakly return. Although the last time he had seen Rella had been during a battle with a sickening evil, her presence brought him some comfort. She was a reminder of a simpler time, when he still counted himself a brother to more than the memory of great men.

Finally, they came upon a precipice that led down into a steep ravine, far from view. There were dozens of rocky outcroppings that formed a sort of twisting pathway down, mired with bushy shrubs and trickling streams that seeped out from among the rocks. It would be a rough trek down, even for one experienced with these mountains. Trent supposed they could make the climb to the bottom, but the Divine Beasts? The ravine itself was barely wide enough to allow their girth, even if Tyr was willing to risk exposure by flying to the bottom. Trent leaned over the edge and tried to scan the cluster of trees at the bottom to see if there was any sign of what they were looking for.

"Should we go around?" he asked.

"The seal we seek is at the bottom," Teo responded, distantly.

"Wait here then," Ren said to the Divine Beasts.

Aion snorted derisively but said nothing. The shaggy creature had been a creature of Samson, Trent had been told. It seemed that the god's disdain for servants of Arra had trickled down into his servants as well. Trent tried to brush the irritation he felt toward the surviving Gods of Light aside. Ahead, Ren and Divinity began the slow descent down the winding path of rock and shrub into the unknown below. Teo and Rella followed quickly behind, with Trent taking up the rear.

*What use are these damn wings if I have to walk everywhere?*

Trent smirked to himself—in that moment the voice in his head belonged to Elise rather than he. Regardless of what he wished they could do, Ren seemed to be forging her own path now, and he did not wish to question her lead. The pathway they had chosen down was a steep, winding slope littered with loose stones that slipped from under their feet and onto the treetops below. Trent found himself thankful he could use his wings to maintain his balance as he made his way down. How the monks were able to fare as well as they were seemed an impossibility. The occasional shrub or small tree blocked their path, forcing Ren to stop and hack away enough branches with her sword that the large cat and others behind her could continue on.

When they were about halfway down, the tops of the giant pines at the bottom of the ravine were nearly close enough to touch. Small black birds flew through the treetops and landed on nests crammed between the brush and boulders that the party traversed. Trent looked back up the distance they had traveled. He could see the edge where their descent had begun, but he couldn't make out the shape of any of the Divine Beasts. Even from this distance, Trent thought he would have seen Tyr or Aion looming over the edge. He hoped they had gone back into the trees where they would not be seen if servants of the enemy were to fly overhead. This thought gave him momentary pause. Where they climbed now was the most exposed they had been since fleeing the village several days prior. So far there had been no sign of Merek or Daniel, nor did any of the traditional Servants of Darkness follow them. Trent prayed that all eyes were focused on the south for the time being.

After another hour of climbing, Ren finally stepped foot upon the level ground at the bottom of the ravine. A large stream cut across the bottom, fed by several smaller tributaries they had crossed on their way down the mountainside. Once all of the group was on the floor of the ravine, Teo stepped back in front of Ren and led the group through the stream toward what must have been the center of the chasm. The light of the sun barely reached them now, turning the world around them into a dull twilight. The forest here was denser than anywhere else they had traveled, likely meaning that none of the three Divine Beasts would have been able fit down here had they flown down in any case.

*How are we going to get whatever we find down here, back out?*

Trent decided to try his luck again and picked up his pace until he was walking alongside Ren. She didn't totally ignore him this time, gingerly taking his hand when he outstretched it. After giving it a light squeeze, she dropped his hand and carried on in silence, leaving Trent to muse over what the gesture meant. He sighed to himself in exasperation. It seemed she was no longer angry with him or, perhaps, no longer angry with herself, but the task at hand still meant more to her than the hurt feelings of her companion.

Soon, Teo brought the party to a halt in the center of the shallow stream. The chill water filled his boots and numbed his feet. At first, it was hard to tell that they stood on it, but after a few moments Trent saw the seal below them. The ground under the stream was smooth as it was elsewhere, but the current had brought several small stones to rest over the seal, hiding its presence somewhat. Teo looked down at the seal and frowned.

"We will need to block the stream somehow," he said matter-of-factly. "There is no other way for my blood to reach the ground itself. The stream will simply wash it away."

Trent looked back upstream, trying to see if there was anything they could do to block the flow of water short of causing a rockslide. Perhaps, if they used their magic to fell some of the trees, they would be able to block the flow for just long enough to get some blood onto the soil. He turned back to suggest the idea to Ren when a dark shape jumped from within the trees. Trent tried to throw up a defensive barrier, but it was too late. Blood-red energy struck him dead in the chest and sent him careening, end over end, into the stream bed. His skin seemed to howl in pain, and his ears rung with a thunderous clap. He landed face-down, stunned. The fresh water filled his mouth and nose, but he was too weak to pull himself up. Water filled his lungs, causing to choke. Distantly, he could hear shouts and the hot crackle of lightning and flame bouncing from the rocks and trees.

A firm hand gripped Trent by the shoulder and pulled him up so that his face was no longer submerged. He belatedly spat and choked out the water, feeling it run down his chin as it sputtered out of his mouth. Blinking, Trent saw the dark shape fighting with Ren, sending bursts of magic this way and that. He could feel the hair on his body standing on end from the massive amounts of energy filling the air. The dazed Seraph turned and saw that it was Teo who had pulled him from the water. The Balance Monk nodded as Trent tried to open his mouth to say his thanks, but only more water sputtered out.

Teo spun away from Trent, joining Rella and Divinity in attacking the creature that had nearly ended Trent. Trent struggled to sit up, his mind still not processing the information around him as quickly as he would have liked. It was as if the water he had ingested had filled his brain as well. He spread his wings and forced himself to take to the air, hoping the sensation would clear his head. Suddenly, Godtaker was in his hand, and he was flying directly at their attacker. The air whipped through his hair, bringing everything back into crystalline focus. As he neared the thing, he recognized it as Daniel. The onetime Champion of Light turned just as a recovered Trent smashed into him with all of his might, striking the twisting creature across the chest with Godtaker. In the moment it made contact, Trent could feel the armor and flesh beneath splitting. Daniel launched backward into a great oak, shattering the tree into a rain of wooden shards. Trent cried out, his voice echoing through the ravine.

*I don't bow that easily.*

Ren was beside him then, her face a mask of rage. She clutched Nightbreaker in her hands like the blade would float away if she loosened her grip. The woman looked at Trent and nodded, turning back to the remnant of the tree where Daniel lay in shock. Both Seraph's raised their swords and used the blades to channel glowing blue lightning that crackled to life up and down the steel. Moments later they were releasing the attacks simultaneously into the forest, each Seraph swinging wildly to send arcs of the magic into Daniel from various angles. The forest ignited, pops of bursting trees and gouts of flame rising over the tree-line. The shape of Daniel disappeared into the smoky haze.

The two Seraphs rushed into the miasma side by side, quickly trying to ferret out the body of the fallen hero so they could finish him. In the onslaught, several of the trees had fallen onto the stream, diverting its flow just enough that the Grey God's seal was exposed behind them.

"Start the ritual!" Ren shouted over her shoulder.

Then Daniel was before them, matching each Seraph blow for blow with his wicked blade. To Trent's chagrin, Daniel seemed to be focusing more of his attacks at Ren rather than Trent. That being said, Trent was hardly spared the monster's assault. Daniel came at them savagely, and without tiring. Trent saw that hate in his hollowed eyes, and he nearly recoiled at it. Ash covered Daniel, nearly turning the black cape he wore the same color as his grey armor. Suddenly, Daniel knocked Trent backward with a mighty swing of his sword, then followed up by clawing Ren across the chest. She stumbled back, crying out as silver and red blood began to leak from the deep rents in her breastplate.

Divinity pounced from outside the smoke, bearing Daniel to the ground. He cried out in rage, raking the tigress with his clawed hands. Before Trent could intervene, he had torn a piece from her neck and cast her aside.

"No!" Trent cried out. "You will suffer for that!"

"How?" Daniel asked, pulling himself to his feet. "How can I suffer? What can you do to me that has not already been done? We are all of us doomed from the day we are born. It is through blood that we enter this world, and blood that we leave it."

The dark figure lunged, stabbing wildly at Trent. Nightbreaker suddenly flashed down, slamming through the steel of Daniel's blade, cleaving it in two. Ren raised the black sword for another strike. Trent tried to rush forward to aid her, but he was a moment too slow. Daniel spun from her attack and jammed the remnant of his weapon into her stomach, punching through the plate like it was cloth.

"It always ends in blood," he hissed.

Trent heard nothing else over his own cries as he grabbed Ren by the shoulders to keep her from falling. Daniel had taken Nightbreaker from her loose grasp, lifting his old sword over his head to finish both Seraph's in a single stroke. Then the earth shook as a giant golden shape landed beside them, nearly toppling the twisted creature. Aion howled with unmatched fury, backhanding Daniel with such a savage force that he was sent flying backward into the smoke and fire of the ravine.

"Don't," Ren choked out, blood covering her chin.

"The choice isn't always yours to make," Trent whispered.

As he felt the healing magic leave his body, he finally understood.

# Chapter XVI

"We leave the Mortal Plane by sunrise one week from today!" Admiral Wyn shouted to the gathered crowd. "Those who helped with the construction of the fleet will be allowed to board first. There are no guarantees for the rest of you."

Even from where he stood in the center of the crowd, Gil could see her words pained her. It was the Ten who spoke through her at this moment. The Admiral's face was drawn and haggard, but she still held herself with all of the required grace of one in her position. In that moment she reminded Gil of the Lady Ren. At her back on the platform stood the Ten, the Paladin brutes that really ran Seatown. Gil seethed at the audacity of these men and women to deny the Lady Ren and abandon the people of Illux and the other villages to ravages of the enemy. Something had to be done, and soon. If Seatown didn't come to the aid of Illux, then who would?

Gil was wearing the baggiest cloak that Alyssa could find for him, hoping to hide his bulk beneath its folds. And his new arm. When he had stumbled back to The Drunken Ox several nights ago, he had nearly been delirious from the pain. Blood and sweat stained him.

When the innkeeper saw he now sported a sword blade where his arm had been, she had nearly fainted. He hadn't fully grasped how much he must have looked like an Accursed until she had pointed it out to him. Since then he had barely left the inn, and when he did so, like this morning, he made sure that his arm was strapped to his body underneath enough fabric to hide its presence from any suspicion. Perhaps, he hadn't made the wisest choice. Impulsiveness was never really his style, but then again, nothing had been the same since Marna burned. And this, this was something he needed to witness.

The crowd was growing restless now, with some rotten vegetables hurling through the air into the direction of the Admiral. To her credit, the woman tried to ignore these projectiles as best she could and simply get on with her speech, though her face twisted into another grimace.

"Soon, the gates will be closed and we will allow no further refugees," she intoned. "Those of you who are still expecting family to arrive had best help us with the last few ships. Exceptions might be made if you provide the most work."

"And what of Illux?" a female voice shouted. "What of my sons trapped there?"

"We cannot leave the Mortal Plane to die!" shouted another.

The Ten started to leave the podium, making their way through the crowd to ferret out the source of the voices. They shouldered their way through the mass of bodies, blades drawn. Gil's stomach began to tighten into a knot. He knew what came next. More of the rotten food began to fly, this time finding its mark on the head of one of the Paladins. The man snarled as he pushed a villager down, casting his eyes about to find where the cabbage had come from. More food began to fly and the shouting took on a renewed frenzy. Across the crowd, the female voice from before began shouting as the woman was dragged by her hair out of the sea of flesh and up to the makeshift gibbet.

"Please!" she sobbed, mucous and tears running down her chin. "I just want to save my sons. I don't believe in the Lady! I don't! They are heretics."

Her half-hearted attempt at reconciliation came a moment too late, for the rope was soon around her neck. The crowd grew even more restless now, with shouts of outrage demanding the woman be freed. Gil felt white hot anger welling up from deep within him to the surface. He tried to suppress the urge to untie his new arm and charge ahead, saving the woman from a fate that was altogether undeserved.

*What then? They would overwhelm me, and then we would both get strung up.*

The cries of the woman turned to choking gasps as she wildly kicked her feet and twisted about in the noose. Some of the Paladins continued to make their way through the crowd toward where Gil was standing. It almost seemed as if they were converging on him. Gil knew that if they got close to him all of this would be over. Slowly, the one-armed Paladin began backing up through the crowd, trying to remain as unremarkable as his large form would allow. He knew he was failing miserably. Then there were more shouts as a man jumped up to the gibbet with a small blade in hand. The man tried to cut the rope that held the still twitching woman. Two Paladins grabbed him by the arms, bearing him to the ground. A sword rose then fell, eliciting screams from the crowd.

Then it was chaos.

Villagers began swarming the Paladins, kicking and punching where they could. Swords sprang to life as more of the unarmed were cut down. Silver flashed and red sprayed. The podium on which Admiral Wyn stood and tried to appease the rioters was quickly overrun. The Admiral was knocked onto her back and covered by the enraged people from below. Though Alyssa claimed that Wyn Thacker was a relatively good woman, she had done nothing to curb the slaughter of her people by the Ten. Gil felt no pleasure at seeing her torn apart. He felt nothing.

His hand fumbled with the cord under his cloak that bound his weapon-arm to his body. If he could undo the rope, he would be able to help the villagers and end this heresy before it resulted in more death. He felt it start to come loose when the pops of blue light began to pepper the crowd. Scorched bodies were flung into the air wildly. In moments, the crowd broke and began to run in opposite directions. Gil was swept up in the retreat and followed the fleeing villagers out of the square. He could feel their bodies pressing against him with such force that he had no chance to move in any direction but that of the crowd. When he looked over his shoulder, Gil saw the Ten cutting down the few villagers who had not made it off the podium and into the streets. Above, Admiral Wyn was a bloody mess, but she appeared to be breathing.

"Did you see what they did to those people?" Lin said in a hushed whisper.

Alyssa cast a wary glance around her establishment, the first time that Gil had seen her do so since he had arrived. The inn was mostly empty, save for a few regulars who sat in various places around the room and stared blankly into their cups. Alyssa, Gil, and Lin where nestled into a corner, discussing the mornings events over some mead. The warmth of the hearth washed over Gil, but he still shivered at Lin's words.

"I saw," Gil replied, even quieter. "I saw and I did nothing."

"How bad was it?" Alyssa asked. She had remained in The Drunken Ox that morning, choosing to ignore the summons to listen to the Admiral. Her inn wouldn't run itself she said, not even for a few hours.

"It was bad," Lin said. "Dozens are dead. It turned into a full-blown riot for a moment, before the Paladins used their magic on the villagers."

"Gods," Alyssa cursed. "They have never resorted to that before. The people must have finally had enough."

"That may be so," Lin replied. "But now they are broken. Whatever you were hoping to accomplish here Gil, I think you missed your chance. After what happened today, there is no way the people can be coaxed into abandoning the Ten."

*No way that they will expect.*

"You might be right," Gil said. "Which is why we have to remove any other option from them. If they cannot leave the Mortal Plane, if they are forced to ignore the Ten, then I can convince them to march on Illux."

"It won't work," Linn said. "You are but one Paladin, they are, well, ten."

"What do you need?" Alyssa asked, ignoring Lin's concerns.

"We need to gather as many people to our cause as we can," Gil replied. "Today might have broken the will of some, but it will surely awaken an anger in others that had been lying dormant until now. We must capitalize on that rage that the slaughter today has caused, and aim it where we want it to go. I did nothing today, and I will regret that for the rest of my life. I'm sure I am not alone in that feeling. Surely, you know of people who either are or were on the edge about the Ten and the denial of the Lady?"

"Most of them are strung up in the square," Lin said, sourly.

"Most," Alyssa agreed. "But not all. I can get some names to you, but we must be careful, many of them will not trust us at first, especially you when they found out what you are. To those who don't know any better, all Paladins are the same."

"Lin, I want you to start getting some supplies together," Gil said. "Weapons, torches, armor, and food if possible."

"Food?" Lin asked, confusion playing across his face.

"I want to prepare The Drunken Ox for a siege if need be," Gil said, coolly. "One way or another we will make sure that this fleet doesn't leave Illux to die alone."

"What are you going to do?" Alyssa asked.

"I need to pay a visit to some new friends."

The sun was slowly setting over the sea when Gil slipped along the wharf. The ships at his left were bobbing gently in the surf, mostly unmanned at this late hour—or so he hoped. There were dozens of them completed, and several more in various stages of construction. Whatever wasn't finished by the time the Admiral gave the word to set sail would most likely be torched to prevent any possibility they would be followed. Gil figured that even for what a waste it seemed, it was a smart plan to start more ships than they could possibly hope to finish in time. It gave the villagers more incentive to work, with the looming fear that if they didn't finish in time, they might be left behind. The more they worked the less chance they would try and rebel against the Ten.

Ahead, overlooking the sea was a tall building that seemed to lean over the waves. Ocean spray flew up at the base of the structure where waves broke against its foundation. Even in the dark the white foam could be seen reflecting the light of the town, followed by the thunderous crashes as the water smote the stone. Alyssa had named this place the Overlook, home to the Admiral. The Ten stayed in the chapel near the center of the town, trying to give off the image of piety and holiness. Living closer to the gods added a legitimacy to their heresy it seemed.

Though he was still cloaked, Gil freed his arm from its binding in case he needed the blade. His range of movement was increased so much by this he nearly forgot that he was missing an appendage—which was unfortunate. More than once he nearly cut himself trying to scratch an itch on his other arm. As he neared the Overlook he began to creep along the dock, darting from shadow to shadow where he could. The moisture in the air began to cling to his skin, making him shiver. Above, light shone in a single window; no doubt the chamber in which the Admiral readied herself for sleep and nursed the wounds she had received earlier that day.

Gil circled around the Overlook, narrowly avoiding two guards making a patrol around the base of the structure. One of the guards spoke as they passed the location where the one-armed Paladin crouched in the shadows.

"I can't believe they didn't roast the last of them, Shae. Did you see how close they came to killing the Admiral?"

"Me either," the familiar voice of the other guard replied. "I don't trust all of these new folk we have been letting in. Not a one. I say that we have enough ships, so we don't need no more bodies to build them, and if we don't have no more bodies then we don't need no more ships."

As the speakers passed by, Gil could see in the moonlight that the one called Shae was the same woman from the gate a few days before. It had been her that had kicked him in the face after taking his horse. Anger swelled within him again.

*I'll repay the favor, if not this night then another.*

Once the two guards had disappeared back toward the front of the building, Gil unhooked the rope and grapnel that Lin had scavenged for him earlier in the day. He wasn't sure how easily he would be able to do this with his left arm, but he would still make the attempt. What choice did he have? Kicking in the front door didn't seem to be the best option. Stepping back from the side of the Overlook, Gil wound up his arm and threw the hooked end of the rope at a window just below the lighted one. He missed by several feet and the metal hook landed on the ground with a loud clang—not quite masked by a crash of the waves.

Scrambling, Gil coiled up the rope and dropped off the pier, holding himself above the waves with only the strength of his left arm. He could feel the weight of the blade on his arm pulling downward toward the sea as if it was called home. The guards quickly returned, scouring the area for the source of the sound.

"What was that?" Shae spat.

"I dunno," her companion replied. "Probably nothing."

The guards disappeared again, and Gil pulled himself back onto the dock, heaving loudly from the exertion. Once he had regained his breath, he returned to his previous position and made the attempt again. This time the hook found purchase. Two quick tugs later and it was set in the opening of the window. Gil twisted the rope about his forearm and planted his feet on the side of the building, pulling himself up. The surface of the structure was wet with mist from the ocean, making it difficult for his feet to stay on the surface of the wall. When he found himself slipping, he dug the point of his sword arm into the stone, halting the gradual sliding of his body back toward the ground. The rope burned as it slid against his arm, but he kept on.

After what seemed like hours, Gil was climbing into the open window and collapsing onto the floor. He could hear the voices of the guards below again, so he quickly pulled the rope up behind him. Moments later it sounded as if they passed directly below him, their voices carrying over the sound of the sea. The Overlook was only three levels high, but the one-armed climb up to the middle level had taken more out of him than he had planned. If he found himself in a fight any time in the next few moments, he would be in serious trouble. The Paladin looked around the darkened room to make sure that there were no others inside, sleeping in the thick darkness. Once he was sure that the quarters were empty, he felt his way for the doorway and into the passage beyond.

*What a large building to sleep one person. I hope I am not wrong about this.*

In the hallway beyond, he found his way through the darkness to the central stairs. Once here a dim light from the candles above led him on. As soon as he stepped upon the first stair, his ears were greeted with a loud creak. Silently cursing, Gil continued to move up to the next landing, trying his best to evenly space out his weight. When he finally neared the top, he slowed and peered up into a large room.

Admiral Wyn Thacker sat at a small wooden desk, flipping through the pages of a large book. The cream-colored pages seemed to glow in the light of her desk candle. She was wearing nothing but a shift, which showed her dark skin through its thinning fabric. Even in the dim light, Gil could see several bruises covered the body of the woman, and her hair was matted with dried blood. The townsfolk had not gone easy on her, even though she was known to be on their side.

Towering beside her desk was a pile of books, many still open at various points, even with other books stacked atop them.

There was no one else in the room, and the nearest weapon to the Admiral was her thin, ornate sword that hung along the wall. Gil pulled his hood over his face and sprang onto the landing, rushing behind the woman as quickly as he was able. In one motion he grabbed her by the back of the neck and threw her onto her bed. Straddling the woman, he clamped his good hand over her mouth and pressed the point of his sword into her belly.

There was no fear in her eyes, only the wet glaze of sadness.

"I don't want to skewer you, Admiral," Gil said, softly. "But I will, gods help me. I just came here to talk, but my patience for those who don't wish the best for our people has run very thin as of late. I wish to make some things clear to you if you are truly the woman they say. And if I am wrong, I will come back here and drown you in that sea you love so much, and no number of Paladins will be able to stop me. Am I clear?"

Gil relaxed then, taking his hand from her mouth, and removing the blade from her body. He swung himself off her and sat down in the chair she had been occupying. Wyn eyed him cautiously and sat up, covering her chest with her crossed arms. Her face had finally taken on a look of annoyance more than anything.

"Who are you?" she asked defiantly.

"I am a servant of the people," Gil said. "Who I am isn't important. I could be a bandit, a soldier, a farmer, a Paladin, the damn Raven Lord returned. It matters not. What matters is what you and the Ten have done to the people of this city. What matters is that your heresies don't go unpunished. What matters, is that the people of Illux are not left to die alone."

"You are the man from the gate the other day, aren't you?" she asked.

"The same."

"I never should have allowed them to let you in," she said, rising up a little. “You barge into my house and accuse me of wrongdoing?”

“I do,” Gil replied. “Did you somehow miss the bloodshed in the streets today? Or have your beliefs in the lack of divinity in the Lady Ren twisted your mind so much that the slaughter of good people is seen as righteous?”

Admiral Wyn sighed then, but her eyes lost none of their defiant luster. She uncrossed her arms for a moment and ran her fingers through the blood-soaked parts of her hair. When she pulled her hands back, she looked at them, staring at the dried crimson flakes that clung to her fingers.

“I did not want that,” she said. “I don’t want to leave any of these people behind. It was me who convinced the Paladins to allow us to build more ships in the first place. The Mortal Plane is lost, but that doesn’t mean that we all have to die with it! Don’t you see? We cannot win this war with the Darkness, not now in any case. But we can survive. We can explore the world and find a new home!”

It was then that Gil looked over at the book she had been reading. Drawn across its pages was a map of the coastline. Beyond that were other smaller bodies of land, hastily sketched in place by a shaky hand. The ink was only just starting to fade. This map wasn’t as old as the book itself appeared to be.

“Our people have been there!” she exclaimed, following his eyes. “My mother made landfall beyond the horizon when I was just a girl. When Seatown was raided by Demons, and later by Bandits led by a rogue Paladin, its people were butchered. My mother searched for somewhere her people could be safe. The High God created more lands than these. Why should we be confined to just this place?”

“Because this is where our people are,” Gil replied sullenly. “I do not disparage your wish to explore and find new lands, especially if they are free of the taint of the Gods of Darkness. But I cannot sit by while the people of Illux and other villages are slaughtered. Nor can I watch as the Paladins of Seatown make a mockery of our faith and butcher the innocent in the streets. I came here to warn you, Admiral. There will not be time for your dreams of a better world, not until this darkness is destroyed. Here and now, people are dying, and that is going to stop. The ship that carries the Ten will sink, Wyn Thacker. Will you be upon it?"

With that final pronouncement, Gil swung his sword arm and cut the flame from the candles on the desk. Once the room was plunged into darkness he was back in the stairwell, making his way toward the lower floors.

After returning to the outside, Gil started his way back to The Drunken Ox. He hoped he had not erred in allowing the Admiral to know that forces moved against the Ten, but he had a gut feeling that she would be more amenable to his cause than theirs. The Ten only wished to leave the Mortal Plane to save themselves, and because starting over somewhere else would allow them to cement their rule as the only true servants of the Gods of Light. The Admiral, on the other hand, seemed not to want power, but to explore the blank edges of the map. That in itself was a noble goal, so long as she didn't try and achieve it at the expense of her people. He hoped she was more like Ren than Castille.

Gil rounded a corner near the central square when he nearly ran headfirst into a Paladin. The hulking brute was half a head higher than Gil, with a thinning beard and even thinner hair upon his head. His breath reeked of ale and fish. The man instinctively gripped at the sword at his side, looking Gil over with hollow eyes. Gil mumbled an apology and tried to sidestep the big man when the Paladin put a strong hand on his arm. Even drunk, the other Paladin's strength was impressive.

"You don't look like a villager to me," the man said, slurring his words. "Nor have I seen you helping with the ships. What is that under your cloak?"

Gil had been trying to keep his arm as unremarkable as possible, but without the cord tying it down, the blade was catching the fabric of his cloak. Without a second thought, the one-armed Paladin used his good hand to remove the grip of his assailant. The drunk Paladin opened his mouth in shock. Gil lifted his sword-arm out of his cloak, slicing upward as he did so. The Seatown Paladin stumbled back, clutching at his face. Blood sprayed out from between his fingers—the cut was deep enough that it was possible that his skull had fractured. Already, a blue glow began to cover his hands and face as he tried to desperately knit the flesh back together. Gil planted a boot in his chest, kicking the man back into the wall of the nearest building. His sword-arm sank deep into the chest of the other Paladin, nearly to the flesh of Gil's elbow. The other Paladin stopped trying to heal himself, staring dumbly at Gil through rivers of blood that poured out of the two halves of his face.

"The Lady Ren is the voice of the gods," Gil said harshly. "And you have betrayed your oath and your people. If you go to the High God's side, I will find you again one day, and you will regret that meeting as much as this one."

He pulled his arm free, leaving the shuddering body of the other man to slide down the wall. Gil turned and ran the rest of the way back to The Drunken Ox.

# CHAPTER XVII

They had gathered a total of six Divine Beasts to their cause: Tyr, Aion, Lythe, Orros, Makar and Yyn. Teo had known each of them by name before they had even fully emerged from their seals. Such power deserved the respect that only knowledge would bring. He and Rella had spent the nights studying the great tomes they had saved from the Grey Temple to refresh their memories and acquaint themselves with their future companions. The moniker seemed wrong—placing these mortals on equal footing with such immortal beings—but in such times, better to be fighting alongside them than against them.

His premonitions had begun to fade after Yyn was freed, leaving him to believe they did not have any more seals that were reachable to them in this part of the Rim. He knew that there were at least dozens of other Divine Beasts scattered around the Mortal Plane, but the High God did not see it fit to show him their resting places yet. Even so, Teo hadn't let the others know this.

Several days ago, the Seraphs had been amenable to the idea of killing Gaxxog and retaking the Grey Temple, but after the near death of Ren, Trent had taken a more single-minded approach to the cause and decided that nothing was more important than getting to Illux. Ren herself, on the other hand, had remained almost comatose since her run-in with Daniel. She had taken to eating alone, and only answered questions with one or two words at a time. He didn't know her well enough to guess whether or not she would recover from the trauma she had gone through recently. Fearing that without their support he wouldn't be able to convince the Divine Beasts to come with them, Teo erred on the side of falsehood to get their group back to the temple to deal with Gaxxog.

*We must restore balance. It is the only way.*

He wished he could speak the truth to the others, but if he did, they would surely make the wrong decision. Fear of losing their own home and their own people led them to think they had no time to avenge his. He didn't like that he was lying to them, it burned his very soul. Only Rella knew the truth. He could not allow that creature to pollute the Grey Temple one further day. Gaxxog was still there, of that Teo was certain.

Divinity sauntered up to the monk and fell into step beside him. He looked down at the great cat for a moment, rubbing her behind the ears. She had nearly died several days ago as well, though her recovery had been swifter than Ren's, for which Teo was abundantly grateful. Something about the creature brought him comfort, just as she seemed to do for all of the party. Different than even the Divine Beasts that aided them, Divinity was not of this world. She was of the same realm as Ravim had been, and that made her more important than Teo could ever say.

Behind Teo and Rella, Trent walked alone, occasionally muttering to himself and playing with the hilt of Godtaker. The male Seraph hadn't been the most approachable member of the group now that Ren almost completely ignored him. Behind him, Ren sullenly walked alone, weaponless and without words.

Bringing up the rear was the now varied assortment of Divine

Beasts, some moving quickly along the ground, while others flew through the air, just over the top of the trees. The very earth shook with their passing, and every living thing in this forest knew for miles they were coming. They had thrown caution to the wind after the Daniel attack, none of them doing as much work to hide their presence from the enemy any longer. Why did it matter when they had been followed this far already?

Orros padded along the fastest, being a great cat not unlike Divinity, but much larger. The Divine Beast had shaggy white mane and silver scales like that of a snake that covered the rest of his body. His eyes flashed with a golden brilliance whenever his gaze fell upon you. Makar hopped from place to place, flashing his bulbous purple tongue at creatures that tried to fly away from him. Yyn was hardest to follow, for the flying blue dragon bobbed and weaved through the air, choosing to fly higher and farther than Tyr or Lythe even dared. Once again, Teo thought on the irony of the fact that it was a servant of the god who had imprisoned these creatures who was the one to awaken them.

*Ravim brought balance to the world by sealing them away, and I restore the balance by freeing them.*

Though most of the animals fled long before they passed through an area, there was always some sign of habitation in these woods. Until now. The wildlife in the area had all but disappeared, a fact that Teo was painfully aware of.

"We must be close," Rella leaned in and whispered. "Don't you think?"

"We are," Teo said somberly. "I expect us to arrive in the next few hours."

"And then what?" she asked.

"And then we win our first victory. The others will come around, I am sure of it."

Teo sounded more confident than he felt. His mind returned again for the second time in the last few days to Jin. The woman he had killed on the slopes of these very mountains. The woman he had loved, in his way. And she had loved him in hers. Why did this lying to his new companions feel like a betrayal of the same magnitude? Was he falling back into his own ways? Was he drifting away from the teaching of Ravim and back toward the Darkness? It wasn't possible. He was bringing balance.

To his surprise, Teo had grown to like the two Seraphs. At the very least, he respected them more than he would have thought it possible for him to respect the dogmatic followers of either of the two warring factions he had been taught to stay between. Trent was bull-headed at times, but he was also a steadfast warrior with a near fanatical drive to protect those around him. Ren was a rock of confidence and wisdom, far beyond her years. Or, she had been. Now the woman was a shell of her former self, shaken and broken by what had been done to her by the former Seraph. Daniel was an unexpected stain upon the heritage of the two Seraphs, which she had not taken well.

History had recorded that the Champion of the Light had been slaughtered by Xyxax over a thousand years ago. It was his death that had galvanized Lio and precipitated his fall. It was Daniel's death that had set all of the events in motion that were even now playing out in this final struggle for dominance between the Gods of Light and the Gods of Darkness. Who would have thought that Xyxax had taken an even more wicked approach to destroying that which Lio had loved? It had been an act so vile that even Ravim had hidden the truth from his followers.

*Light and Darkness destroy each other. That is why we must walk the middle path.*

They continued on for the next several hours, passing between trees and around small boulders. Teo tried to be aware of their location from what he remembered of these parts of the mountains. If he aimed them right, they would come across the Temple without first passing through the burned remnants of the fields. If they want through that killing ground first, he risked them realizing exactly where it was they were. In order to pull this off, Teo needed to keep the others from learning where they were actually headed for as long as possible.

As if reading his thoughts, Trent ambled up and spoke.

"Are you sure we will find another seal today?" he asked. "We have gone farther between awakenings than we ever have before."

"It shouldn't be much longer," Teo said sternly, walking ahead.

Divinity stayed behind with the Seraph, growling deep in her throat. Teo didn't think that the tigress was growling at him, but the scent of Gaxxog. At least that is what he hoped. And if she could smell it... The Divine Beasts had begun to act uneasy over the past hour, but none of them spoke of what had caused the change. Perhaps, they did not yet know themselves. He knew they would smell or sense the presence of the giant lizard long before any of the mortals would, and even Teo thought he could feel its taint in the land around them. It was in the nature of Divine Beasts that followed him to destroy such a creature. They had to know it was close. Hopefully, that wouldn't mean they were onto Teo's duplicity yet.

Overhead, Yyn let out a high-pitched roar that split the heavens, echoing from peak to peak across the Rim. She let out a gout of blame flame before spiraling down toward where they walked. Teo knew she must have spotted something. Within moments Yyn rocketed onto the ground before him, knocking trees down as she did so. The dragon loomed over him, her blue scales and forked silver antlers shimmered from the scattered rays of the sun. A light breeze ruffled the thin mane that encircled her shoulders. None of the Divine Beasts had a true gender, but Yyn spoke with the voice of a woman, while at the same time sounding serpentine and guttural.

"Where are you taking us, Servant of Ravim?" she hissed. "I see the ruins of a large fortress just beyond the tree line. I sense Gaxxog as well. Have you led us astray? Is this a trap?"

"I am merely making sure that the purpose you were awakened for is fulfilled," Teo said, calmly.

Yyn roared in his face, covering his body with sizzling spittle from behind her white fangs. Teo removed his staff from the strap that held it to his back and tossed it aside. He gazed defiantly back at the Divine Beast, never averting his gaze. He could see the rage in her dark eyes—rage, borne of a grudge that was over a thousand years old. Upon hearing the words of the dragon, the other Divine Beasts gathered around, surrounding Teo and Rella in a tight circle. Aion beat his chest and bared his teeth, while Tyr beside him fluttered his wings wildly. These creatures were giants, looming over Teo like he was a mere ant. In that moment, without the aid of his god to strengthen him, Teo felt truly insignificant. He looked up at each of them in turn, trying to keep his gaze steady.

"Trent, don't!" Rella screamed.

Godtaker touched Teo on the neck, drawing blood.

"You told us we were headed to another seal!" the Seraph spat. "You told me that we were close! You lied to us!"

"You agreed with me several days ago," Teo whispered.

"Things were different then," Trent said. "That was before we knew they could find us so easily. That was before you lied!"

"You are right," Teo replied, still whispering. He needed to rely on methods he would have used in his old life. Half-truths and a honeyed-tongue had served him well once. They needed to once more. They had to. "This isn't just about restoring balance, Trent. You and I might disagree about the reason for this fight, but our goal is the same. We need a victory, Trent. We are losing our momentum. Ren needs a victory. Look at her, Trent, she is lost. We outnumber Gaxxog six to one. This won't even be a battle, but it will be a victory. She needs this."

Trent eyed him suspiciously but lowered Godtaker to his side. Behind him, Ren stood outside the perimeter of the Divine Beasts. She was watching, but her expression was distant. Teo had kept his voice low enough that none but Trent could hear him. Beside them, Rella had her hands up, ready to fight if need be, though Teo knew it would have not been easy for her to battle this man with whom she shared so much history.

"Can I trust you?" Trent asked. "Are we on the same side?"

"Yes," Teo lied. "You can trust me."

*I fight to restore the balance. That is all I have ever done.*

"I stand with Teo!" Trent yelled. "We will go and finish Gaxxog."

"After this one misled us?" Tyr said.

"This servant of Ravim?" Orros roared. "A God of Darkness?"

"The God of Balance," Rella corrected.

"Not by my recollection," Makar croaked.

"Enough! Aion bellowed. "I have been opposed to this venture since this monk first suggested it. The people we were created to protect are cowering behind their walls, praying for salvation. We have no time for such detours. But now, here we stand on the edge of doing battle with one of our oldest foes. I don't know about the rest of you, but I thirst for blood!" The Divine Beast beat his chest again, for emphasis.

"Be warned, mortals," Tyr interjected. "Though you may have killed Akklor alone, do not expect the rest of our brethren to go so easily. Luck was on your side then, but this next battle will take all of us."

"Agreed," Lythe hissed. "Let usss be done with this. I haven't seen sssuch indecision since Ash Company existed."

Teo bent to pick up his staff—no one stopped him. The Balance Monk walked under the legs of the blue dragon Yyn and made his way through the trees at her back. Many of the trees had been scorched by flames, none had leaves or needles adorning them any longer. Minutes later, he stood at the edge of the clearing that marked the domain of the Grey Temple. The landscape had been turned into an abattoir. Bits and pieces of human and Demon alike were scattered around the countryside; all were parts small enough to evade Gaxxog's hunger, but large enough to be identifiable to the group. Giant rents in the earth made the plain anything but. As for the temple itself, it looked to be nothing more than a hollow shell, gutted of anything beyond its outer walls.

He was so overcome with emotion that he nearly collapsed to his knees. Behind him, the rest of the part filtered out into the clearing. Rella opened her mouth and let out a silent cry. Teo could see his own agony reflected in her face. They had fled from the beast so quickly that they hadn't allowed themselves to see how badly the damage from the creature had been. This was their home no longer. Pools of putrid urine and boulder-sized dung lay scattered near them, but of Gaxxog itself there was no sign.

"He isss close by," Lythe hissed. "I can feel it."

"Let us finish this," Teo croaked.

He led the others forward, carefully navigating the now uneven terrain toward the ruins of the temple. The walls quickly rose up before them, cracked open like the shell of an egg. The stench of the grave filled this place, stronger even than it had been when the creature had been present. The rot and decay clung to them with thin fingers that Teo felt dance across his exposed flesh. In front of what was left of the gates were large claw-marks. Teo himself had been running from Gaxxog when it had nearly killed Rella, but had taken an initiate in her place, right there.

"Mica," Rella whispered, tears flowing freely.

The iron doors hung askew, knocked in by the Demons when they had laid siege to the temple. Teo stepped through the entryway, carefully stepping over bits of rubble nearly as large as Divinity. There would be no hope of rebuilding any of this once the war was finally over. Inside the central chamber, the floor was nothing more than pulverized masonry. There was nearly nothing left of the roof that had once been overhead; it looked as if Gaxxog had shorn the entire top half of the structure off. The puddles and piles of excrement were more common here, but still there was no sign of Gaxxog having freshly been here.

*Has the creature moved on finally? Have I broken their trust for nothing?*

The Divine Beasts were outside the temple still, each of the giant beings clearly on edge. Trent, Ren, and Divinity had followed behind

Teo and Rella, neither of the two Seraphs any more composed than the Balance Monks. Teo was almost surprised at the way that the carnage was having an effect on the two Champions of Light. Would he have felt the same way if this wreckage had been Illux?

"Another of the powerful places in the world has been destroyed," Ren said, softly. "This could be the Grand Cathedral."

There was a flurry of motion from behind them on the outside of the temple as Tyr, Lythe, and Yyn took to the air. The owl, snake, and dragon spread out, scanning the countryside for any signs of Gaxxog the Incorrigible. Teo gripped his staff until his hands ached. He could feel a scream building in his lungs, and it took every ounce of his training to hold it in. He failed.

"Show yourself!" Teo shouted. "Answer for what you have done to this sacred place!"

As if in answer to his summons, the sound of a small rockslide caused every head to look up. High above the temple, on one of the cliffs that remained of the mountain peak from before Ravim built this place, the menace known as Gaxxog clambered down toward them. Six legs pulled the mottled green and purple beast down the cliffside, its forked tongue sliding out to greet them. The razor-tipped tail thrashed impatiently as it made its descent. Suddenly, the Divine Beast launched directly at them, jaws wide. It was nearly half the size of the massive chamber they stood in. It would crush them in an instant.

A golden blur struck Gaxxog from the side, knocking the beast into the far wall of the Grey Temple. The mortals gathered within ran from the cloud of dust and silt that plumed into the air. Aion stood from within the cloud, growling and beating his silver hands upon the back of the lizard. Each blow cracked like thunder. He climbed onto the top of Gaxxog, gripping the creature by the neck and twisting. Then Aion arched his back and howled in pain. The blade-like tail of the behemoth lizard emerged from his chest. Gaxxog cast Aion aside like a doll, springing back to its feet. It jumped the wall of the temple and landed just outside—visible through a giant opening that it had no doubt made when the temple had been under siege.

Orros sprung from the side, roaring as he did so. Claws raked Gaxxog, causing the lizard to hiss in pain. It bit down hard on Orros, tearing upward—removing a large chunk of flesh. Makar leapt into the temple, his purple tongue wrapping around the neck of Gaxxog and tightened. Makar was large and bulbous, covered in warts and bumps of various sizes and colors. Teo thought for a fleeting moment that this Divine Beast resembled a toad or a frog more now than it ever had before. Gaxxog's tail lashed out again, but not before ice froze the blade-tip solid, causing it to crash to the ground, just short of Makar. Lythe had returned from scouting.

Trent took to the air, flying toward the creature. He let out a battle cry that echoed through the chamber as he wielded his god-killing blade. Flashes of blue-energy flew from his outstretched hand, hammering into the exposed throat of Gaxxog. Teo tried to run after him, but an outstretched hand from Rella gripped his shoulder and stopped him.

"Wait," she said. "This is a matter for those of Divine Blood. There is nothing we can do."

Teo nodded and relented, relaxing his body for the time being. She was right of course. His suicide would do nothing to help restore the balance. Beside them, Ren looked indecisive for a few moments before igniting the energy that flowed around her weaponless hands and taking to the air as well. She still didn't look like herself, but at least she was fighting. Her coarse, white hair fluttered around her face as she blew past them.

Gaxxog hissed loudly again, standing upon the back four of its legs. Swiping with its front two claws, it yanked Makar close with a jerk of its neck before tearing one of his eyes from its socket. The toad-like Divine Beast let out a croak, half stumbling, half hopping, backward to where it collapsed into another wall of the temple its tongue loosening from around Gaxxog's neck. Lythe swung by, blowing frigid air onto Gaxxog, freezing its legs. The lizard smashed its tail onto the ground again and again, until finally enough of the sharp end was free for it to be dangerous once more. The blade lashed out, knocking one of the Seraphs from the air. Then Gaxxog snapped at Lythe, catching the snake in its jaws. It flung her away, broken and bloodied. The lizard leapt and buried its claws in Makar, tearing his other eye from his head.

"No!" Rella cried out.

*This is my fault. I can't just stand here.*

Teo broke away from Rella and Divinity, charging toward where the giant monsters did battle. His speed was not what it had once been while Ravim lent him power, but he covered much ground all the same. Ahead of him, Gaxxog was rolling and tearing at Orros now, while Makar's corpse lay twitching within the temple. Within moments, Teo was near the fallen Seraph, who was alive but unconscious. It was Trent. One of his wings was broken, but he looked otherwise unharmed. Thank Ravim for that. Without a second thought, Teo grabbed Godtaker from where it was lodged in-between the rubble of the temple and kept running.

Once he was outside the temple walls, the battling of the Divine Beasts shook the earth so much he could barely run. Finally, when he was within range of Gaxxog, Teo jumped into the air, as high as he could. The ground fell away, and then returned just as quickly. He felt foolish when he realized he wouldn't have made it much higher than the top of the monster's foot. Thankfully, two hands gripped him under the arms and carried him high into the air, near the head of the beast.

"Where do you want to be?" Ren yelled over the wind whipping through his ears.

"The top of his head!" Teo shouted back.

The Seraph took him just to the top of the Divine Beast's eyes, dropping the Balance Monk when he was within several feet of the scales. Somewhat gracefully, Teo tumbled upon impact, rolling, and jumping to his feet in one fluid motion. Orros tore into the side of Gaxxog, slicing through scales into the softer flesh beneath. The giant lizard shuddered with every blow, nearly throwing Teo off. The Balance Monk tried to make his way to one of the monster's eyes, but a quick shake of its head sent him rolling down its snout. He nearly tumbled into the abyss but, at the last moment, he shoved Godtaker through one of the nostrils of the creature; the blade pierced through to the other side, holding him fast. Gaxxog howled in pain.

As Teo hung on for his life, he noticed two shapes barreling down at them from above. Tyr and Yyn were returning. This battle would soon be over. But now, thanks to his own stupidity, the Balance Monk might not be around long enough to see Gaxxog perish. The forked tongue of the Divine Beast licked up at him, trying desperately to dislodge the little man that was somehow causing it so much pain. Suddenly, Gaxxog twisted its neck, throwing Teo into the air. He fell back toward its gullet, the fetid odor of decay washing over him.

He thought it was over.

Then Ren was there once more, snatching him out of the air at the last moment, carrying him away from the creature just as fire from the mouths of both Tyr and Yyn washed over it. Gaxxog roared defiantly until the last, when the hungry beast was no more than a smoldering, twitching carcass.

Later that day, the group buried Makar the Imminent under a pile of rubble from the Grey Temple. Aion, Lythe, and Orros would all survive, though the Divine Beasts would need at least a few days to heal. While Divine Beasts carried the blood of the gods, their healing powers were much weaker than those of their Seraph counterparts. This defect balanced the sheer power that was imbued in every other facet of their being. Trent healed his wing and retrieved his sword from what was left of Gaxxog while Teo and Rella searched what was left of the library.

They had decided to return the books they had saved, storing them in the room in which transcribing had usually taken place. That room was possibly the most secure place left in the entire temple. Most of the other books within the library had been destroyed by the fighting and nesting of Gaxxog, but they were able to find some worth preserving, which they tucked away with the others.

"What will we do with them when we are through?" Rella asked, looking over a tome on the flora native to the Rim.

"I don't know," Teo said, softly.

He couldn't get the image of Makar's twitching corpse from his mind. His duplicity had gotten the Divine Beast killed. Even though Gaxxog had been destroyed and the Grey Temple cleansed, he didn't feel right about it. If they had simply left the creature to continue polluting this holy place, Makar would still be alive. How many in Illux would die now because of the delay that this had caused?

"We must rebuild," Rella said at last. "Using these books, these grounds. We must restart the order. You said it yourself before, even without Ravim, we can still follow his teachings. There must always be Balance Monks in the world."

"You are right," Teo said. "It is our duty, to all of those who have died, to carry on."

He hid the lone tear from her as they made their way back to the central chamber where the others had gathered. Once they arrived, they found the Seraphs discussing the next steps of their plan with the Divine Beasts. The group stopped talking as they approached. Forgiveness would not come easily it seemed. It was Trent who spoke first.

"You aren't going to lead anymore," he said. "I am."

"Understood," Teo replied.

"We are trying to decide what to do next," Trent continued. "Aion, Lythe and Orros need a few days to rest. I was thinking that we would take the others and make for Illux now. Do you think there are any more seals between here and there?"

Teo wracked his brain for a moment, trying to see if he could feel any further premonitions. He could not.

"I am not certain," he said. "I won't know until we start."

"Then we depart at first light," Trent said.

"Wait," Ren spoke up. "We cannot go back to Illux, not yet."

"What do you suggest?" Trent said in a huff. "We cannot afford to waste more time."

"Nor shall we," she replied. "But we cannot go back to the City of Light with just five Divine Beasts. There is no telling what the enemy has in store for us. We need an army as well."

"Where are we going to find an army?" Rella asked.

"Seatown."

# Chapter XVIII

They were calling them Demigods—Tess and her band of survivors from the Lady Ren's army. Each of them claimed to have imbibed the blood of the Goddess Arra, when she had intervened in the battle. It was a miraculous story for sure, and one that was immediately met with doubt. Why would one of the Gods of Light have broken the Pact? And how would it be that Arra would have been wounded in the first place? And yet, this story had physical evidence in the powers exhibited by these Demigods. The name for them had come from the guards, those who had believed Tess's story at any rate. From there, the moniker had spread like wildfire, and now it seemed the only name that made sense. Even though the name was now commonplace, not everyone trusted that the Demigods had any true divine connection, not to the Gods of Light at least. This meant that Tess's story about the outcome of the battle was doubted by some as well.

Castille had not taken kindly to these interlopers who claimed to hold the blood of a god in their veins, something he had very publicly wished for himself for years. That being said, the narrative of the Lady

Ren falling in battle and being carried away by Arra was one that he couldn't discount in its entirety, for it only served to solidify his position as the highest-ranking mortal left on the Plane. Given the situation, Castille couldn't afford to openly discredit Tess and her small army, no matter how much he distrusted them. The fact that some villagers and certain members of the slums had begun to worship the Demigods as they would have worshipped Ren only served to complicate matters.

Edmund, on the other hand, had been impressed from the start. He had seen to it that Tess and her people were placed under his personal protection. None of the Paladins or any of Castille's people could even look at a Demigod without first going through a loyalist from the City Watch. The street on which they set up the City Watch headquarters had been completely cleared out, allowing for the Demigods to take refuge if they did not have homes elsewhere in the city to return to. Tess was given quarters directly next to Edmund. He knew he needed her close by if he was to use the Demigods in the coming siege. And the siege was coming.

"Scouts are reporting a massive force making its way up from the south, no more than a few days away at the most," the man was saying. "They are several thousand strong at least. Demons and Accursed like we have never seen. Giant creatures march with them as well. Monsters out of myth. Some think even the Gods of Darkness walk with them."

*So, Tess was proven right again.*

"Those must be more Divine Beasts, like the one that attacked the army under the Lady," Edmund replied. "As for the reports of the Gods of Darkness on the march, I would chalk that up to simple fear. If they walked the Mortal Plane again we would have already have fallen—or our own gods would be here now. Still, we need to adjust our preparations at once. Go to the inner city and see how the engineers are getting along with the construction of the siege devices."

"Anything else sir?" the courier asked.

"Yes," Edmund said. "Send Tess in on your way out."

The man nodded and left the room. Edmund stood in the common room of the inn, alone for the first time in weeks. A map of the city was spread out on the table before him, half-emptied goblets of wine and candles burnt low were scattered its surface. Several circles were drawn on the map with red ink, marking the known entrances to the catacombs beneath the city where the dead were interred. The walls of Illux were tall, and to Edmund's knowledge, they had not been breached since the gods had walked the earth. Yet a siege would cripple the city, food was already running low. If Edmund's fears of what was coming proved true, then the walls would finally be breached, and what happened after that was more important than what happened before. Castille's wall dividing the inner city from the slums was nearly complete, serving as a second fallback once the Forces of Darkness made it into the city. At least, that was how Edmund planned to use them. Castille intended to protect the families of the inner city by keeping the refugees and citizens of the slums out. Edmund wasn't going to allow that to happen.

"Edmund," Tess said, as she entered the room. "You needed something?"

*You.*

"Yes," Edmund said. "I wanted to talk to you about what I can expect from the Demigods in the coming siege."

"You sound certain that there will be a siege. What I saw in the field says different. There isn't an army of the enemy left."

"The man who just sent you in here brought word from our scouts. There is an army of Demons and Accursed several thousand strong that is marching directly toward Illux from the south. Even with the army to the west being crushed by Arra, it seems that the Gods of Darkness are taking at least one more chance to destroy us, once and for all. What's more, there are more Divine Beasts with them this time."

To her credit, Tess hid whatever shock she must have had behind her steely visage. She walked over to the table and eyed the map of the city, tracing the line around the inner city with her fingers. The worn paper crinkled under the pressure from her hand. After a few moments she looked up at Edmund again. Her dusky skin and brown eyes were captivating to him. Even the white streak in her hair stirred his body. She gave him feelings he hadn't had for a woman in quite some time. Still, he knew from asking around that she preferred the touch of a woman to that of a man. He would have to search elsewhere for love, then.

"What would you have of us?" she asked. "I do speak for the others, it's true. Though referring to us Demigods as one cohesive force is stretching things a bit. Now that we have returned to the city my command over them has waned. I led them in the field because I was the highest ranked officer, and the meanest. I killed any of the bastards who spoke out. The more civilized manners that Illux requires don't do much to keep the troops in line."

"How many could you muster together? For old times' sake?"

She laughed at his joke. His heart raced.

"At least half. Those who are truly loyal number at least that much. The others will fight when they have to, but certainly not before. The horrors that we lived through were enough to fill even the blackest of hearts with enough bloodshed for a lifetime. And there are those of the army that survived and did not drink the blood of the goddess. I'm sure that many of them could still prove useful."

"Half should be enough," Edmund said. "We have no Divine Beasts of our own, nor do we have any others besides you and yours with Divine Blood. We need something that can match the power of the enemy."

"Not all of us are powerful enough to stand up to one of those monsters," Tess replied, sullenly. "Some of my people can only heal or read thoughts. Some control fire, or ice, some can fly, some have strength that could shatter the gates of the city, while others could whip up a storm that would blow the Grand Cathedral over. But, not all of them are weapons, Edmund."

"I will need each and every one of them. Not all of the needs of the city will be based on defending the walls. What have you heard of Castille and the political climate of the city since you have been gone?"

"Some," she replied, pacing around the table. "I know that old son of a bitch decided to finally take the opportunity to enforce his notion of inner city superiority. It was his cronies that shut the gate and locked us out, remember? I've heard he shut out refugees before us, as well. And that wall..."

"You have the right of it. The man is drunk with power, especially now that you confirmed what he had been assuming all along. I don't care if her corpse is strung up at the front of that army bearing down on us. Until the gods see fit to make another Seraph, the Lady Ren is the light and leadership of this city, and I will honor her wishes, not his. I have commanded my men to disregard any command to defend the inner city. We have spent our resources setting up stations along the walls and preparing homes inside the slums from a breach. Even so, I plan to use the wall that Castille has built for a fallback position if the situation outside gets too dire. We have mapped out the catacombs so we can get people from the slums inside the inner wall quickly. Make no mistake, the enemy will get inside Illux. And when they do, I need people I can rely on to attack those inside the inner city if need be. I will not allow that man's classist rhetoric lead to the deaths of thousands of good people. Can I count on your people to back me on this?"

*If not, we are all lost.*

Tess pulled a dagger from her waist and thumbed the blade, twirling the point between her fingertips. When she was done, she planted the point directly into the fourth spire.

"I will make sure that we do what needs to be done," she said, solemnly. "I cannot speak for all of us, but I know enough will back me. Some of our soldiers, especially those who were Paladins, came from families of the inner city. I cannot ask them to battle their families, but I can make sure that we hold the walls long enough to evacuate the slums. Will there be enough room?"

"No," Edmund said. "There will not be. But if we can fill the Grand Cathedral and the Paladin Barracks with those too old or infirm to fight, then the others will be able to defend the second wall. Taking into account the casualties we will sustain during the retreat, we will have to make them fit in the inner city. I would stage a coup now, with your backing, but I don't want to risk losing the will of the people. Part of me hopes that Castille will come to his senses when he sees how the siege is going."

"And why are you sure that the walls will be breached in the first place?" she asked.

"A feeling," he said. "A sense of dread that has hung over me since I was promoted to Captain. They have several Divine Beasts. After what you told me the one did to our army, I am sure that we will suffer losses of a magnitude that Illux hasn't seen since the Purge. We have no army, just an assortment of City Watch, refugees, and some Paladins who aren't loyal to anyone but themselves."

"And what would you have done to stave off the Divine Beasts without my support?" Tess asked. "You don't strike me as the type to lay down and let the people under his command die."

Edmund smiled.

The weapon he showed Tess was kept secret from all but the Paladin command, his most trusted City Watchmen, and himself. It was a giant crossbow, nearly the size of a building. It fired bolts as large as trees and was powered by a series of cranks and pulleys operated by a team of men. The engineers had dubbed it a ballista. It had been based on old plans found in the archives. It seemed that it had been planned during the Northern Campaign but abandoned when that conflict had wound down. Edmund hadn't originally planned for Divine Beasts to be a factor in the siege, but he had ordered the engineers of the inner city to begin the construction of siege weapons that could take out large groups of Demons and Accursed at the same time. This had been what they had crafted.

Eight in total had been cobbled together over the last few weeks, one for each side of the four gates. Now that Edmund knew they faced Divine Beasts as well as the rank and file of the enemy forces, he marveled at his own foresight. Each ballista would be manned by a team of several men and women, who could be counted on to think clearly in the heat of battle. He wanted to be sure that nothing went wrong with their operation. Edmund wasn't deluded into thinking these would completely turn the tide of battle, but he held out hope they would be able to remove at least a few of the Divine Beasts from the fray before they were overrun.

"I want a Demigod stationed with each team," Edmund said. "Pick eight that you can trust, with abilities that you think will serve us best in this situation. Can you have them here by the end of the day to learn the operation of the machines?"

One of the teams launched a test bolt. The projectile shattered a makeshift brick wall and embedded itself into the building behind it.

"Yes," she replied. "I already have several in mind. Edmund, why do you trust me?"

"Should I not?"

"You hardly know me. I certainly didn't trust you, not at first."

"I took a gamble," Edmund replied. "I will do whatever it takes to protect the people of the city, and I sense you would do the same. I had someone tell me that the city needed men like me once, and I plan to prove him right."

Suddenly, Edmund saw several Paladins approaching him from the corners of his vision. He immediately recognized one of them as Hunt. The glowering Paladin drew his sword and motioned for the others to spread out and surround the pair. Several of the guards working at the ballistae drew their weapons and tried to get to Edmund first.

"What the hell are you doing?" Edmund shouted, pulling free his sword.

Already, ice was forming on Tess's body, her arms encased in sharp frozen blades. Once again, her skin began to pale and her eyes glossed over an icy blue.

"Under the command of Castille, Holy Leader of Illux, you are to be arrested on charges of treason!" Hunt shouted. "Your siege weapons are to be confiscated and used at the discretion of the Fourth Spire."

The Paladins and City Watch stood at opposite sides now, each waiting for the word to strike. Edmund looked around them, seeing they were truly outnumbered, if not in bodies, then certainly in power.

*You son of a bitch, Castille.*

Edmund sighed and cast his sword onto the ground. It clattered away from him dismissively. He felt the overwhelming surge of defeat. What would become of the people in the slums? What of Elise and Ajax? But he couldn't throw away the lives of those gathered here. Not for his own sake. He just hoped that Castille would show him mercy, but deep down he knew that wasn't going to happen.

"Stand down," he said. "Put away your weapons."

"Would you men fight and die for this man?" Tess said, her voice deeper than it had been before she had iced over.

"We would!" a man shouted.

"Then get him somewhere safe!" she shouted.

Ice ripped forth from her body, freezing Hunt solid and then shattering his body into a shower of jagged, red shards just as quickly. The other Paladins shouted in fear and broke rank as she followed through with another barrage of frost targeting them. Flashes of blue light sprang into existence, trying to stave off the blizzard. That was when the chaos truly began. The air around them dropped in temperature as shards of ice flew through the air, killing all they touched.

Buildings began to ignite from the Paladin-fire as Edmund was dragged away from the scene by his men. The last he saw of Tess was at the swirling heart of snow and ice. Of the Paladins there was no sign.

# CHAPTER XIX

The men and women that surrounded him were possibly the most ragged group of individuals he had ever seen. They weren't much to look at, but they were loyal to the Lady Ren, and they were the best that Lin and Alyssa could get together on such short notice. Some were refugees from the other villages, some had lived in Seatown their whole lives; some had loved ones stuck in Illux, some had no friends or family to speak of, but they had a conscience that ached at the thought of leaving the Mortal Plane to ruin. These were men and women who were willing to chance death in one loud act of defiance against the Ten. Gil shuddered at the thought that he was damning these gathered few, but there was no other way. Death for them might mean life for thousands more.

Lin silently handed out the torches he had spent the last day gathering the materials for. Gil looked from face to face, making sure he saw no second thoughts. He had already decided before any of them had filed into the room that he would kill anyone who he thought would endanger his plan. There was no time for second thoughts, no chance for mistakes this night. The fate of the Mortal Plane rested on their shoulders. It was a burden he had carried his entire time he had been a Paladin, but never of this magnitude.

"I want to thank all of you for braving the streets after the curfew to meet here," Gil said, quietly.

*The curfew I created.*

After the body of the Paladin was found, summary executions had increased tenfold. So too had the number of dead guards found in the streets multiplied, many with the words "For the Lady" written in their blood or carved into their flesh. The city was reaching its breaking point, and tonight, Gil planned to ignite the blaze. He just hoped that those gathered here would be enough, and that the warning he had given Admiral Wyn had brought her over to his way of thinking. With her support, the rest of the city would turn on the Ten with little confrontation, but without her…

"Whatever happens tonight, the Mortal Plane will never be the same," he continued. "The Ten will not continue their heresy in new lands, nor will they abandon Illux in her time of need. We stand before a tide that wishes to wash away our way of life. We cannot allow it to do so. That means that some of us have to die, and more of us have to kill. Is anyone here opposed to these stakes?"

He looked over the room one final time, praying silently to himself that no one would stand to leave. He didn't want to risk turning the others against him by striking any of them down, but he would, to keep this mission secret and safe. Gods, he didn't want it to come to that.

"Just remember," Alyssa spoke up, "we aren't fighting the Forces of Darkness this day. These are men and women who once served the Light just as we all do. High God help us, most of them have been deluded into thinking they still do. Don't kill if you don't have to, some of these people who will stand against us can be saved."

Gil nodded grimly but said nothing. He was beyond mercy. When had his heart been hardened so? Once he would have spat on any Paladin that thought of any Mortals in such terms. Even the slick blood of bandits upon his blade had never brought him joy. What had become of that man?

*Jaina.*

He motioned for the group to follow him, exiting The Drunken Ox and into the night beyond. The group was no more than thirty, each armed with swords and unlit torches. They moved through the darkness like a gentle wave from the ocean, washing over each street on their way toward the docks. The air was damp and cold. It sent shivers down more than one spine. A guard swung about a corner, stopping short at the sight of the armed mob. Lin grabbed the man by the neck and clamped a hand over his mouth. Gil approached and stuck his sword-arm through the man's chest. He shuddered violently and went still. They lowered the dead guard into the shadow of a doorway and continued on their way. Behind them Gil could hear Alyssa sigh, defeated.

Overhead, a thin skein of cloud floated in front of the full moon. Aenna was there as usual, but beside the bright moon Gil could tell that the window to the heavens was dimmer than it had been for most of his life. Had he noticed this before in his delirium outside Marna? How many gods had fallen? What was the state of the world beyond the battle that raged tonight?

They reached the docks without many more incidents, though a string of dead guards littered the walkway leading back to The Drunken Ox. Gil adjusted the cloak he always wore, pulling free a torch. He motioned for Lin and Alyssa to come closer. Lin pulled free a flint and struck it, igniting Gil's torch. The Paladin dipped the head of the flaming beacon, igniting the torches of his two companions. They each turned about-face and lit the torches of the rest of the mob. One by one the points of yellow and orange sprang to life, spotting the silver light of the moon like so many stars.

"Burn every board, every scrap of cloth!" Gil shouted. "Don't step back onto land until this fleet is in ashes!"

Thirty torches were raised high, and thirty voices shouted back in affirmation. Gil broke into a run, jumping from the dock onto the nearest of the ships anchored there. It took him a moment to gain his footing under the gentle undulating of the ship as it bobbed on the surf. He reached the rope ladder leading higher up the mast, pulling himself up rung by rung, carrying his torch precariously in his mouth. Sweat began to run down the left side of his face as the heat washed over him. Once he was near the furled sails, he held the torch out to the cloth, keeping it there until it caught fire. The heat was instant, nearly smothering him with its intensity. The flames spread up the sail quicker even than he imagined. Realizing he suddenly had little time, Gil grabbed the end of a rope that wasn't fully fastened to the rigging, wrapping it around his sword arm and waist. Without a second thought, he jumped from the mast and swung through the air, touching the torch everywhere he could as he made his way downward.

By the time his feet where back on the deck and the rope about his waist was cut, the flames had taken on a life of their own. They sprang from cloth to wood, jumping here and there with impunity. Gil had assumed that the moisture in the air would have prevented the ships from igniting so quickly, but he was pleasantly surprised. Already, smoke mixed with salt and burned his throat as he breathed. Turning around, Gil saw that the others had had similar levels of success. The entire wharf was lit by yellow and orange light. It wouldn't be long now before the Ten and their cronies arrived. He cast a glance at the Overlook. The windows of the upper level came alive with their own faded yellow light.

Suddenly, the door to the cabin burst open and two groggy men rushed out brandishing swords. Gil sprang into them before they had a chance to figure out what was going on. The first man fell before his sword stroke, clutching at the bloody stump of a leg. The scent of copper joined the smoke and salt. The second man recovered himself long enough to parry Gil's attacks. The Paladin let the magic in his body spring to life, hammering the man overboard into the dark grave below. While trying to push the thoughts of the man slowly drowning out of mind, Gil kept the magic flowing, ripping through the mast and rigging, toppling the burning tower onto the rest of the ship with a torrent of blue flame.

He turned and jumped from the ship, landing back on the dock. Standing before him, shadows cast from the flames dancing across her features, was a member of the Ten.

"What have you done?" the woman shouted, pulling free her sword. "This is madness!"

"This is your doing," Gil spat, casting the torch aside.

She rushed him, hacking with savage strokes that seemed to unbalance her. She was clearly shaken by the surprise attack on the fleet. Gil used her rage against her, blocking as deftly as he could, sidestepping her attacks whenever possible. He thought back to the way he had seen Balance Monks fight Demons, using the strength and size of the brutes against them. Until he had gotten used to having only one arm he would be disadvantaged against other Paladins, unless he could outsmart them.

After a few minutes of blocking and dodging the woman, she began to slow, giving him the opening he needed to press his own attack. Gil hammered into her with offensive magic. The blue energy pounded into her defenses, pushing her farther and farther back upon the dock. Gil jumped at her, swinging his sword-arm in a large arc. The Paladin woman stepped backward onto the edge of the dock, narrowly avoiding his stroke but losing her footing on the wet planks. He raised his good hand and sent her into the water with a blast of blue fire. The armor she wore was too heavy, dropping her beneath the waves like a stone.

Gil quickly looked around, seeing that the rest of Seatown had finally begun to stir. It wouldn't be much longer before the rest of the Paladins and guards rushed to stop the burning of the ships. Now was the time for the others with him to take part in the fighting and dying. He bent and picked up his torch before turning back to look at the rest of the fleet. The ocean was lit with oranges and reds the likes of which he had never seen before. Every third ship was burning, with the others soon to follow. Embers floated through the night sky on the ocean breeze. Hungry flames danced and jumped from mast to rigging, decks were ablaze and frightened sailors jumped overboard. It was chaos. Chaos he had orchestrated.

*Is this what madness I have wrought? Surely the Gods of Darkness laugh at us this night.*

"No!" a now familiar voice screamed from his right.

Gil turned to see Admiral Wyn collapsing to her knees. Already more of the ships caught flame; what little work those stationed on them had done to defend them being for naught. When her eyes met his, the reflected flames illuminated hate the like of which he had never seen. In the back of his mind Gil thought this might not have been the first time this woman had seen Seatown attacked by Paladins. Was she old enough to have lived through Cecilia's raid?

"There were people on those ships!" she cried. "Good people. My people. You burned them alive!"

"Some people deserve to burn," Gil said coldly. "Those were your people the Ten hung up in the square every day. Where were your tears then? Or did these ships mean more to you than the people who built them?"

"This is evil," she rasped. "I thought you were different than this. You spoke to me in my room, I should have known. I-I am responsible."

"You want to see evil?" he asked. "Look no further than there." Gil pointed with his sword arm in the direction of the town square. "How noble of you to make sure they hung them where you didn't have to see them from the Overlook. I was the fool for leaving you alive when I came to your room. I thought that you could be made to see reason. I was wrong."

"The Ten will stop you."

"There are only eight of them now."

A burst of shouts reached his ears. Gil spun, seeing the mob swarming from within the city. The rest of the Ten were at the front of an armed cadre of guards and villagers. The rest of Gil's band of dissenters quickly gathered around him, leaving the rest of the fleet to its own demise. The hissing and spitting of the flames were quickly drowned out by the sounds of the approaching crowd. The Admiral stayed where she was, silently staring at the burning wreckage of her power. With no ships to command, the rule of Seatown was now truly in the hands of the Ten, for what use was an Admiral with no fleet?

Gil looked at those gathered close to him. Alyssa looked grim but determined. Lin tried to keep his face neutral, but his facade was cracking. The others didn't appear much better. Some were covered in blood and other grime; most had a sheen of soot on them. If Gil couldn't convince the people of Seatown that what he had done was the right course of action, they would all die. There was no way that this paltry force could withstand that which gathered before them. Once again, he wondered if he had made a terrible mistake.

When the mob came to a halt, they stood just at the edge of the dock, staring at Gil and his companions. The eight Paladins at the front of the column had their weapons drawn, but none stepped forward to challenge Gil. He stared down each of them in turn, trying to find a weakness among them. There seemed to be none. The Ten were a monolith. Beside them, the guard woman Shae glowered at him with her flinty eyes.

*I haven't forgotten you.*

"People of Seatown!" Gil shouted. "Why do you follow these false Paladins? We were entrusted by the Gods of Light to serve mankind, not to rule over them. What they have done here is not the true path, but heresy. They have defied Illux and profaned the name of the Lady Ren! Does that not burn your very souls? They strung up innocents for no crime greater than speaking their minds! Has that not filled you with rage?"

The Ten remained silent, letting him continue to speak for some reason he could not fathom. The crowd began to grow restless, with nods and grumbles of approval filtering across some of the faces he could see, illuminated by the flames behind him. He nearly had them, it wouldn't take much more for his plan to succeed.

"I served the Lady in Illux, then Rinwaithe to the north. Finally, I was stationed at Marna," he continued. "I was there when the enemy, the true enemy, burned the village. I watched as every man, woman, and child was butchered. It was there that I lost my arm to that evil as I tried to stop it. I lost my soul. This is more than heresy at work here. This is cowardice. That same evil that burned Marna is heading for Illux. It may be that some of you are destined to travel the world and discover new lands, but not at the expense of innocent lives. Those who are not cowards, those who serve the true Light of this land, stand with me. March with me to Illux and save our people. I am from the villages, I know how Illux treats us, but they are servants of the Light as well, we cannot abandon them!"

It was then that one of the Paladins stepped forward, raising his voice so that all could hear.

"Do not listen to this man. He is no Paladin, look at his deformity, he is more Accursed than man. He dares to speak of heresy while speaking the praises of Ren? If she truly spoke for the Gods of Light, they would not have allowed her and her army to be crushed in the wilderness. Where is the Light in that? Look behind him, those are your ships he has burned. Each of you had a brother or a daughter aboard those ships, and he has burned them all as well. Those standing here are the cowards, cowards who have robbed you of the salvation we had promised. They deserve the only real justice that exists in these dark times—the end of a rope."

It was then that Gil first noticed the extreme heat washing over his back. He knew he had lost the crowd. They no longer looked convinced of his words. Few, in fact, seemed even confused any longer. All expressed the bloodlust and hate he had seen in the face of the Admiral. He had been wrong.

"Gods," Alyssa whispered.

The mob surged forward, shouting for blood. Gil reacted mechanically, raising his good arm, and firing a blast of energy at Shae, incinerating the woman before he even tried to attack any of the others. The Ten converged on him almost instantly, knocking down his defenses and cutting into his flesh. He saw through the confusion that Lin had fallen, his throat slit from end to end. Alyssa was overpowered and forced to the ground—what happened to her next he could not see. As for Gil himself, he collapsed within moments, taking only one other Paladin with him, a man he had stabbed through the eye. Gil's legs gave out under his own weight.

The other Paladins gripped him by the arms, restraining him from doing any further damage, though, in truth, they simply were preventing him from falling to the ground. Around him, all of his companions were likewise killed or subdued. It was over. His gambit had failed, and he had lost more innocent lives.

As the Ten carried him away, Gil looked over and saw Admiral Wyn, standing now, looking at him with fierce determination. He struggled against his captors for a moment to stop them from dragging him forward.

"I may have lost my place beside the High God," he shouted at her, "but know this, whatever fate awaits me at the end of that rope, awaits you as well. Whatever dark my spark journeys to, I will surely see you there."

The last thing he noticed before the mailed fist took the light from his eyes were the tears running down her face.

# Chapter XX

The settlement of Seatown spread out beneath them, a brown smudge on the sandy shore. The sky was hazy. Black smoke twisted and curled along the horizon. White gulls spotted the air like bits of falling snow. Trent was instantly reminded of the burning cathedral on the day that Terric died. Snow and ash didn't actually mingle and fall this day, but the smell was the same. He grimaced at the scent of fire, urging the horse they had corralled from the hills below the Grey Temple onward. Something evil had happened in this place, he was sure of it. Fire rarely signaled something good had happened.

*I just hope that we are not too late to gather an army of some sort. What chance does Illux have otherwise?*

The betrayal of the Balance Monk Teo had angered Trent at first, but eventually he had come to understand. If he had been given a chance to avenge the deaths of Gil or Terric he would have done the same. If he had not slain Akklor the Unbidden the very day that it had ended Devin he would have hunted that creature to the ends of the Mortal Plane, Illux be damned. Had that Divine Beast still drawn breath Trent would have lied to his companions a thousand times over to get close enough to slit the beast's throat. Even though Makar the Imminent had died in the attempt, a scion of the Gods of Darkness had fallen as well. Bittersweet as it was, they had won their first victory against the Fallen One. If the High God was willing, they would win several more before the end.

The ride south had happened with little incident. Ren was still as sullen as she had been since the run-in with Daniel. Trent had hardly been able to get her to speak to him, let alone repeat the physical contact they had shared before she had lost her sword. It was as if they were even less acquainted than they had been when he had been a simple Paladin serving under her. He knew that until she regained that fabled blade, she would be a stranger to them all. Something about losing the symbol of her office had stripped her of everything she had been. The thought of going up against Daniel again didn't appeal to him, but that seemed to be the only way he would regain the woman he loved.

After several minutes of riding, they finally began heading down the gradual slope into the town. Trent had only been to Seatown a handful of times, and most of those had been when he was barely a man, a fresh Paladin under the command of Broderick Breaksword, the man who had personally saved this very settlement from a rogue Paladin once upon a time. That had been a lifetime ago now, it seemed. Devin and Gil had ridden with them then, both as green as Trent had been. Devin had never truly forgiven himself for what had happened to Breaksword. It had been a lesson to them all about humility and the need to follow orders. Now Trent was one of the ones giving orders, and he wasn't sure he liked it. Broderick certainly never had.

"How do you think they will take to two Seraphs?" he mused aloud.

"They barely listened to one," Ren said, distantly.

She rode behind him to his left, a good deal behind him. Divinity padded along beside her, staying in line with the horses. The two

Balance Monks followed in the rear, keeping their distance physically and emotionally as well. Though he had understood why they had lied, and even forgiven them, they had not forgiven themselves. Trent was more isolated now than he had ever been. He longed to see Elise again, or even the man Edmund, whom he had charged with keeping her safe. Someone who would talk to him, who didn't feel the need to keep their distance due to failure or falsehood. He patted his horse on the neck.

*At least you haven't bucked me off yet. That's something.*

Ahead, the small gates to the city were barred. Outside, there were no signs of any watch or guardsmen on duty. The wall surrounding Seatown paled in comparison to that of Illux, but it still would prevent the party from entering without flying over. When they reached the gate, Trent approached it and pounded his gauntleted fist against the timbers. Each blow rang out in the silence like the crash of waves on the opposite end of the town.

There was no response.

"Have you ever known a fortification like this to go unmanned?" he asked.

"I have not," Teo replied, pulling his horse up beside the Seraph. "What do we do now? Fly over the wall?"

When the other man finished speaking, Trent noticed a noise carried on the wind: the sounds of a crowd milling about somewhere past the gate. It was the dull roar of a people who were about to witness something exciting. Perhaps, this was connected to that smoke they had noticed from the rise above.

Trent nodded and hitched his horse to a post just to the right of the gate. The others did the same. It was quickly decided that Divinity would be left to guard the other animals as she would be the most difficult to carry over the wall. She didn't seem to mind for she curled up beside the horses and closed her eyes. Trent wrapped his arms around Teo while Ren did the same for Rella. In a matter of moments, the Seraphs had taken to the air, bearing their charges over the wall and on to the street below. While they were above the wall, Trent saw what had caused the smoke: a massive fleet of ships lay in a smoldering ruin, broken and blackened hulls and masts poking above the surface of the waves. Some looked to have crashed into the wharf, while others floated out further to sea. He also noticed there was a crowd of a hundred gathered in the central square of the town.

After landing, they continued their way toward the center of the Seatown, making their way through the winding streets that would have given the slums of Illux a run for their money. Seatown, it seemed, had been planned even less in advance than Illux had as it had grown and expanded over the years since Arendt had founded it. As they passed small shops and smaller houses, they didn't see a single sign of life. Trent could only assume they were heading in the correct direction because of the sounds of the crowd that grew louder as they progressed. He hoped that their plea for an army would not fall on deaf ears. He did not want to resort to conscription, especially not when the citizens of Seatown already despised the rule of the Seraphs so much. The town had been pillaged and nearly razed to the ground twice under Jerrok, and although this had not continued under Ren, those who remembered those days had not forgiven Illux. Even so, he decided they would not leave this place without getting what they came for.

*They will see reason.*

Finally, the buildings began to part, revealing a massive square, filled from one side to the other with people. The first thing that Trent noticed were the bodies hanging from gibbets around the perimeter. Crows and other carrion birds pecked at the faces and necks of the bloated morsels that swung in the breeze. The gulls that circled overhead suddenly took on a far more menacing timber in their *caws*. He had never seen such a thing in all his life. Hanging was a rare punishment under the rule of the Seraphs. Those who were not banished from Illux were usually executed by the sword. Seatown and the smaller villages would hang bandits from time to time, but never in numbers such as these.

"This isn't normal, not even for Seatown," Rella whispered. "What is going on here?"

The group stood at the rear of the crowd, waiting to see what was going on before making themselves known. It wouldn't take more than a glance for those gathered to see that the Seraphs had joined them. Ren and Trent had done nothing to disguise their identities from these people. Trent hadn't thought there was any need. After looking at the bodies that ringed the square, he wasn't so sure. He found himself looking at the faces to see if he had somehow known any of the victims, to see if any of them were his father.

Luckily, the crowd was too enthralled with those gathered on a large platform at the far end of the square to notice the newcomers. The raised platform currently held nearly two dozen figures. Trent could tell that at least seven of them were Paladins, even from this distance. The others, save one, looked to be beaten and bloody prisoners, the largest of which was bound with his arms behind his back and a rope around his neck. The only other non-Paladin who clearly wasn't one of the prisoners was a rather regal looking woman with an ornate cloak spun from greens and blues. She stood to the side of the prisoners, just behind the Paladins. Trent could tell that this woman was important, but it was clear who really was in control here.

"You have come for justice, have you not?" one of the Paladins called out. "You have come to see this man receive the justice of the gods?"

The crowd made several conflicting sounds in response. It didn't seem that all of them held the same opinion on the matter.

"These heretics burned our fleet. They killed your brothers and sisters. They killed three of the Ten! They have brought sin into Seatown, a black stain they would have brought to our new worlds, and what is worse, they have shown no remorse for their actions. For that, they must die!"

"Shouldn't we stop this?" Rella asked.

"Maybe..." Trent trailed off.

He couldn't take his eyes off the large man with the noose around his neck. Something about him was familiar. The man's face was so bruised and bloody that he was nearly unrecognizable. Even his own mother would have had a hard time telling him from another prisoner. He wore clothing of no special note, and his hair was a mix of blond, blood, and dirt. Yet Trent felt an innate connection to the man, as if he knew him intimately like a brother. For a moment, Trent's gaze wandered onto the woman in the ornate cloak. Even from here, he could tell she was uncomfortable with the entire affair.

Trent was preparing to do something when the Paladin who had been speaking pulled a lever, dropping the man far enough down that the rope pulled taught. The familiar looking man twitched and spun, flailing his feet wildly as the air left his lungs. Trent couldn't bear to watch, casting his eyes at the ground momentarily. Then a woman on the platform stumbled forward, crying.

"Gil!" she shouted. "No!"

*It can't be.*

But it was. Trent knew with complete certainty that the man who was losing his life before them was one of his greatest friends. He saw the look of shock on the faces of Ren and Rella, both women who had known the man, but by then, Trent was no longer thinking clearly. Godtaker appeared in his hand, and the ground fell away from his feet. He flew directly at the rope, preparing to sever it in one stroke. The crowd erupted into shouts of fear and awe as he passed over them, clearly startled by the flying creature that had materialized in their midst. Trent never made it to the rope though, for he was knocked from the sky by multiple flashes of blue light from the platform.

The Paladins had struck first.

"The heretics from Illux have come to save their own!" one of them shouted.

Trent was up again, roaring like an animal from the middle of the mob. One of the Paladins jumped from the platform, clearing away the crowd as he landed. Men and women scattered to give room to the fighters, afraid they too would lose their lives. Within seconds, the rest of the Paladins were on the ground surrounding the Seraph with weapons drawn.

Trent barely saw them. He looked back up at the platform. The woman in the bright cloak pulled free a thin sword and sliced through the rope, dropping Gil to the ground beneath the platform. From there she moved to free the bound prisoners, barking orders to the guards, who had started up the steps to the platform. The guards paused, torn between listening to this woman and enforcing the order of the Paladins.

The first Paladin who had jumped down to face Trent lunged at him, but he knocked him away with Godtaker, removing one of the man's fingers as he did so. The next attack came from a pair, each jumping with weapons high above their heads. Trent tried to block them, but bursts of energy from behind knocked him into his attackers. He hacked with Godtaker, savagely and single-mindedly attacking those who would have hung his friend, his friend who had somehow survived the razing of his village, his last living friend.

Two Paladins fell, crumpling into ash from a burst of lightning. Ren landed beside Trent, gripping one of the Paladins he grappled with and tossing the woman aside like a doll. She snarled like Trent did, clawing at each of their assailants with fingers curled into points. Hot blood sprayed her face from a throat the she tore out in one smooth movement. Distantly, Trent could hear the sounds of more fighting, no doubt the Balance Monks trying to make their way through the crowd to the Seraphs. Another Paladin fell from a cut from Godtaker so deep that it nearly split the man in two. Blood sprayed over the seraph, covering his wings with a crimson mist.

"Stand down!" Ren shouted over the din. "We command you! I am the Lady Ren!"

"Heretic!" one of the last Paladins spat. "You do not speak for the gods!"

Ren was taken aback by this, reflexively stepping backward. Trent didn't allow the Paladin to press his advantage. Trent lifted a fist and channeled so much fire that he smashed through the weak shield that the other Paladin threw up at the last moment and the man began to boil in his armor. When the smoke cleared, Trent looked around to see that nearly all of the Paladins were dead, and those two who weren't, moaned in pain on the ground. Likewise, it seemed that Teo and Rella had dispatched half a dozen guards on their way to the pair. Below the platform, Gil's head was being cradled in the lap of one of the other prisoners.

Since the guards that had tried to rush them had been dispatched by Teo and Rella, the rest gathered around the woman in the green and blue robes protectively. She stepped toward the edge of the platform and looked over the crowd, shouting her words as she did so:

"Our people will no longer be under the yoke of those who wield their power against the weak! I have failed you until now, but I will do so no longer!"

"What of the Seraphs? Either of them?" a woman shouted. "Are they here to rule us? Are they really the enemy of the Light?"

Trent lifted Godtaker defensively, but Ren put a hand on him to stay his sword. These were her people, even if they would rather not be. There was no way she would turn on them unless absolutely necessary. Trent had no such compunction, not after what they had allowed to happen to Gil.

"We have not come to rule over you!" Ren shouted, a bit of confidence returning to her voice. "We have come to ask you to come to the aid of Illux. The Forces of Darkness march on the city as we speak. If we do nothing, the city will fall, and then Seatown will follow. If we do not stand together, we will all die. I know that Seatown has not always liked being under the thumb of the city, and I know that Illux has failed to protect you in the past, but I promise we have never meant to mistreat you."

"Prove your worth!" a man shouted.

"Why are there two of you now?" yelled another. "Was one not enough?"

"Show us Nightbreaker!"

"I—" Ren began, "I cannot. I lost the blade."

The crowd took a negative turn. Shouts became more aggressive. Trent looked over his shoulder at Gil. His longtime friend was sitting up and staring at him, clearly confused. If only they had time to talk. Trent turned back to address the crowd when a crash and the sound of rushing water drowned out all of the other noises. He again looked over his shoulder, this time gazing out at the sea behind them.

More than one shape was rising from beneath its surface.

# CHAPTER XXI

The inside of Elise's dark hovel was not unlike his childhood home: dark, small, and dirty. Edmund had been in hiding here for the better part of a week, waiting for some sign that he could venture back into the city without immediately running into some Paladins that wanted him dead. Before they had tried to arrest him, the relationship between Castille's loyalists and those of Edmund's City Watch had been strained at best, but since then, the city had been on the verge of a civil war. Edmund wasn't just hiding because he feared what Castille would do to him, but also because he feared what his people would do in response. The City Watch itself was now divided between those who supported Edmund, and those who either were loyal to Castille or who distrusted the Demigods with which Edmund now found himself aligned.

Tess had murdered several Paladins and Castille loyalists. What had actually happened after that, Edmund wasn't sure. What few reports he had received were a garbled mess of hearsay and rumor. Some claimed that two entire city blocks were still frozen around the site of the battle, while others claimed that no Paladins had died except for Hunt. Most of the reports agreed that Tess was dead, however, either as a result of her uncontrollable powers, or a rush of Paladins who overcame her. Edmund doubted that to be true. She was a woman of far more resilience than that. Like Edmund, the remaining Demigods had gone into hiding as well, scorned by the loyalists, and feared by most of the common folk. It seemed their blessing had become a curse.

*When is that not the case?*

Elise was humming quietly to Ajax while Edmund worked at washing the clothes from the surrounding houses. Music soothed the boy in a way that nothing else could. Perhaps, his mother, or even father, had the gift of song? Sadly, they would never know now. Even so, Ajax had begun doing remarkably better now that he was in the care of the old crone. Edmund was amazed at first, but then he realized that the love the boy's mother had shown him was finally reflected in someone else. She had taken him in as her own, just as she had done once before… There had been at least one good thing he had done since becoming Captain of the City Watch.

A rapid pounding at the door alerted Edmund. He dropped the laundry into the wash bucket with a slosh and pulled free his sword.

"It's Liara!" a familiar voice called out.

"Hurry up before you are seen!" Elise replied.

Quickly, the guard woman opened the door and slipped inside. Her face was a mask of grave concern. Edmund could see sweat glistening on her almond-colored forehead. She wasn't one to scare easy. Something was wrong.

"What is it?" Edmund asked, dismissing her weak salute.

"They are here," she said, almost in a whisper. "The army of the enemy is outside our gates."

"For how long?" Edmund asked.

"I left as soon as they arrived," she said. "It's been the better part of an hour."

Edmund began to gather his belongings, strapping on his boots as he looked at Elise and Liara. Ajax began to cry again.

"And what of Castille's preparations?" Edmund asked. "The siege weapons?"

"The Paladins retreated to the inner city once the army was spotted. They left the care of the slums to the Watch. We have moved the ballistae to the walls on either side of the gates as you requested. What are you planning to do?"

"It is as you said, the Paladins are not concerned with the slums or the outer walls. I am. That is where I need to be, and where I need to be seen. I won't hide here while the city falls under siege. I am no coward, not matter what Castille thinks."

Fully armed and armored, Edmund stood and made his way for the door. A sudden flight of fancy made him return to the old woman and the baby. He kissed Ajax on the cheek and hugged Elise tight. She eyed him carefully, but not harshly.

"Keep us safe," she whispered. "At least until my Trent arrives."

*I will.*

For all of the bad news that had come back to Illux in the preceding weeks, Elise had never given up hope that Trent would return. Edmund nodded and followed Liara out the door in a rush. Once outside they began making their way toward the southern gate, urging all regular citizens they encountered to return to their homes. Edmund had wanted to make sure that all of them were armed before this day, but his plans had fallen apart once he had gone into hiding.

"Divine Beasts?" Edmund asked, his tongue drying out.

"I'm not sure, sir," Liara replied. "But there are thousands of Demons, they said. Thousands."

"High God help us," Edmund muttered. "We are truly facing the end of the world." He laughed. "Gods, I wanted none of this. I should have ignored Trent and become a Paladin. That way I'd either be dead or hiding behind two sets of walls instead of one."

Liara tried to smile, but her eyes fell. The sounds of the city were quieter than usual, though a low rumble of some kind undercut all of the other noises. Edmund feared they were in for a rough night—and possibly no dawn if they couldn't muster a valiant defense. Demons could see in the dark, and men could not. Even with the pitch and torches he had equipped the archers with, they had no hope of doing any real damage to the enemy after nightfall. The same could not be said for what the Demons could do to them if they scaled the wall. And this didn't even account for the Divine Beasts that were surely out there, waiting to end this engagement before it even began.

Suddenly, three hooded figures fell into line behind the two guards. Edmund and Liara both dropped their hands to the hilts of their blades, but not before one of the figures removed the hood from her head, showing the familiar dusky complexion and flash of white hair in a shock of dark.

"Tess!" Edmund blurted out. "I feared you had—"

"Had what?" Tess interrupted. "Had frozen solid? Not possible. And I don't let people who are hunting me find me. Nor do you, it seems. It took my men the last three days to figure out where you were hiding. Who is that old woman?"

"A friend," Edmund replied. "I am glad you're all right. And your people?"

They turned further southward, the wall quickly looming above them.

"More united now than before my little stunt. They are scared, and people are scared of them. That does wonders for our unity. I have already sent my best to help the crews on your siege engines. The rest are gathering not far from the southern gate, waiting for my orders. And yours."

Edmund nodded again, his confidence building. Perhaps, they did have a chance, now.

They reached the gate. Hundreds of City Watch and armed civilians ran back and forth, milling about behind the gate with no order. Someone had taken the initiative to round up as many citizens and refugees who could fight as possible but had done nothing beyond that to get them into any kind of formation. Edmund started barking orders like he hadn't been in hiding, and to his surprise the people listened. Within a few minutes he had all of those gathered below following him through the gatehouse and up the stair to the top of the wall.

As soon as Edmund stepped out onto the battlement, he lost his breath at what he saw scattered out below them. The earth was blackened with thousands of Demons and Accursed, spread out nearly to the horizon. Farther back he could see dozens of larger creatures, many in the shape of twisted animals. These must have been the Divine Beasts, not unlike the one that Tess had spoken of. They looked as if they had crawled straight out of the stories he had been told as a child. His guts began to ache. Edmund looked to his right. On each side of the gate was one of the giant crossbows, loaded and aimed at the mass below. He noticed the white streaks of hair that marked the Demigods present at each of the weapons.

*Good. This will give us a chance.*

Then, a small shape began to rise from the field below. As it got closer, Edmund could make out the red wings and skin that marked the thing. Surely this was the new Herald, sent to replace the one that the Goddess Arra had killed. When the creature was level with the top of the wall, it hovered in the air, eyeing the defenders with an unbridled wickedness. In one hand it held a weapon that looked akin to a giant butcher's cleaver.

"Let the leader of this city come forth!" the creature shouted. "Your people shall fall before the might of Lio, the Fallen One. We will butcher your children and condemn your men and women to an eternity of damnation in our service. Come forth, and you alone might be spared. You alone will meet a swift death so you may rejoin your High God."

"Spear!" Edmund shouted.

A man placed the weapon in his hand. Edmund leaned back and threw it as hard as he could at the Herald. His aim was poor and the weapon fell short, but the effect was the same. The creature twisted away, hissing in distaste. Tess stepped to the edge of the wall and stuck out her exposed arms, filling the air between them and the fleeing beast with frost.

"You will find no cowards here! She shouted after the creature. "Fly back to your master. If he was truly a god, he would face us himself!"

The rumble they had heard earlier grew louder as the dark mass from below rushed the wall, slamming against it like a black tide. Edmund motioned to his archers who began firing flaming arrows into the mass of bodies below. Once the Demons reached the base of the wall they began to climb its smooth surface as if it were as easy as using the rungs of a ladder. Tess and her handful of Demigods leaned over the edge, shooting flame and ice and wind down below, trying to knock as many of the dark shapes free as they could. Boiling oil was quickly carried to the wall and dumped into the abyss.

When Edmund looked up again, he saw that the Divine Beasts had begun to charge the walls as well. The crews at each ballista quickly rotated their weapons and sighted them in. They would launch the massive bolts only when the creatures were truly within range. They couldn't afford to waste a single bolt, not with what bore down on them. Edmund counted in his head, waiting until he reached five before he gave the signal to launch.

A roar twisted him about, just as yellowed talons raked across the battlement. Most of those gathered beside Edmund were able to jump out of the way, though some fell off the wall to their deaths, screaming the entire way down. The Captain of the Guard himself rolled out of the way at the last possible moment. A Divine Beast in the shape of some carrion bird, nearly twice the size of one of the ballistae had gotten close while they had been distracted. As it was turning back in for another strike, Tess jumped up and hammered at its face with shards of ice. The archers quickly followed her attack, filling the sky with black and orange. The beasts roared again, slipping through the wall of arrows and back out over its army.

Edmund nodded to the ballista crews, and they launched. The first bolt missed its target, though dozens of Demons and Accursed were ground into the dirt. The second bolt struck home, hitting the carrion bird in the wing. The force of the blow sent the large creature into a death spiral, spinning end over end until it collapsed in a heap—killing another score of the enemy as it landed.

"What is that?" a man shouted, pointing to the southwest.

Edmund stood and looked back over the wall.

A second army of what had to be more Demons and Accursed was approaching, this one smaller than the first, but moving at greater speed.

*Gods have mercy. We are doomed.*

Those gathered on the wall looked on in horror for what seemed like hours. Then the second force quickly met the first, but the result was not what any of them would have expected. Bodies smashed into one-another, and the assaulting Forces of Darkness quickly wheeled about to meet this new threat. Even most of the Demons still scaling the walls dropped back to the ground, trying to join their fellows to prevent the attack on their flank.

"They are attacking each other!" a woman yelled. "What does this mean?"

"It means we have been given an opportunity!" Tess said, excitedly. "Edmund, open the western gate."

"What?" Edmund said, confused.

"Let my people go out there and attack them while they are distracted. No army can win on two fronts. We won't be out there long. Just give us enough time to break their flank, then we come back in. Before the Divine Beasts make it to us."

Already the two forces had become fully entangled with each other. The Divine Beasts were battling with new Divine Beasts. Four-legged creatures of some kind washed over the Demons and Accursed of the initial army, running them down like some imitation of cavalry. Edmund shivered at the sight. Something terrible was happening below. He even thought he saw flashes of light in the sky where three winged figures were doing battle near the center of the fighting. Tess was right. They needed to take advantage of this opportunity somehow, but he didn't feel like sending their best weapon outside of the wall was a wise idea. What was he to do?

"Edmund!" Tess said, harshly.

"Now!" Edmund snapped. "Follow me!"

The Captain of the City Watch of Illux spun around and led the Demigods back down the steps into the guardhouse. Tess told Edmund which direction her people were gathering on the streets below. He sent a runner to tell them to make for the western gate. Once they reached the ground he began to jog along the wall, for they had no time to waste. The High God smiled on them for this briefest of moments, and there was no telling how long this opportunity would last. The second army wasn't as large as the first, and even with the element of surprise, it was unlikely they would last long in an open engagement.

The city was as quiet as the catacombs and smelled even worse. The slums nearest to the wall had taken the brunt of the refugee camps, which had now been cleared out enough to give the Watch the room to run back and forth. Dozens of hungry eyes watched the group as they passed, sunken faces that hid from within the shadows of houses and tents. Edmund tried to ignore them, tried to remind himself they were what he was fighting for. He wished he could bring Castille to justice for the conditions they had been subjected to, but he didn't even expect that he would see that bastard again, let alone arrest him.

Once they reached the gate, Edmund got his men to prepare to open it. Minutes later the Demigods began to gather, filing into battalions like they were back in the army again. Tess had removed her cloak, revealing the armor she wore underneath. She no longer wore the simple armor of an army officer, but the ornate plate that would befit a Paladin. It wasn't bulky like true Paladin armor, though, but slim and fitted to her. The plate was enameled in a mix of blues and whites. Already, frost was forming on her neck and shoulders. A short sword was strapped to her side, and her bow had been removed to make sure that the wood wasn't damaged from the extreme cold.

The gates ground open with a metallic scrape. Once they had swung as wide as they were able, Tess nodded to Edmund and charged through the opening to the outside, her Demigods following behind while retaining their formation. Once they were past the gate, Edmund motioned for them to be closed again. As soon as the gates were closed enough that only a single file line could fit through, he held up his hand to stop the men from closing it any further. This would have to be good enough. If the gates were closed completely, it would take too long to open them to allow the Demigods to get back through in time.

*I hope she is right about this.*

"Close that gate!" a voice shouted.

Edmund spun and saw Yan and a cadre of Paladins standing behind him.

"By order of Castille, close that gate!" Yan yelled again. It was as if he didn't even see Edmund.

Edmund drew his sword. They would not close the gate while he drew breath. Suddenly the Paladins struck, igniting their hands with blue magic, blasting at the City Watch as they ran back to the gatehouse. Edmund tried to intercept them, but Yan turned on him, knocking Edmund aside with a blast of magic. The Captain of the City Watch tumbled to the ground, knocking his head against the paving stones. The force of the impact stole his breath for a few moments.

His ears rung oddly as he tried to stand, the world spinning madly beneath him. He could see the gate closing in the distance, his men massacred before him as if they were the enemy and not citizens of Illux. Rough hands pulled him to feet and bound his arms behind his back. The cord they tied him with burned at his flesh.

"Castille said not to open any of the gates again," a voice said. "Let the abominations die out there."

Edmund tried to find the speaker, his words tumbling out. "You aren't safe in the inner city. None of you are safe when they make it in here. We might die first, but they will come for you all the same!"

A black bag was dropped over his head.

# CHAPTER XXII

"It's time," she whispered to him.

A hiss from the lava outside the tower punctuated her words. Vardic nodded and gripped his spear tighter, looking out the window to his tower. He could see the black bell on the central isle of Infernaak below them. Acrid smoke belched from the red rivers, rising, and filling the air between the isles with a dark haze. They had been conspiring together in this room for hours, waiting for the right time to summon Lio to his death. The Fallen One could not see their attack coming, so they had decided to strike just before their forces on the Mortal Plane intercepted his at the gates of Illux. They would surprise him and his servants at the same moment, just as he had done to Ravim. Once Lio was dead, the Demons and Divine Beasts under his control would fall into line and follow their Heralds as they crushed Illux once and for all.

The God of Darkness looked back over his shoulder at the naked body of his grey companion. Generations of mortals had been born and died in the amount of time between couplings of these two. Rhenaris hadn't wanted him since the Purge at least. Nor had he wanted her, truth be told. Solitude was a kinder companion than any other god could ever be. This time was different somehow, the excitement of the near completion of their plan was euphoric; it had awakened a lust in him he had nearly lost. Soon they would rid themselves of the greatest failure that the Gods of Darkness had ever allowed. After that, it was only a matter of time until the last two Gods of Light fell. Samson and Luna were weak. They would put up little resistance with Illux gone. Perhaps, then the High God would return.

Rhenaris began strapping on her armor, eyeing him as she did so. Her spines began to shiver slightly in anticipation. This plan had been her idea, hatched in the days since their return from the Mortal Plane. With each of them controlling their own Herald's, it made sense to create their own army and awaken their own Divine Beasts, which would have no loyalty to Lio. Just as they had not realized he had begun freeing these ancient beasts, so, too, had he not noticed when they had done the same. While the Fallen One had curated a force from Xyxax's Demons to the south, they had taken to gathering the remainder of their army that had been scattered by Arra. The Demons and Accursed that had survived that encounter had fled in many directions, but none had gone too far to be brought back into line. It hadn't taken much for the new Heralds to convince them the Fallen One was actually their enemy. He had promised them the destruction of the Light. He had lied.

When she was done dressing herself, the dark goddess grabbed her flails and left the room, expecting Vardic to follow. The way in which she had taken command over him was infuriating. He would need to remind her who was Xyxax's true successor when this war was over.

*Perhaps, there needs to be only one God of Darkness.*

He followed her out the door and down the steps to the landing below. The torches that lined the stairwell flickered as he walked past, acknowledging the power that radiated off him. Vardic knew he needed to use caution in the coming moments, lest he underestimate the power of his foe. Vardic was proud, but he wasn't stupid. Lio had killed Xyxax after all, and Ravim. If they misjudged the correct time to strike, it would mean both of their deaths. Who knew what would become of the world then? Perhaps, Lio didn't truly scorn the Gods of Light like he claimed. Maybe Arra was the only one he sought vengeance against? What if Lio planned to align with Samson and Luna all along?

The great door to the outside swung open, letting the hot air flood the room with a hiss. Rhenaris twisted her wrists, working her flails in wide circles before stepping out onto the island. She hid her feelings well, but Vardic knew she too was afraid. Though this had been her plan, he was the one most prepared to carry it out. His grip tightened on the shaft of his barbed spear. He reached behind his head with his free hand, making sure that the red ribbon that held back his black hair was still in place. Taking a deep breath, Vardic stepped out into Infernaak behind his companion.

They crossed the small bridge to the central isle with purpose, neither stopping now that they were exposed and in the open. For all they knew Lio was lying in wait, planning to attack at the first moment they showed themselves. They reached the bell where it lay upon the ground, a small crater rimming its edge. Vardic beat the haft of his spear against the side of the bell again and again, causing reverberations that echoed from tower to tower. The sound was nothing compared to what the ringing of the bell had once sounded like, but it would quickly gain the attention of the Fallen One nonetheless.

He did not disappoint. Lio opened the door to his tower and made his way toward them, showing no signs of urgency as he did so. Why would he? What did he have to fear from the likes of them? He had shown them who was in charge when he had struck Rhenaris on the Mortal Plane. His arrogance was nearly palpable; it floated on the hot air over to where Vardic was standing, enraging him in a way that would make his attacks uncontrolled. The God of Darkness took several deep breaths to steady himself, casting a wary glance at his companion. Rhenaris's entire body was rigid; the muscles in her arms, legs, and abdomen clenched tightly. The spines on her head and neck pulsed expectantly while she slowly twisted her flails.

*Closer. Just over the bridge.*

As if reading his mind, the Fallen One stopped just short of the isle, gazing at the pair expectantly.

"Why have you disturbed my rest?" he asked flatly.

"We wished to discuss your plans," Rhenaris responded. "How will Xyx carry out the siege? Should we be preparing to attack Samson and Luna at the same time?"

"You brought me out here to ask me that?" Lio asked. His face began to warp into a snarl. "I do not answer to the two of you, you answer to me. I will tell you what I want you to do, and when I want you to do it!"

Vardic felt his silver blood boiling. He would not allow this false god to address them this way. He could not allow this cretin to stand there a moment longer. He had waited for this long enough. Plans be damned. Suddenly, the expression on Lio's face changed to one of shock. Clearly Xyx or one of the Divine Beasts had told him the news. Their army had engaged his.

His spear whistled through the air in the blink of an eye, slicing Lio across the side of his head. Silver blood spurted out and sizzled on the hot stones of the bridge. Beside Vardic, Rhenaris was cursing his stupidity for not waiting for their enemy to get closer. It mattered not. They had lost the element of surprise. The dark goddess raised her flails and ran across the distance between them, reaching Lio nearly as quickly as the spear had. She spun at the last moment, each skull-headed flail slamming into the chest of the Fallen One with a resounding crunch. The false god staggered sideways, nearly toppling into the lava. Lio still seemed as if he hadn't quite registered what was happening. His arrogance had been his undoing.

Vardic smiled before sprinting to the edge of the bridge and vaulting past the two gods, landing behind them where his spear had embedded itself in the stone. He gripped the weapon tightly and pulled it free, spinning around to finish their enemy once and for all. With Lio stunned in such a way, this would have been easier than he ever would have hoped.

A sword stroke cleaved the left horn from his head. He screamed in agony, silver blood blinding him. A gauntleted hand gripped him by the throat and lifted him into the air, throwing him back onto the central isle. He crashed into the fallen bell with a resounding *clang*. His ears reverberated for several moments before he was able to regain his bearings. Slowly pulling himself to his feet, Vardic wiped the blood from his eyes. Before him, Rhenaris was nowhere to be seen. Vardic assumed the worst. Although his breastplate was nearly caved in, Lio marched toward him defiantly, sword raised high. Vardic gripped his spear with both hands, crying out as he did so.

"You were never one of us!" he shouted. "You are nothing but a rejected God of Light, a coward who pretended to have real power."

Lio said nothing, parrying each thrust of the spear with his sword. Vardic grew more enraged with each attack that was deflected, stabbing harder and harder at his opponent's midsection. Red light swirled around the pair, flashing out of the fists of each. The gods twisted and leapt over each other, moving in a flurry of motion no mortal eyes would have been able to follow. Vardic felt pain from the loss of his horn, but he remained otherwise unharmed. The same could not be said for his enemy. Already, the Fallen One began to slow, his arms struggling to exhibit the same range of motion they were used to now that his armor was caved in. Rivulets of silver blood trailed down his chin and cheek from the corners of his mouth and his lifeless eye. Vardic pressed his advantage, pushing his enemy back toward the molten rock that flowed behind him. Another few steps, and he would be near enough to knock Lio back into the abyss once and for all. There was no recovering from that, even for a god.

The Fallen One lunged at Vardic, his sword making it past the spear. The cut wasn't deep, but it was enough to enrage Vardic beyond all rational thought. He swung the haft of his spear in a wide arc, cracking Lio across the skull with such force that the weapon shattered. Ebony shards sliced through the air, many tipped with sparkling silver blood. The Fallen One staggered back, nearly falling into the lava. He tried to steady himself, but it was too late. Vardic jammed what was left of his weapon into the thigh of his enemy, cutting off any further chance of escape.

"Now you know what Xyxax felt," Vardic hissed. "What Ravim felt. Your army will fall to mine. Then Illux after that. It won't be long before I am not only the single God of Darkness, but the only god on either plane."

Vardic placed his foot on Lio's chest. One push and his lifetime enemy would plummet to his ultimate demise. Everything was building to this moment. Vardic felt a pang of regret that Rhenaris wasn't going to see this, but only for a moment.

Silver blood sprayed out of Vardic's throat. A pain like he had never felt before ripped through him. Numbly, his hand went to his neck. His fingers brushed the barbed end of an arrow.

Tumbling, end over end, the last God of Darkness fell into the lava. As the hot surface of the molten rock rose up to meet him, he belatedly noticed that only one of the three towers sunk beneath its surface.

# Chapter XXIII

Samson had seen this forest more times in the last few weeks than he had since the Divine Plane had been created. Walking back and forth to the Basin and the High God's Throne had never been of interest to him. Before the Pact, Samson had taken to walking the Mortal Plane as much as possible. It had been good to be amongst the people he had sworn to love and protect. He had preferred direct battle to the strategizing and machinations of the others in any case. Since he had been robbed of that pleasure, he had stayed in Ayyslid almost exclusively, leaving the pointless sojourns to Arra. What good did it do him to wander through these woods when there was nothing for him to fight or defend?

*Once Lio is dead, I will go back to the Mortal Plane and save Illux myself.*

Luna followed behind him, her warhammer strapped across her back. She had remained quiet since he had announced that today was the day to strike, killing Lio and possibly Vardic and Rhenaris once and for all. Ren had stopped communicating with them altogether since her run-in with Daniel. Lio's old pet had survived whatever it was Xyxax had done to him, living through the ages imprisoned like a Divine Beast. Had Arra known this, he wondered. And now that Merek had shown himself as well, it was clear that Fiora had failed to kill him all those years ago. Another Seraph chosen by Arra who had turned out to be a failure. The only positive piece of information they had gathered before Ren had gone silent was that several more Divine Beasts were being awakened. Samson had spoken with Aion once he had been freed. Samson had actually felt some modicum of joy during that interaction.

The forest fell away behind them as they passed into the dominion of the High God. The smooth stone that separated them from the Gods of Darkness seemed to stretch on forever. There was endless light here, possibly the last true light that either of them would gaze upon. Samson remembered the darkness of Infernaak—and endless night that was only lit from the glow of the rivers of lava and the faint light of the horizon. Smoke filled the air there, and yet one could see as if it were day… He had only been there once, when Lio and Xyxax had battled below, but the landscape had been burned into his mind. If he was being honest with himself, he had hoped to never return. The death of one God of Darkness had precipitated that last visit to that wasteland, and he hoped that it did so this time as well.

His mind wandered as they walked, images of Arra passing before him. He even thought of Lio from before his fall. Samson had been jealous of him them, though he was loath to admit it. While Samson had fought bravely in the battles on the Mortal Plane, and had led thousands of warriors to death or victory, he knew who truly held the power of the Light. Lio had been the mightiest of them, every ounce as just as Xyxax had been wicked. Or so they had thought. Somehow, Lio had found himself in love with a mortal, hardly a godly desire. For all of his own weakness of the flesh, Samson had never taken to bed with a mortal. Somehow Xyxax had found out. Once that secret had been revealed, it had only been a matter of time before Lio's true colors had been seen. He was weak, cowardly, and a fool. The High

God had been sure to reward him for that...

Before them the empty throne of the High God rose out of the horizon, a monolithic reminder of the past. The High God had abandoned them, left them to this war as if nothing else could be done for this world. The other realms of creation had a better chance of salvation than this one that Samson lorded over. In the past, the High God had left them for brief periods to walk the realms, returning with stories of other worlds completely different from the Mortal Plane. Surely, that was where he resided now. As Samson walked past the throne, his eyes fell to the Basin of Aenna. Luna walked around him, breaking the surface of the silver blood with her fingertips. The liquid shimmered and changed, showing the walls of Illux below. The city was besieged by an army the like of which the Mortal Plane had not seen in hundreds of years.

*They are doomed. Even if we succeed, there is no hope for the City of Light now. The Seraphs have failed us. We have failed.*

The thought made him shiver. He had loved them once. He had fought beside them, cared for them, even respected some of them. That had been a long time ago. Now, he was more puzzled by his failure to prevent Lio from getting this far. Luna sighed as she stood beside him, staring into the image, and stroking the blood again as she did so. The ripples from her fingers cascaded to the edges of the basin, bouncing back in on themselves and changing the vision below as they did so.

The Seraphs appeared, riding into Seatown. Though Ren had gone silent, ignoring their attempts to command her, this destination was not completely unexpected. The Paladins of Seatown had grown blasphemous as of late, and needed to be corrected. If they ignored the edicts of the God's Chosen, then how long before they began to ignore the gods? Ren had resisted the idea, vainly hoping she would be able to come up with some sort of peaceful resolution. She foolishly thought they would be able to rally together in their time of need. No doubt that was what she hoped for now, reinforcements to help them save the city. Little good that would do, even if the Paladins came around. And it did not seem that the Divine Beasts were with them. Perhaps, they had decided to abandon her as well? He would have to reach out to Aion after this was over and find out what had happened.

It was Samson that reached out then, the Divine Blood warming his fingers even through his armor. The scene changed back to Illux again. He wanted to look over the city one final time, before the stain of Darkness was fully upon it. It would remind him of better days, he hoped. Something was different this time. There was another horde about to attack Lio's army. Another force of Demons and Accursed was moving in to strike.

*How could this be?*

"They turn on themselves!" Luna shouted. "There is still time, we must hurry!"

Without a second glance, the goddess turned and broke into a run toward Infernaak. Samson belatedly began to follow her, his eyes lingering on the image of the city a moment longer. Was she right? Was there still a chance to save the city? If they killed Lio and got Vardic and Rhenaris to agree to a truce, they could order the remnants of the Army of Darkness to pull back from the city and spare those gathered within. They could return to a tenuous balance of some sort. It was a foolish hope, but something made Samson wish for it more than he had wished for anything for as long as he could remember. Arra would have smiled.

The two gods moved quickly, covering the smooth stone that separated the Light of the Divine Plane from the Darkness in a matter of minutes. The jagged stones that jutted out of the ground at odd angles were just ahead, beyond the line of night. Luna nearly jumped over the boundary into the darkness, springing past the first line of rocks as if they were nothing. She must have been holding onto the same hope he was. Perhaps, they had not lost their way after all. Samson sprang after her, pulling an arrow from his quiver. It would be a while yet before they were in sight of the fiery fortress, but Luna's newfound enthusiasm was infectious. With his other hand, he pulled free his bow, carrying it by his side.

They jumped from stone to stone, weaving between the largest of the jagged sentinels as if they would come alive and bar them entry from this wicked landscape. The night was endless, and there were no stars above like there would have been on the Mortal Plane. He was sure that the sky was actually blanketed by a thick skein of smoke and cloud. Samson shivered again, the second time he had noticed the sensation that he could remember. They were surely heading toward the death of a god. He could feel it.

*But which one?*

Finally, there was a light on the horizon, an orange glow that radiated not from above but from below. They had arrived. Luna would have continued her sprint had Samson not headed her off and motioned for her to stop. They could not lose the element of surprise, not now. He would not allow the Gods of Darkness to overwhelm them. Dropping low, the two Gods of Light crept along the ground, moving closer to the hissing rivers of Infernaak. Soon they could see it, the three towers that encircled a large, central island. What was on that central island caught Samson's breath in his throat.

The Gods of Darkness were engaged in a fierce confrontation. It seemed that Lio was pitted alone against Vardic and Rhenaris. Though the odds were against the Fallen One, it seemed they were in fact evenly matched. Even after Rhenaris caved in Lio's breast plate with one of her flails, he blasted her away with such a large gout of flame from his fist that she flew backward nearly to the edge of the isle. Vardic soon followed her, thrown by a strong hand. The horned god landed in a heap next to the remnants of something made of black metal.

"We must get closer," Luna whispered. "You must wait for the right moment."

Samson nodded and crept closer to the edge of the molten river that separated the mainland from the central isle where the trio did battle. Without warning, the dark shape of Rhenaris shot past where they crouched. Either the dark goddess did not notice them, or she did not care, for Rhenaris didn't stop or even spare them a single glance. She looked truly afraid, an expression that Samson had never seen on her face before. He looked up again, seeing that the tide had finally turned. Lio was on his knees, nearly at the edge of the molten rock. Vardic stuck what was left of his spear into the fallen god's thigh.

Samson stood, nocked his arrow, and prepared to finish Lio. Anticipating what he was about to do, Luna was in his ear, warning against it.

"Don't," she breathed. "Not Lio. He is already defeated. Kill Vardic while we still have the element of surprise. Then we can finish Lio."

He didn't have time to question her. His arrow left his bow and buried itself in the back of Vardic's neck. The God of Darkness twisted and flopped over the edge of the island, plummeting into the river. Before Vardic was even fully over the edge, one of the keeps was already sinking beneath the surface of the lava, just as one had a thousand years before. Moments later, the Divine Plane grew dimmer.

Luna sprinted again, bounding across the bridge toward where Lio had slumped over. Whatever burst of energy she hadn't used up getting here she surely used now. Samson tried to keep pace with her, but she was to their fallen enemy before he was even at the remains of the blackened bell that lay on the ground between them. The air was thick and smelled of sulfur down here, slowing his advance. When she reached him, she cradled his head against her breast. Samson stopped short of them.

*What is this?*

Had she lost her mind? Perhaps, the sight of their old companion nearly dead had simply overcome her with emotion. Either way, Samson didn't like it. He approached them slowly, pulling free another arrow. Now wasn't the time for sentimentality. Now was the time to finish this war once and for all. Rhenaris could die or hide for the rest of time, it didn't matter which. This war was finally over.

"Step aside," Samson said.

Luna was whispering in Lio's ear. She looked up defiantly. "We can bring him back."

"No, we cannot. He killed our sister. Do you not remember?"

"I'm sorry, my love," she said. "This is all my fault. Forgive me. I didn't know what he would do. What any of them would do. I didn't know. Forgive me."

Samson lowered his bow. Her eyes were almost unfocused. She wasn't truly looking at him or Lio. Clearly something had happened to make her lose her mind. He would pull her away and finish Lio by himself. They could sort the rest out later. He gripped her by the shoulders, pulling her to her feet. Her unfocused eyes finally met his, tears forming at their corners. Lio's sword sank deep into his stomach.

When Samson looked down, he saw that it was Luna's hand that gripped it.

# CHAPTER XXIV

Water poured off the great beast as it pulled itself from the ocean. Barnacles encrusted its oily black shell. Tentacles and arms of various lengths and shades of green protruded from inside the armored carapace of the thing, reaching out and tearing at the wreckage of the ships and nearby buildings. Pincers shattered masts and large suckers ripped the walls from houses. This monstrous being was only the first of several Divine Beasts that were making their way inland. Behind the crustacean was the long head of a serpent, the mouth of which opened sideways as it snapped back and forth. Still farther back, a larger shape pressed against the surface of the water, but did not yet break free. It was as if the ocean itself was coming to life in an attempt to destroy those who had hoped to conquer it.

The townsfolk ran back and forth in panic, with no leadership to hold them fast. Trent tried to bark orders, but with the Paladins that had, until moments ago, ruled here having been felled by his hand, they chose not to listen. The Seraph wasn't sure whose timing had been worse, his or the Divine Beasts that now bore down on them.

Even he stared at the approaching threat in muted shock, not at all prepared for the severity of the situation. Though only Ren had been a Seraph at the time when they had defeated Akklor, they now faced three creatures of such magnitude. Even with two Seraphs how could they hope to handle that?

*How can we possibly overcome three of them? We cannot.*

"The first one is Zad the Petulant," Teo whispered, appearing out of nowhere. "Behind him is Tolkash the Iniquitous, and the large one that hasn't broken from the surface I would guess is Rullug the Murk."

"I don't care," Trent replied. "How do we stop them? Three of them at once?"

"Should we flee?" Rella asked. "Surely, they won't be able to follow us inland. These were of the stock intended to battle each other out at sea. They were never meant to come inland and attack the armies of Light directly. The Fallen One probably sent them to destroy the fleet that was here, to prevent the chance of any mortals escaping his wrath."

As if in answer to her suggestion, a bloody scream cut through all of the other sounds in the cacophony that was Seatown. Trent turned and saw the shattered form of Daniel holding Nightbreaker before him. A man was impaled on the end of the sacred blade, twitching slightly before he was tossed aside. The former Seraph looked crazed—filled with bloodlust even. There was scarlet blood splattered across his face, which he slowly licked off his lips.

Trent raised Godtaker, looking to Ren to see how she would react. To his surprise, she was already bristling with energy, her white hair swirling about her as the air crackled with sparks. Even from where he stood, Trent could feel the hair on his arms begin to stand on end. Both of Ren's fists launched out, sending lightning arcing into where Daniel had been standing. The dark figure leapt away at the last moment, sending a gout of black flame back at them.

Trent took to the air, flying right where he anticipated the former Seraph would land. A blade clipped his wing from above, sending him spiraling into a heap on the ground. Silver and red blood welled up out of the wound, staining the white plumage of his wing. When Trent looked up, he saw Merek descending after him. Trent jumped to his feet, hammering the enemy Seraph with a blast of blue energy. Then Daniel was at his back, hacking at him with Nightbreaker. It was only a quick pivot that allowed Trent to protect himself from the first few attacks, but his defenses quickly slowed. He was nearly overwhelmed when Divinity and Rella slammed into Daniel at nearly the same time, knocking him back long enough to give Trent the time to return to the air. In that moment, Ren flew by in a blur, following the others after Daniel.

*Someone must have opened the gate.*

Even in the midst of battle, Trent nearly chuckled aloud at the thought of the white tigress charging into Seatown just as frightened townspeople were attempting to flee. No doubt, several of them had soiled themselves in shock.

Merek flew away from the fighting, heading out to the Divine Beasts. Somehow these two had awakened these creatures and brought them here—they must have, for as far as they knew no new Herald had yet risen. Daniel and Merek would have been better suited to send a land creature to force them into the sea. Rella was right, the townspeople would be able to flee into the wilderness without the Divine Beasts being able to effectively follow them. Now that Trent was no longer surprised, he was able to realize that though this attack was unexpected, it wouldn't be as damaging as it could have been. In the distance, the final Divine Beast finally pulled itself free from the waves.

It was a gargantuan, amorphous thing, seemingly made more of slime and algae than flesh. It looked as if it had absorbed the murkiest parts of the ocean into itself while it had been imprisoned below. From within its central globule came the shape of two long arms that helped to pull it ashore. The arms receded back into the mass and the Divine Beast began to slide over the buildings on the shore, absorbing them as it did so. Trent swallowed hard. It seemed that Rullug would take little notice of steel, even if it came from a god-killing sword. He started to follow Merek in any case, hoping to catch his enemy before the other Seraph could command the Divine Beasts toward whatever purpose they were charged.

The cries of the townsfolk reached a crescendo suddenly, and Trent whirled in midair. It seemed that Merek and Daniel had not been as shortsighted as they could have hoped. A thick-bodied wolf-like creature ran along the border of the town, killing those who got too close to any of the exits and shepherding the rest back toward the sea. They had not erred in who they had awakened after all.

*Gods help us.*

Trent knew they would have no victory today without the aid of their own Divine Beasts. And they had left them in the Rim within the ruins of the Grey Temple to lick their wounds. Little good they would do for these people up there. Ignoring Merek for the moment, Trent flew back toward the ground, looking desperately for Ren. He had an idea, and it would require her Divine Blood. He found her trying to harry Daniel from above, launching her magic at him from nearly every angle imaginable. Sweat poured off her snarling face as she lanced fire and lightning toward the ground in waves of destructive energy. The twisted creature was able to deflect or dodge most of her attacks, all the while parrying the blows of the two Balance Monks and the great tigress.

"Ren!" Trent cried out.

His companion looked at him, then back at Daniel below her. After a moment of thinking over her options, Ren let off her attack and made her way through the air to where Trent waited for her. She looked nearly feral as she approached him, her eyes wild with the same bloodlust that Trent had seen in Daniel just moments before.

"What?" she nearly spat. "We almost have him. We almost have my sword back."

"Do you hear yourself?" Trent asked, sadness creeping into his voice. "You are not him, Ren. You are not that damned sword. You are the Seraph of Illux, and right now your people need you! Look around! The People of Seatown are being slaughtered. We cannot destroy these Divine Beasts alone. You need to break your silence with Samson and Luna, you must tell them to contact the Divine Beasts and send them to our aid. With any luck they can be here before all of us are dead. Even more importantly than that, we need you back. I need you back."

"I—" she began.

Trent cut her off, "You are stronger than any of us. You should be the one leading, not me. Stop doubting yourself, stop analyzing your failures and stop keeping me locked out. At least until this is over. Please."

Ren's expression softened somewhat as she stared at him, her eyes closing slightly. She was clearly reaching out to the gods, passing on the message that Trent had asked her to. At least she was listening to him again. Suddenly, her eyes snapped open, and she nearly dropped out of the sky. Trent moved in close and grabbed her, keeping her from falling all the way to the ground.

"What is it?" he asked.

"T-they have turned on each other. Samson and Luna. S-she stabbed him Trent! Luna stabbed Samson. She is with Lio now. We cannot expect them to help us."

As her words tumbled out, Trent looked up instinctively. To him, Aenna looked dimmer than it had before. He nodded dumbly at her and relaxed his grip. Everything was falling apart again. They had been so close to turning the tide he had thought. But now…

"What do we do then?" he asked.

Ren shook her head and looked back down at Daniel. "You try and bring some order to the townspeople before they all get killed. See if you can find a way to break past that wolf and get them to safety. I will try and help the others break away from Daniel so that we can see to Merek and the other creatures. They are the true threat."

Trent started to move away when Ren grabbed him by the hand, spinning him in a circle in the air. When he was facing her again, she pulled him close and kissed him hard.

"Trent," Ren said. "I love you. Thank you for not giving up on me."

Then she was gone, returning to the battle below where their companions fought for their lives. Trent nearly followed her, ignoring the orders she had given him moments before. She said she loved him, and like that, he had to watch her go. When he finally returned to his senses, he remembered that there was another friend of his who needed seeing to. Someone who could help him round up the townsfolk and stop this madness.

*Gil.*

Zad was farther inland now, as was Rullug. The two creatures had nearly destroyed the entire wharf, removing any signs that there had even been any ships or docks there. Trent tried to ignore their progress, searching now for his long lost-friend in the crowds that tried to run from the wolfish beast prowling the streets at the landlocked edge of the city. It howled before each kill, urging him onward as fast as his wings could carry him through the salt-tinged air.

Trent winged his way toward the largest group of townspeople, at the head of which was the woman who had cut Gil down earlier. She had her rapier held out before her, while her colored garb swirled behind as she ran. Trent quickly gained on her, the words she shouted to those behind her quickly filtered up to his ears.

"We must stick together! This beast cannot take us all!" she shouted.

Trent dropped beside her, keeping pace with the woman as she ran. It seemed like she was taking the group to the edge of town while the beast attacked those who fled from the other side.

"Where is Gil?" he asked.

"Who?" she wheezed, never stopping.

"My friend who the Paladins tried to hang!"

"The last I saw of him, he was headed for the beast. What do you hope to do?"

"Together, he and I will kill that thing!" Trent shouted, returning higher to the air. "Don't try and leave town, it would overwhelm you. Lead it back toward the square if you can."

Trent left the woman and the ground behind, making his way toward where the wolf-thing prowled at the far edge of town. As he got closer, he saw that it was smaller than most of its brethren, yet it still towered nearly three times the height of a man. Its mangy fur was brown and grey, intermixed with bristling spines that dripped purple venom. They seemed to quiver slightly as Trent approached, as if they sensed a change in the air. A woman hung in its jaws. With one snap she was shorn in two, each half dropping to the ground with a wet thump.

*You better not die on me twice. I won't let that happen. I can't. For Devin, I won't.*

He looked around for signs of his friend, but saw none. Then, a cloaked figure jumped from Trent's left, springing from one of the taller building and settling on top of the wolf, nestled between the spines, which bristled sharply. The wolf howled in rage, but the cloaked figure could not be shaken free. Trent swooped in low to aid the man, who he knew instinctively to be his friend, channeling lightning through the blade of Godtaker. The silver steel crackled to life with blue energy. The wolf lunged through the air, its slathering jaws snapping wildly at Trent. The Seraph spun sideways, narrowly avoiding certain death from the mouth of the creature. One of the black spines sliced his cheek, burning the very flesh beneath. Trent recoiled in pain, falling to the ground. When he looked up, the wolf had rounded a corner and disappeared farther into the city.

"Trent?" a familiar voice asked. "How? Can it be?"

Trent's face was hot, and he felt bile rising in his throat. He tried to push himself up from the ground but nearly collapsed back into the dirt. He settled for rolling onto his back so he could see his old friend.

"It's me," he rasped. "And you never thought I'd amount to anything."

Gil's laugh was weak, but it brought Trent some happiness, however fleeting it might have been. He tried to work his healing magic on the wound on his face, but he couldn't make it do anything—couldn't stop the burning or the tightness. It seemed that the poison of the creature was resistant to such measures. The burning feeling intensified and spread throughout his neck. He winced.

"I'd shake your hand to congratulate you but..." Gil trailed off. "Gods, what happened to your face?"

"That thing poisoned me. How bad is it? I can only feel burning. My magic won't make it stop."

"The skin is turning purple and grey. Let me see what I can do. We don't have time to sit here and feel sorry for your face, those people need us."

Trent sat up, truly taking Gil in for the first time since he had recognized him. His old friend looked worn now, his blond braid was loose and tinged with silver that hadn't been there before. One arm was missing, replaced with a sword not unlike that of an Accursed. He was less whole than he been when Trent and Devin had seen him last. No doubt he had been through just as much if not more than Trent had.

The Paladin stepped forward and placed his good hand on Trent's face. A blue glow nearly blinded Trent as Gil worked, cursing quietly after a few moments. The burning sensation dissipated, but Trent still felt a tightness in the skin that hadn't been there before. Gods, even his jaw ached.

"I've stopped the spread," Gil said. "This will take more power than mine to dispel I'm afraid. Can you stand? Better yet, can you fly? I think that thing is heading back to the center of town."

Trent stood, flexing his wings. Without another word, he grabbed Gil under his armpits and lifted him into the air, making their way toward the center of town. Gil was right, of course. The Divine Beast ran up and down the twisted streets of Seatown, picking off the fleeing townspeople that Trent had stopped and spoken with earlier. Had he not told them to stay within the city they might have actually had a better chance. Of the woman who had been leading them there was no sign; the entire crowd ran back and forth in disarray. Some tried to stand and fight, but they were torn to shreds in an instant.

The Seraph swung low, bringing Gil just over the top of the creature. Its spines flared, some of them swollen and gorged with so much of the purple venom that they frothed and fountained the garish liquid. It would do them no good to attack the wolf directly. Trent wasn't sure he had the energy for a magical assault either. The venom had sapped most of his strength. In the distance, he saw that Rullug and Zad were nearly to the center of the town. At first, this filled him with despair. Then it gave him an idea.

Sometimes evil could be used to destroy evil.

"I'm going to drop you behind that thing. Try and get as many of these people out of the city as possible. I know how to kill it."

"Are you sure?" Gil asked, his voice nearly lost in the wind.

"It's the only way."

Gil nodded. Moments later, Trent dropped his old friend to the ground and sped ahead, getting in front of the world, and turning to look at it. The Divine Beast had noticed him, but it refrained from following him, choosing instead to continue to pick off the townspeople that ran in its wake. Trent pulled free Godtaker and lanced flame down the surface of the blade, singeing the fur on its snout. The smell of burnt hair filled his nostrils. The Seraph slowed, bringing himself even with the haunches of the creature when he swung his blade, severing one of the spines. The purple fluid sprayed out, burning everything it touched. Trent barely avoided the deadly stream, returning to the front of the wolf. It howled in rage and sprinted after him.

Trent cut left around a corner, then right around the next. The wolf-thing howled again, crashing through the buildings that separated them. Even for as fast as Trent was able to fly, this Divine Beast could run nearly the same. It barreled after him with a ferocity he would only be able to outpace for a little while longer. Trent knew that if he miscalculated his plan in any way, it would catch him. The venom from its spine had done enough damage that he would lag behind very soon. Another right turn steered him in the direction he wanted to go. Over the top of the buildings he could see Zad and Rullug.

*Just a little farther.*

Godtaker lashed out again, sending blue lightning arcing into the front paws of the wolf, enraging it further. Saliva fell off its jaws in massive globules that sizzled and hissed as they landed on the paving stones. Trent struck it again and again with lightning. Each haphazard blast of magic sapped him of more of his strength and slowed him even more. Ahead, the winding streets continued, never quite terminating in the end he hoped for. One more turn. That's all it would take. One more turn. Above them, the murky bulk of Rullug loomed.

*Where is Merek?*

Trent swung left. The wolf blasted through the nearest building again, springing after Trent with a feral momentum that it hadn't before shown. That was exactly what Trent had hoped for. He flew upward, directly along the gelatinous mass of Rullug. The wolf slammed into the other Divine Beast, sinking into its surface silently. The Seraph pulled back, watching in horror as one Divine Beast silently consumed another. The wolf dissolved in a matter of moments. It didn't struggle or cry out, almost as if it had died the moment it had made contact with Rullug. Trent was glad his plan had worked, but he was horrified at the implications. How could they possibly hope to destroy Rullug the Murk? This thing seemed to be impervious to any physical assault.

He turned to make his way back toward the center of Seatown. Trent needed to find Ren and the others, and quickly. They all needed to get out of here as soon as possible.

A green tentacle wrapped around him, tightening until his wings began to crack. Trent cried out as he was pulled back into the shell of Zad. The putrid stink of rotten fish washed over him. Before he was enveloped in darkness, he saw a glimpse of something large on the horizon. He wasn't sure if his mind was playing tricks on him as he died.

It looked like it was Tyr.

# CHAPTER XXV

She grabbed him by his thin white hair, pulling it free in matted, bloody clumps. The creature that had once been Daniel howled in agonizing pain, trying to rake at her face with his taloned fingers. Ren found herself laughing as she kicked away from him, sending the misshapen monster to his knees. There was no fear anymore. He could do nothing to her. She was herself again. She was fighting for her life but she was herself.

And he had her sword.

*Not for long.*

The others were scattered around the street, trying to stand. Divinity was sulking in the doorway to a building, licking her wounds and casting weary glances at the battle. Rella and Teo had each stepped back to try and recover from a multitude of injuries that the dark Seraph had inflicted upon them. Daniel was stronger than any of them individually. Stronger than she was. Stronger than she had been when she had doubted herself, anyways. Now, none of them had her strength. None of them could.

Ren hovered in the air above him; flames swirled about her right hand, while lightning crackled up and down her left arm. She was a righteous fury now unbridled from the weight of guilt and self-doubt. She was the Light manifest. Ren pointed her fists at Daniel and released all of the energy gathered in her body. Every ounce of rage, every bit of bitterness and sadness and self-defeating pity emptied out of her body with the magic, slamming into the former Seraph with such ferocity that he crumpled into the ground at the center of a smoldering crater. Dirt and paving stones flew into the air; nearby pillars supporting the roofs of houses buckled.

"You are not worthy of your legacy!" she shouted over the roar of her magic. "You are not worthy of the Light! You are not worthy to be a Seraph! What happened to you was evil and cruel, but you have chosen to lose yourself to it. I am not like you. I will not allow the Darkness to make me lose who I am. I am not you! I will not become you! I won't!"

Daniel tried to throw up a barrier of protective magic, but it did him no good. Ren shattered through it like it was nothing, sending up yet another cloud of smoke and ash and stones. The air began to boil from the heat emanating outward from where Daniel had been standing. When the swirling malaise finally cleared, there was no sign of him. Nightbreaker laid there, untouched save for a skein of ash that covered its black blade. Ren lowered herself and grabbed the sword, thrusting it high above her head. She shouted. She cried. Tears ran down her face, but they felt restorative. They felt empowering.

She was back.

*Trent.*

Ren flew over to her companions, lending each of them a dose of healing magic. It wasn't much. Even for all of her newfound confidence and euphoria, she could feel her energy waning. She had expended almost all of it to destroy Daniel. What was left of him, in any case. She sighed. Samson and Luna would no longer be of any assistance either. Gods, if only Arra had survived.

Divinity limped over to her and licked her fingers.

"I'm sorry girl," she whispered. "I can't heal you yet. I need to conserve my strength. I need to find Trent. We still have the Divine Beasts to deal with. And Merek. I need you to stay safe until I can make you better."

"Trent flew back to the front of the city," Teo said. "Rella and I are going to get closer to Zad and Rullug. We need to see if there are any weaknesses to exploit. These are some of the most powerful Divine Beasts in all of creation, Ren. We need all of the help that we can get. If Tyr and the others leave now, they might be able to get here before…"

"I—" Ren began. She hadn't told them about the Gods of Light yet. "I will see what I can do."

Teo and Rella nodded, turning, and making their way toward the waterfront. Ren rubbed Divinity behind the ears and returned to the air, winging her way toward the front gates of Seatown. When she got there, she didn't see any sign of Trent. Bodies that looked to be half-eaten were strewn about the gate and inner roads of the town. Small fires had started to crop up inside various buildings. It was chaos.

Just beyond the wall on the outside of Seatown was a small crowd of townspeople. At their lead was the woman who had cut Gil down earlier. It took her a moment, but Ren remembered she was the Admiral of Seatown, a position of civilian leadership that had been created by Arendt when he had founded the settlement over five hundred years before. To her inner shame, she could not remember the woman's name.

Ren landed in front of the woman, still clutching Nightbreaker tightly in front of herself.

"Tell me your name, Admiral," she commanded.

"Admiral Wyn Thacker," the woman replied, standing slightly taller than she had a moment before.

"I command here now, is that understood?" Ren asked.

"It is."

"Good," Ren said. "What happened out here? Where is Trent, the other Seraph?"

"He is fighting the wolf-creature in the city," a man said.

Ren turned and saw Gil running up to meet them, a trail of townsfolk following behind him.

"Alone?" Ren demanded, already lifting into the air.

"He wanted me to get these people out here, to safety," he continued. "He said he had a plan. My Lady, I don't know if he can do it alone."

*He can. But not if I want to see him again.*

"Gather the survivors and prepare to march," Ren ordered. "Once we deal with this threat, we are all headed for Illux. They need our help."

"No!" Admiral Thacker shouted. "I will not send my people to die for yours!"

"We are all one people," Gil said. "They need us in Illux!"

*We don't have time for this.*

"I respect your desire to keep your townspeople safe, but if Illux falls, the Mortal Plane falls. What will it take for you to help us?" Ren asked, quietly. "Name your price, Admiral."

"You will relinquish all claim to the people of Seatown. If we come to the aid of your city, then we shall be free after it is done. And you must promise me it can be saved. I will not bring my people on a suicide mission to satisfy your sense of duty. That is my price."

Ren tightened her grip on Nightbreaker, lowering herself to eye level with Wyn. The two women locked eyes, neither backing down. It would be so easy to behead this pretender and take control of these people. Much easier than compromise would be. But Luna had stabbed Samson. The Light was tearing itself apart. She didn't want to splinter her people. Nor did she wish to strike down a woman who simply wanted what Ren wanted: to keep her people safe.

"I could kill you right now, and your price would be meaningless," Ren said, coldly. "I am tired of bloodshed. We are one people, but we don't have to be. Seatown can make its own destiny. I agree to your price, Admiral. And I give you my word, we march to save Illux, not to die outside her walls. Soon, you will understand."

She took to the air, refusing to look back at the expressions of those below her. Then a voice shouted up at her, giving her pause.

"Wait! Seraph!"

Ren looked back down at the man speaking to her. She nearly caught herself thinking that it was Trent himself looking back up at hear, albeit Trent with an extra thirty years of hard living under his belt.

"Yes," she replied, coming lower.

"Did you say that the other Seraph was named Trent?" he asked.

"I did. What of it?"

The man didn't answer but broke into a run, heading back into the town. Ren was perplexed for a moment but returned to her journey. She would have time to ponder who that man had been later. Her thoughts returned to the promise she had made to the Admiral. Whatever she had done, she was committed now. A small smile crossed her face when she thought of Castille's expression when he heard the news. She had undone in a single moment what generations of Seraphs since the time of Arendt had worked to preserve. What difference did it make? The Gods of Light had turned on each other.

Samson had told her that Luna had betrayed him, stabbing him in the gut when they had the chance to destroy Lio once and for all. He had barely survived, though Vardic was dead by his hand. Now, Samson was wounded and holed up in Ayyslid, awaiting the inevitable attack Lio and Luna would bring. As soon as Ren heard the news, she closed her mind off to all Divine intrusion, concerned that Luna would attempt to use their connection to progress the dark god's plans. So far, the fallen goddess had not made the attempt, but Ren was not convinced that it wouldn't come. In a way, she thought she knew how the Forsaken Ones had felt, for just a moment.

*We will make our own way. The Gods of Light were nothing without Arra, in any case.*

As her thoughts drifted to the Gods of Light, Ren missed the winged shape that came at her from above. She nearly would have died in that moment had some sixth sense not caused her to drop through the air just as Merek slammed into the empty space where she had just been. Her pulse quickened when she realized how close she had come. Ren spun around, seeing the enemy Seraph inhabiting the patch of sky just behind her. He had his swords drawn, and his face was a mask of smug assurance.

"This is all over, you know," he said calmly. "What a fitting place for it to end, too. It was nearly this spot where Fiora was thought to have killed me. Instead, it was she who died, while I escaped. Now that I am finally able to come out of hiding, I may do it here as well. Surely, that means this was ordained by the High God himself."

*Herself.*

Ren noticed the shapes of Divine Beasts in the distance, flying toward the city. Her heart skipped a beat for a moment, then she recognized those shapes that made their way toward them: Tyr, Yyn, and Lythe, the larger two of whom looked to be carrying Orros and Aion. She smiled. Her change in expression clearly unsettled Merek for the briefest of moments.

"You seem so sure of your victory for someone who just became outnumbered," she said.

Merek spun, gazing at the shapes that winged their way toward his position. He cursed aloud, turning back toward Ren. She was already on him by then, hacking wildly with Nightbreaker. Her sudden ferocity forced him backward through the air, keeping him on the defensive. The blade felt good in her hand, and she wielded it like it had never left. Each cut was more savage than the last, breaking any concentration that the other Seraph could have hoped to hold.

"You are an oathbreaker!" Ren shouted over the clatter of steel. "You vowed to serve the Light! Look at what you have become. At least Daniel was cursed to become the twisted thing he was. You don't have such an excuse. I pitied him, but I despise you."

Merek cursed through gritted teeth, no longer giving up as much ground. "You are right, Daniel was given a sickness by Xyxax, but he would have made the same choices I did had our roles been reversed. Who can say I was not loyal? I swore an oath to serve Lio, and in response, I had to watch as my brothers and sisters were executed for likewise loyal service. I was hunted like an animal by a woman whom I had called friend, all because I was loyal to the wrong god? That is madness."

The male Seraph batted Ren back with the pommel of one of his swords, following up with a backhand across her face. She cried out as she spun through the air, Nightbreaker tight in her grip. She would give her life before she was parted from it again. Ren regained her bearings just as Merek followed up his physical assault with a magical one. She twisted and weaved through the air, narrowly avoiding the bursts of lightning that chased after her. He couldn't hit her, but neither could she stop dodging long enough to return the attack.

Ren decided to disengage, flying closer to the town below them while making her way toward the sea. Merek continued to curse as he followed behind, never quite catching up to her. She flew up higher as she passed over the Divine Beasts that lay siege to the waterfront, looking in every direction for Trent, but seeing no signs of him. The amorphous blob had absorbed nearly half of the docks, while the shelled-beast used its tentacles to feel inside buildings for life that it could consume. Once it had finished rummaging through an area it would wipe away all structures that were still standing. The third being, the serpent-like creature that had not come onto land, patrolled the shoreline, though with no ships, this was a wasted effort. Ren continued to fly until the ground gave way to ocean and there was nothing below the two Seraphs but water.

The salt air blew across her face in the form of a cool breeze. It was nearly silent up here, for even the gulls had fled once the monsters had started rising from the ocean depths. She thought for a moment that it was peaceful. A sharp blow struck her in the back at Merek slammed into her, his arms wrapping around her torso with an iron grip. For some reason he had sheathed his swords, a mistake she would make him regret. She elbowed him in the face, shattering the bridge of his nose. Together, they plummeted toward the murky depths. As they fell, Ren could see out of the corner of her eye that the sea snake was rapidly approaching their direction, likely to finish one or both of them as soon as they broke the surface of the waves.

Ren gripped Nightbreaker with all of her remaining strength and swung upward, breaking Merek's grip and cutting both of them across the shoulder. White hot pain and warm blood exploded out of her. Merek fell backward while Ren spread her wings just wide enough to catch herself right before she would have fallen into the water.

The serpent burst from the water, snapping its jaws, and nearly catching her. As it swung its head in a circle, it unwittingly struck Merek, sending him crashing into the ocean. He sank under a spray of water and foam. Ren swooped back in, cutting across the side of the Divine Beasts face with Nightbreaker before heading back toward land. She would have to ignore Merek for now, it seemed.

The serpent chased after her along the surface of the water, keeping pace with her as best as it was able. She knew she should have headed higher into the air, but she was tiring too quickly. The Divine Beast launched itself upward at her, leaving the water with the majority of its orange and tan bulk. Right before its jaws closed around Ren, Tyr, and Yyn struck it from different angles, each gripping the snake with talons and claws. They twisted and pulled in opposite directions, ripping the sea serpent in half. Both followed up the attack with gouts of flame from their open mouths, turning the remnants into smoldering husks, which sizzled as they dropped back into the water.

"Quickly, Seraph!" Tyr thundered. "We need to finish this quickly, before Rullug and Zad can do any further damage."

"Did all of you make it?" Ren asked, loudly.

"Yes," Tyr replied. "Yyn and I carried Aion and Orros between us. It was no easy task, but we made do."

"How did you know that we needed you?"

"We decided to come closer to make our march to the city take less time. Once we recognized Luna's treachery, we made all haste to get here, lest you were also under attack. It was not the wrong decision, it seems."

"It was not," Ren replied.

They returned to the town, joining the other three Divine Beasts as they did battle with the shelled Divine Beast. Tyr had told Ren that this creature was called Zad, and the other Rullug. Wisely they had focused their attack on Zad, for any of them could have easily been absorbed by the murky mass of Rullug. Aion was on the shell of Zad, pounding both great silver fists on the carapace in an attempt to break through. All the while, Orros tried to distract the claws and tentacles to give Aion time to break through. Each thunderous contact between fist and shell rang out down the coastline with a crack.

Lythe flitted back and forth, freezing any of the appendages that made it past Orros to Aion. Zad was flailing each limb wildly in an attempt to shake off Aion. Ren immediately dropped into the mass of swirling tentacles, slicing left and right at the nearly infinite amount that besieged them. A tentacle made it past her defenses and tightened around her, nearly causing Nightbreaker to drop to the ground below. The large suckers attached to her chest and back, clinging to her armor and wings. The grip of the Divine Beast tightened at an alarming rate. She would have been snapped in two had Orros not sank his jaws into the tentacle, tearing it loose from the main body of the creature. Ren fell to the ground where she was able to wriggle free once the suction cups loosened in death.

Aion hammered again and again until finally a resounding *crack* thundered louder than all of the others. Without warning, the golden figure leapt from the back of the other Divine Beast just as Yyn and Tyr filled the newly made hole with fire. The inside of Zad hissed and popped while all of the tentacles writhed and twisted, and the claws snapped open and closed manically. Ren pulled herself to her feet and sprang to the air, flying away from the shuddering remnant of Zad as it collapsed to the earth.

Behind her, Orros started to roar triumphantly was but was instantly silenced. The white lion suddenly had half of its body enveloped in the amorphous mass of Rullug the Murk. The half of the Divine Beast that had not yet been absorbed did not move or shudder even once as it was slowly sucked into the bulk of the larger being where it was quickly dissolved.

"No!" Ren shouted, tears forming in her eyes.

Aion bellowed and beat his chest but stayed back at a safe range, lest he meet the same fate. There was nothing he would be able to do against the such a creature. Lythe, Tyr, and Yyn took to the air, circling Rullug with open mouths, sending streams of fire and ice into its algae covered mass in a blinding assortment of oranges, blues, whites, and reds. The flames boiled the surface of the Divine Beast, causing giant bubbles and pustules to form and burst. The ice froze swaths of the gelatinous murk solid, after which it would shatter under its own weight. The large clawed arms Rullug had used to pull itself ashore broke free of its amorphous center, vainly reaching up and swatting at the fliers who stayed just out of reach. A reptilian head emerged from the center of the thing in its final moments, wailing in a deep rumble that sounded akin to a horn blast.

Finally, it was done.

There was nothing left of Rullug the Murk but a few puddles of goo that seemed to be slowly moving back toward the sea of their own accord. Concerned it would somehow reconstitute itself, Tyr flew over the remains, bathing what was left with fire until there was nothing left. When he was finished, Tyr and the other Divine Beasts made their way toward the outskirts of the city. Ren, however, looked back at the sea.

*Merek.*

She lifted into the air for what her body hoped would be the final time, and flew back to where she had last seen the rogue Seraph, scanning the area for any signs of him. It was likely that his armor had weighed him down enough that he had sunk to the ocean floor.

Yet, he had been thought dead a thousand years before when he had likewise fallen into the sea, and she would not allow that mistake to be made a second time. Eventually, she saw him, floating in the surf like a discarded piece of driftwood, clinging to a piece of the dead sea snake. Ren cautiously landed in the water, lifting the other Seraph into her arms, and returning to the air with him. When she was back to her preferred altitude, she looked him over. Merek still lived, though his breathing was ragged. His eyes fluttered open as the breeze jostled his white hair. They widened with shock as Nightbreaker plunged into his chest.

"I am not my forebears," she said coldly. "I will not make the same mistake."

She pulled Nightbreaker free and sheathed her sword, carrying the nearly limp Seraph tightly in her grasp. His silver and red blood covered her breast in a slick sheen. Soon, they were over the land again when Ren let go of her burden. The man who had once been a Champion of the Light and a leader among Seraphs tumbled downward to his ultimate demise. This man had once been the leader of Ash Company, and even fought directly alongside Lythe in those days. Now, he was nothing more than a meal for the gulls once they returned. Ren took no pleasure in the act of killing him, but she could not allow such a man to pollute the Light another moment.

"You dishonor our station," she whispered as he fell. "I will not let you dishonor me."

The Seraph turned and flew back to the large gathering of people outside the walls of Seatown. It looked as though a few thousand had survived, at least. The population of Seatown had swelled with refugees from the villages. They were far from an army, but they would have to do. Two Balance Monks, four Divine Beasts, two Seraphs, and this group of unseasoned soldiers would have to be enough. They had no other choice.

*Two Seraphs.*

Ren suddenly realized she couldn't remember the last time she had actually seen Trent. Quickly, she flew back and forth over the heads of those gathered there, searching face to face, looking for any sign of the man she loved. She saw no white hair, no wings, no Trent. Finally, she landed beside Teo and Rella, desperately searching their expressions for any sign of what had happened to Trent.

It was Rella who spoke first. "I am sorry, my Lady," she said. "We saw Trent swallowed by Zad. The beast took him inside just as we arrived to look for a weakness."

Ren fell to her knees and let out a wail so loud she was sure those on the Divine Plane could hear it. Tears streaked her face, and her throat began to burn. The man who she had loved for this short time was dead. The crowd had turned in on her, many kneeling out of respect. When she was finished, she stood, pulling Nightbreaker free and pointing the blade to the west. There was no time for grief. She needed to harden her heart,

"We cannot delay," she said, loud enough for all around to hear. "We march on Illux. If we wait to bury the dead, we will never stop digging graves."

# EPILOGUE

The forces of the enemy tore each other apart below where he stood on the battlements. Scattered out across the field were three factions, two from the Gods of Darkness, and one from the City of Light. All three factions were his enemies. With any luck, they would destroy themselves before his forces were required to get involved. It mattered not, they wouldn't breach these walls, nor would he give the command to open the gates.

Castille Denost stood above the western gate of Illux, watching as those who would strive to take power from him slaughtered each other just outside his walls. For these were his walls now, just as they should have been for the last twenty years. No one else lived who could claim to control Illux. It had been several hours since Castille had arrested Edmund and locked the abominations outside the city he was charged with protecting. He hadn't taken kindly to the idea that even more unworthy bearers now held Divine Blood while he did not, even if they had not truly become Seraphs.

Scowling, Castille turned and walked back down the steps to the street below. As he left the wall he was saluted by men and women still loyal to him. These loyalists were all that remained, manning the walls and siege weapons that Edmund had commissioned. The rebels who had sided with Edmund had either been imprisoned or gone into hiding among the refugees, those who hadn't been executed, in any case. Castille had tried to keep the wholesale slaughter of members of the City Watch to a minimum, lest the city break into a full-scale civil war. For some reason, the wretches in the slums were more inclined to support the Watch than the Paladins, at least for now. He wasn't about to let that fact go unpunished, however. Castille knew he needed an iron fist to keep the city safe, an iron fist he would use to smash any and all who stood in his way.

*I am not weak like that woman we called a Seraph. I will see us through this siege.*

Once he was back on the ground, Yan and a group of several other Paladins fell into line behind him, following closely at his heels just in case he was attacked. Castille Denost was no coward, but he would not be caught unawares. After Hunt was killed in that Demigod attack, Castille had heightened his own security significantly. It seemed the abominations were a volatile group, and not one to be trifled with. That was why it had been such an easy to decision to lock the majority of them outside, though he knew some still roamed the city streets. Castille's spies had quickly brought him word that the Captain of the City Watch was planning to release the Demigods beyond the wall in a vain hope they could use the strife between the two enemy factions to deal a deathblow. It had been a valiant plan, even one that Castille respected. But that did not mean he would not take advantage of it.

"What should we do with the prisoner, my lord?" Yan asked as they neared the barricade that marked the division between the inner city and the slums.

*Too bad those animals killed Redrick. He was a man worthy of leading the Watch.*

"I would execute him in the morning myself," Castille replied, "but I will not make a martyr of him. Keep him in his cell for tonight, and then move him to a secure location in the slums tomorrow. If the wall falls, I won't waste any manpower keeping him alive. Make sure that you store him somewhere that the Demons are sure to find him if they make it in, and only guard him with men who can be trusted to keep their mouths shut. The last thing we need is some abomination helping him escape."

"If they breach the walls?" Yan asked,

"I am no fool, Yan," Castille said, firmly. "The abominations won't be able to do much more than superficial damage to the larger force, even less if they get pulled into attacking the smaller one. In the end, the original army that marched on us will be smaller than it was, but it will be whole and with a single purpose. Once that happens, they will do everything in their power to breach these walls. They may very well succeed. Is that not why we have reinforced the inner city? The refugees will slow them down, making them easy for our Paladins to crush them when they reach the fallback positions."

The junior Paladin nodded and fell back into line. Castille was less confident than he let on, even less confident than he had been when he stood on the wall a few minutes ago. Reality was setting in. He did not believe that whether or not the wall was breached made any difference. So long as the Grand Cathedral still stood as the last bastion of the Light, then they would live on. The city did not need some Seraph pretender or her two favored heroes to stand against the hordes of the enemy. All Castille needed was a few pious men. Truth be told, that was all he had.

They passed through the barrier into the inner city, winding their way through the paved streets toward the Grand Cathedral and the Fourth Spire. It hadn't taken long for him to solidify his power once it was clear that Ren wasn't coming back. Most of the Paladins who had returned with the Demigods had joined with those already under Castille's command. He had been ordered by Ren to only keep the few Paladins in the city that had been in her final war council where she had rebuked him, the rest were to go out and fight with her in the wilderness. Of course, he had done everything in his power to subvert that command and was left with a larger number than she had known. As for the City Watch, that had been harder to take hold of, since those men and women were still loyal to Edmund for some reason Castille didn't understand.

Or did he?

*Jerrok.*

Castille had loved and respected the previous Seraph in the way he expected the City Watch respected and loved Edmund. Jerrok had been brave, a truly powerful warrior and expert tactician on the battlefield. He was a Seraph in the tradition of Arendt. Together, Jerrok and Castille had made plans to wipe the Forces of Darkness from the face of the Mortal Plane, Balance Monks be damned. They would have succeeded had the Demons not made it over the wall and murdered him. Even though Castille had been saddened and enraged, he had also been hopeful. Expectant. He was the natural choice to be the next Seraph—the only Paladin fit to be Jerrok's successor. In the greatest embarrassment of his life, he had gathered together a great ceremony for the Gods of Light to bestow upon him their silver blood.

And instead, they had given it to Ren.

He had never forgiven her, or himself. He never would. In those hours before she had been transformed, he had her arrested and had made plans for her execution for her part in Jerrok's death. If only he hadn't delayed… Even now, he somehow held out hope that she was truly dead, and he would become the next Seraph. He hoped he would finally be given the chance for glory he had earned through years of pious service. The things he could do as a Seraph. He would save this city. He would bring those wretches in Seatown into line. He would destroy the Forces of Darkness once and for all.

They entered the plaza that surrounded the Fourth Spire. All of the Paladins not currently stationed at a post were gathered here, waiting for orders. Castille walked up the steps into the cathedral, nodding and waving when necessary. He left Yan and the others at the door, passing through into the chapel that had once been dedicated to the worship of Lio. Castille walked past rows of empty pews and braziers that burned incense, entering one of the doors at the rear of chapel.

The long walk up the many flights of stairs kept him in shape in ways that hours of training and drilling never could. He knew he was old, even for a Paladin, and that if he didn't get promoted to Seraph soon, he wouldn't be able to climb these steps for much longer. Castille had co-opted the rooms at the top of the spire that had belonged to the Lady Ren, making them his own relatively quickly after she had gone missing. He wanted to make the transition to leader of the city as easy for the others as possible. If they saw him living and acting like he was the new Seraph, soon, they would start to believe it.

After several minutes of climbing, Castille entered into his chambers and began taking off his armor. He knew this could very well be the last night's sleep he could expect for several weeks. As such he would enjoy every minute of it. While the siege was stalled outside, there was no reason for him to live like it was in full swing. The giant bed in the center of the chamber was round and covered in silk sheets. The mattress was filled with down from the geese that nested below the Rim. The grizzled Paladin commander fell into the mattress, allowing its comfort to absorb him. He closed his eyes and tried to drift off to sleep.

Suddenly, the room was filled with a blinding white light that burned his eyes even through his eyelids. Castille covered his face and swore, falling out of bed as he groped for his sword to defend himself. Surely, one of the abominations had come to assassinate him. He cut himself on the exposed blade beside his bed as his hands felt for the hilt. As he turned to face the center of the light, he nearly dropped the sword from the slickness of his blood. Before him was a glowing statue he instantly recognized.

"Luna!" he shouted, falling to his knees and prostrating himself.

*This is impossible. This must be a dream.*

Though his face was cast down at the floor, he had seen enough of her that her image was burned into his mind. She looked just like her statues in the plaza below. Her glowing skin was radiant, and her hair was the crispest white. The binding light that filled the room came directly from her armor. It reflected all colors and no colors at once. She was so beautiful that he found himself crying.

"Oh, Castille," her musical voice thundered, filling the room. "My sweet champion. You hurt yourself."

"It is nothing, my Lady," Castille stammered. "I would die from a thousand cuts just to see your radiance one more time."

Suddenly, he felt the wound healing. His hand no longer felt any pain.

"You may look upon me," Luna said.

He looked up and took her all in, nearly losing himself again. She was everything he had always wanted her to be.

"I have need of you, my champion," Luna said. "Are you up to the task?"

"Yes, my Lady, anything, anything."

"We stand on the edge of darkness, Castille. It is up to you to remain strong. Samson and I have struck a fateful blow against the Gods of Darkness. Vardic lies dead. But Samson has gone mad. He lost himself to his grief for Arra. They killed her after her foolish entry to the Mortal Plane. I hope that when this war ends there will again be two Gods of Light, but right now there is but one. The Seraphs are coming for you, Castille. I need you to stand against them."

"Seraphs, my Lady?" Castille said, swallowing hard.

"You were always to be next in line, my champion," Luna continued. "We chose Ren to test your resolve. It was to be you next, but as I said, Samson has gone mad, and he made Trent a Seraph as well, because he thought it was what Arra would have wanted. But they have turned against the Light, Castille. Trent and Ren have joined with the heretics of Seatown, and they are marching on you now. You will weather this siege, of that I am sure. But can you survive what comes after? Can you strike down Ren and Trent when the time comes?"

"I can, my Lady," he whispered. "I long for it."

"Then rise," Luna said, raising her arms. "Rise and take my blood."

# ABOUT THE AUTHOR

Kris Jerome was born in the middle of a snowstorm in Pendleton, Oregon, several decades ago. Since then he moved the great distance across the state to study at Willamette University. He obtained a BFA in Digital Communication Arts in June of 2016 from Oregon State University. Kris enjoys reading books while drinking Canadian whisky and watching classic films on his projector while eating American popcorn. He currently lives in Albany, Oregon with his wife, son, two dogs, and three cats, two of whom are named after epic fantasy characters.

# ALSO FROM DARK TIDINGS PRESS

## The Gods and Men Cycle

By Kristopher Jerome

### The Broken Pact Trilogy

- Wrath of the Fallen
- Cries of the Forsaken
- Tears of the Godless (Forthcoming)

A Bandit's Balance

The Nightbreaker

A Voice from the Darkness

## Dark Ocean

By Caleb Chandler

A Memory of Solstice

## Unsettling Accounts

By Bryan Babel

A Grave on Deacon's Peak

CPSIA information can be obtained
at www.ICGtesting.com
Printed in the USA
FSHW021956091119
63843FS

9 781951 138028